COMING AROUND AGAIN

COMING AROUND AGAIN

BETH BURNETT

SAPPHIRE BOOKS

SALINAS, CALIFORNIA

Editor - Heather Flournoy
Book Design - LJ Reynolds
Cover Design - Treehouse Studio

Sapphire Books Publishing, LLC
P.O. Box 8142
Salinas, CA 93912
www.sapphirebooks.com

Printed in the United States of America
First Edition – August 2018

This and other Sapphire Books titles can be found at
www.sapphirebooks.com

Dedication

To Joy Van Stralen, for more than this writer can put into words.

Acknowledgments

This book came to life with the help of several amazing people:

Chris Svendsen. I'm eternally grateful for the continued love and support. Sapphire Books has been my publishing home since 2012, and hopefully will keep putting out my books until I'm 98.

Heather Flournoy. Awesome editor. Thank you for getting me.

Aschlie Lake. She keeps beta reading for me, despite my penchant for fade-to-black sex scenes.

Darla Baker. She is a staunch supporter of lesfic writers, myself included.

Ann McMan. Please do all of my covers for the rest of my life.

Yvonne LeFave. Dear friend, soul sister. She stepped in (with groceries!) when I was writing so solidly, I didn't go to the grocery store for a month.

Joy Van Stralen. My love. She never ceases to amaze me with her unwavering support and unconditional love. And she is always willing to fold the laundry so I have a place to sleep when the writing day is over.

Chapter One

Karma Miller fumbled blindly for the lighter she knew was on the bedside table. With the black paper taped over the window, the bedroom was near-perfect darkness, but she still couldn't bring herself to open her eyes. She felt around the bedside table, knocking coins, a comb, and a half-eaten sandwich to the floor before finally wrapping her fingers around the familiar smooth sides of a lighter. She grabbed it and brought it to the joint in her mouth. Inhaling deeply, she let the smoke fill her lungs. She held it as long as she could before exhaling with a rush. A coughing fit forced her into a sitting position. She stubbed the joint out on the side of a coffee cup and wrapped her arms around her body. Coughing hard, she put her head down on her knees. A strong gag brought the taste of last night's pizza into her throat, and she winced. When she finally got herself under control, she ran a hand across her mouth and realized she had a glob of drool making its way down the side of her chin. *Gross,* she thought, wiping her hand on the blanket. Sitting up, she debated lighting the joint again. Her lungs were still clogged from last night. The party had been at some guy's studio apartment. She remembered the air being so thick with cigarette and pot smoke that she could barely see. Already stoned by the time she got to the party, the cramped, crowded apartment had launched her into a panic attack. She had turned to Crash, her girlfriend of nine months, and asked if they could leave.

Crash had laughed, eyes wide and sparkling. Crash was practically thrumming with frenetic energy. "Hell no," she had shouted over the music. Karma wasn't sure, but she thought Crash had done coke with her friends before they left the bar to come to the party. Hours later, Karma was lost in the maze of people. Drunk, stoned, and peering through the smoke, she had been unable to find Crash. Finally, she left the party and made her own way home. As she trudged through the streets of Lansing in the middle of the night, Karma vowed to quit smoking pot, to quit drinking, and to quit Crash.

Smiling bitterly, Karma acknowledged that she had already broken one vow. She wiped a hand across her face again. She was clammy and hot. The headache that had inspired her to fire up the joint in the first place was abating, but her throat was so dry, she couldn't believe she had managed to drool. Swinging her legs over the side of the bed, Karma tested herself by slowly standing. When the dizziness passed, she took a tentative step forward. She paused, waiting to see if the wave of dizziness would return. *Fuck, I'm hungover. Seriously, I'm done with all of it. I can't do it anymore.* She stumbled into the bathroom and sat on the edge of the tub, hovering slightly over the toilet in case she had to puke. The toilet looked disgusting. Karma couldn't remember the last time she had cleaned it. She knew Crash hadn't done it. Crash didn't do housework. She thought cooking and cleaning was the province of femmes. Karma didn't know she was a femme until she met Crash. Of course, she had known she liked girls since the first time little Janice Farlow with her mess of golden curls stomped her foot down onto Karma's and said, "You pretend to be the dad and I'll pretend to be the mom. That means you have to do everything I say."

When the urge to puke had passed, Karma stood again and leaned over the sink, throwing cold water on her face. Crash hadn't come home last night. Karma wondered if she had just passed out at the party or if she had gone home with another woman. Karma was almost sure that Crash slept with other women, but when she questioned her about it, Crash always made her feel as if Karma herself was cruel for even implying such a thing.

Looking in the mirror, Karma was shocked at how old she looked. Her bottom eyelids were puffy, and her skin was so pale, the dark circles under her eyes looked almost purple. Even her lips were pale. *Happy twenty-first birthday to me.*

After a shower, she dragged herself through getting dressed. She ate a piece of toast with peanut butter even though it made her feel sick. Swallowing repeatedly to keep from throwing up, Karma finished the toast and drank a full glass of room-temperature water. She thought she might live.

She wanted to leave, maybe head over to Bancroft park and walk in the trees for a while. She hadn't been to the park in months. She closed her eyes, thinking of the trees overhead and the ducks in the pond. Fresh air therapy and greenery would help clear her head. But the bathroom needed to be cleaned. Maybe Crash would be happy if the bathroom was clean. When Crash was happy, the whole world seemed happier. She bought little trinkets for Karma and she held hands with her when they walked down the street, even when people stared. She'd lean close when Karma was talking, listening intently to every word. When Crash was happy with Karma, it felt as if nothing could ever be wrong again. Karma knew she had to be better behaved to keep Crash happy. If she didn't drink too much, if she didn't question Crash too much, if she kept the house clean enough. Sometimes Karma felt as if she was walking on eggshells just to keep Crash from being mad at her. But it was worth it. It was worth it. When Crash got mad at her, it was Karma's fault for being so inexperienced at being a girlfriend. Crash was teaching her.

After scrubbing the bathroom, Karma cleaned the kitchen. Pacing, she tried to stop herself from going into the bedroom for the rest of that joint. A little hit would do wonders to calm her nerves right now. Crash didn't like for her to smoke pot before 2:00 p.m., though. She looked at the clock. If Crash didn't come home soon, Karma would take a walk over to the park. She needed some fresh air.

She paced around the phone. Who could she even call? She wasn't sure she remembered the name of the guy who gave the party, let alone his number. She could call Angela, one of Crash's drinking buddies. She dug around in the papers on the phone table, looking for a scrap that had Angela's number on it. Karma finally picked up her phone. As she was hovering her finger over the keys, her girlfriend banged through the front door. Karma smiled at her. She focused on keeping any hint of nagging out of her voice. "Hi, love."

"Hey," Crash said. "Anything to eat, babe? I'm starving."

"I haven't made anything," Karma said. "But I can fix something really quick."

"I'm about to pass out from hunger." Crash

pushed past Karma into the kitchen.

Karma, arms outstretched for a hug, dropped them after Crash passed her. She followed Crash into the kitchen. "Want me to make you an omelet?"

Crash was rummaging around in the fridge. Karma wondered if she should have started some soup or something before Crash got home. But she didn't know when she was going to be here. Crash was making a bologna sandwich. Karma reached out to touch her back, but Crash didn't turn.

"I couldn't find you last night," Karma said. "I was sick, and I needed to leave and I couldn't find you."

"Babe, I was partying. We were all supposed to be partying. You drank too much and had to cut out early. Is that my fault?"

"No," Karma said. "I just wondered where you were. I was hoping you would take me home."

"I was making important connections for us," Crash said through a mouthful of sandwich. "I found a woman who needs a bass player for her band. I hung out with her all night talking about what we both want from our musical careers."

Karma nodded. "When do you start?"

"It's always about the small picture with you, Kars. We didn't hash out the details like it's some nine-to-five office job. We were looking at the grand scheme, the big picture. We're going to be huge. We have the same ideals. This is good for you, too, babe. Don't you want us to be successful?"

"Yes, I do," Karma insisted. "I really do. I'm happy for you. I just didn't know where you were."

Crash shoved the last bite of sandwich into her mouth. Even with her cheeks bulging, she was a gorgeous woman. Karma, who saw herself as nothing but knees and elbows and long hair, marveled at the lean and hard muscles of Crash's body. The first time Karma had seen her, she had fallen in love. She had never seen a woman as tall and self-assured as Crash. The dark clothing and deeply intense stare was so different from Karma and her own hippie sense of fashion. Karma rarely bought anything new, preferring instead to raid her mother's closet. Some of the clothes in there were vintage hippie, actual outfits from the 60's passed down from Karma's grandmother. Karma's mom was voluptuous and tall and her tiny grandmother was the same size as Karma. Between the two of them, she could have new-to-her clothing for years and never wear the same thing twice. Wearing the clothes of her elders felt safe to Karma, like she was wrapped in their love every time she got dressed.

Now Karma wondered if she was really in love with Crash. Sometimes, when Crash was holding her, she felt safe and protected from all the cares of the world. Other times, she was terrified that Crash would turn on her and become sullen and angry, or worse— yell.

Crash put her arms around Karma and pulled her in close. Karma relaxed into her lover, breathing in the scent of Crash's cologne mixed with smoke and whiskey and a little bit of body odor. Karma breathed in for a few minutes, listening to the hard and steady thump of Crash's heart.

"I love you, Crash," Karma whispered.

"Love you, too, babe."

"Crash, you haven't forgotten it's my birthday today, have you?"

Crash pulled away abruptly, pushing Karma back against the kitchen counter. "For fuck's sake, babe.

You're always pressuring me."

Karma rubbed her hip where it hit the counter. Bewildered, she held up her hands. "I'm sorry, I'm so sorry. I didn't mean you forgot."

"I didn't forget," Crash yelled. "Jesus. I've barely been home for five minutes and you're already nagging me."

"I'm not nagging," Karma said. "Please don't be mad. I didn't mean anything by it."

Crash relaxed a bit. "Babe, I would never forget your birthday. I just hadn't said anything yet. Why does everything always have to be about you?"

Karma shook her head. Why couldn't she let Crash relax for five minutes without pressuring her about something? "I don't know. I'm sorry I'm so selfish."

Crash reached out to touch her shoulder. "I'm sorry I got mad."

She missed the feeling of Crash's arms around her. "It's not your fault," Karma whispered, trying not to cry.

"No, it isn't. But I should be a little more patient with you."

Karma smiled up at Crash. "I'm learning."

"You are," Crash said, kissing her on the top of the head. "You are."

Karma leaned her head back hoping for a kiss. Crash obliged, pressing her lips lightly down on Karma's, letting her tongue slip over the sensitive skin of Karma's upper lip.

"I love your kiss." Karma's body arched toward Crash, wanting to feel the strength and warmth of Crash's solid body against hers.

"I'm going to take you out for your birthday," Crash said. "To the best restaurant in town."

"We're going to my parents' for dinner, remember?"

"God dammit," Crash muttered. "Cancel. We can go there tomorrow. Tonight, we celebrate in our style."

Karma steeled her shoulders. She knew Crash didn't like her parents, but she had promised them that she would come over for her birthday dinner. She had cancelled on them several times over the last few months, and she knew her mother was hurt that she hadn't seen Karma in so long.

"I can't, Crash. I can't. We've cancelled on them so many times lately."

Crash turned her back and Karma could tell by the set of her shoulders that she was mad. Torn between wanting to keep the peace and wanting to see her parents, Karma reached out to place a hand on Crash's back. "Please, my love," she said, hating the pleading tone in her voice. "Please. They're my parents and I miss them."

"Do you ever think of how I feel?" Crash replied. "They obviously hate me. No matter what I do, they hate me. Do you have any idea how it feels to have to sit there being polite, knowing how they're judging me?"

Karma stroked Crash's back. She couldn't argue. Her mother didn't like Crash at all. Her father tried to be warm and friendly for the sake of politeness, but her mother thought Crash was a bad influence on Karma. Though her parents were quite liberal in a lot of ways, they didn't like the idea of Karma smoking so much pot and drinking all the time. Karma's mom blamed that on Crash. It had to feel awkward and hurtful to be judged.

"Okay," she finally said. "I'll postpone with my

parents. We can go out tonight. But not to a fancy restaurant. We can't afford it."

Crash turned around to look at Karma. She was smiling, and Karma was relieved. "Excellent, babe. Maybe we can order a pizza and get some beer and have a private birthday celebration just for us."

"Sounds great," Karma said. "Sounds really fantastic."

"Awesome. I'm going to get some sleep. I'm fucking exhausted."

She kissed Karma lightly on the cheek and brushed past her, heading toward the bedroom.

Karma leaned back against the counter and closed her eyes. They had an argument but had come to a compromise. Why did she feel so sad? She remembered her resolution last night to quit all the dangerous habits in her life. Crash was so good to her sometimes but other times, she made Karma feel like shit. This is what it meant to be in a relationship. Argument and compromise. She vowed to pick up another book on communication the next time she was at the library.

Karma decided to head over to her parents' house while Crash was sleeping. If nothing else, she could cancel on them in person. She knew her mother was going to be upset, but the least Karma could do was face her when she canceled. She peeked into the bedroom and determined that Crash was passed out in their bed. Karma scrawled a quick note on a piece of paper and attached it to the fridge. With any luck, she would be back before Crash woke up, but just in case, at least she would know where to find her. Crash hated when she didn't know where Karma was.

Standing on the porch of her parents' house, Karma smiled. She loved coming home. In school, the other kids used to make fun of the shabby house with its wild and overflowing garden, but Karma was in love with it. She used to spend hours in the backyard when the weather was nice, scrawling bad teenage poetry into one of her many journals. Karma's parents had a lot of friends, who would come over on Saturdays and spend the day working in the big back garden, harvesting shared vegetables, and at night, they would all sit on the back porch drinking wine and laughing. Karma never had a regular bedtime, and she would often curl up on one of the outdoor chairs and drift off to the sound of gentle adult voices.

She opened the front door and stepped into the hall. The photographs lining the walls were in haphazard order, but they somehow all seemed to fit. She paused in front of the picture of her grandmother in a wedding dress. Karma looked just like her grandmother, only Grandma was so much prettier than Karma could ever hope to be.

She poked her head in the living room. Some things never changed. Her dad was asleep on the couch, a book open on his chest. Karma tiptoed over to see what he was reading. Never without a book, her father would pick up anything in reach rather than be without something to read. He read everything from classic literature to the latest science fiction to the *Good Housekeeping* magazine that came to their house by accident. She gently moved his hand to peek at the title. *The Book Thief.* She smiled. Dad had read this book to her when she was a kid and it had wrapped itself forever around her heart. She kissed him on the forehead and he opened his eyes.

"Sweetpea," he murmured. "You're early."

"Something came up, Dad," Karma replied. "Where's Mom?"

"I'm here, darling." Her mother swept into the room. Larger than life and glowing with love, Henna Miller pulled Karma into her arms. "Oh, my baby. You're so skinny. Have you been eating at all?"

Karma pressed her face against her mother's soft shoulder, breathing in the faint scent of lavender. "Mom, you smell good."

"It's my newest soap. Lavender oatmeal. I thought it would help with your dad's scratchy elbows."

Karma laughed. Her dad, Frank, was as skinny as she was and they both had the same problem of poking through the elbows and knees of clothing. She freed one arm from her mom's clutches and held the elbow up for inspection. "What about mine?"

"A travesty," her mother said. "I'll ruin your birthday surprise by telling you I've got some soap wrapped up for you."

Laughing, Karma wrapped herself back into her mother's arms. "I've missed you, Mom."

Frank sat up with a sigh. "I don't know how a man is supposed to sleep with you two yapping away."

Hearing the love and laughter in her dad's voice, Karma looked up at her mom's face to see her smiling at Frank. Karma didn't remember ever seeing her parents fighting with each other. Karma's parents were open about everything, and Karma often sat with them as they discussed important decisions regarding the house or Karma's schooling. It wasn't that they never disagreed with each other, it was just that she didn't remember them ever being mean to each other. She was sure she had never heard them raise their voices in anger. And she could say without a doubt that she had never heard either of them call the other a name. She thought back to the night Crash had said, "Karma, you're so clingy. Why do you have to be such a nag?" Once, Karma had heard Crash on the phone saying, "I'm sorry about that. My girlfriend can be a real bitch." She had cried for hours, wondering what she had done so wrong that her own girlfriend felt that way about her.

Releasing her mother, Karma sat down on the couch next to her dad. He put his arm around her and they leaned back on the couch together. She remembered when her parents got this couch, the first new piece of furniture she could recall them buying. It was squishy in all the right places and big enough for Karma and her dad to take opposite ends when they wanted to read or nap.

Henna sat on the ottoman and took Karma's hand. "You're early, darling. And—where's Crash?"

"She's sick," Karma said, looking down. "She's too sick to make it for dinner. I thought I'd come over early and spend a couple of hours before going back to take care of her."

Staring at her hands, Karma waited for one of her parents to say something. Finally, Frank cleared his throat. "Your mother has been working hard to make a meal that both you and Crash would enjoy."

Frank's voice was gentle, but Karma could hear the disappointment. She knew she would start crying if she opened her mouth, so she continued staring down. When she felt her mother's hand on her chin, she had no choice but to look up. Henna's eyes were bright with tears and Karma's guilt shot into her stomach. Clasping a hand over her belly, she bent forward, pressing her forehead down against her mother's arm. Karma felt her dad's hand, warm and solid, on her back as her mother stroked her hair. She knew she was hurting them, but they loved her too much to yell at her. She finally looked back up at her mom.

"I'm worried about you, Karma," Henna said. "I'm worried that Crash isn't treating you as well as you deserve."

"Not all relationships are like yours and Dad's," Karma said.

"All good ones are," Frank answered. "If you aren't being treated kindly and with respect, you are in the wrong relationship."

"But I love her," Karma pleaded.

"Oh, sweetpea," her dad said, tightening his arm around her. "Love isn't supposed to hurt."

Henna sighed. "Your grandmother is going to be disappointed. She hasn't seen you in months."

Frank rubbed Karma's back. "It's okay, we understand. We just want you to be happy."

Karma reached for her mother's hand and sat between the two of them, basking in the feeling of being cared for with such tenderness. It was different for her parents. They didn't know what it was like to be with Crash. They didn't understand the exhilaration of being on her good side. Crash was so good to Karma sometimes, making her feel so special, so above the rest of the world. And when they kissed, it felt like magic. Karma had only kissed one other person in her life. Jimmy Lanham had kissed her at the senior prom and Karma had let him slip his tongue in her mouth. She was curious to find out if there was anything exciting about it. There was not. Jimmy went home disappointed in his lack of action after prom, but Karma wasn't interested in going any further when his kiss felt like a dying fish flopping in her mouth. Still, she owed her parents an explanation. They had been incredibly supportive when Karma told them she had fallen in love with a woman.

"It isn't like that," Karma said. "She's so good to me."

"Is she?" Henna asked. "Is she good to you?"

Karma stared at her mother. "Sometimes."

"Sometimes isn't enough, darling."

Several hours later, Karma left her parents' house laden with goodies. In addition to her birthday presents, which included, of course, several books and several bars of her mother's homemade soap, she had a couple of large servings of her mother's famous lasagna, made with a two-day sauce that Karma was sure she'd kill for. Driving back across town, she wondered if Crash was going to be pissed that she had been gone for so long. Maybe she was still sleeping. If not, maybe the gift of homemade lasagna would appease her. It meant they didn't have to spend money on a pizza. Karma smiled, thinking of putting a candle into the pieces of birthday cake her mother had wrapped up for her, but her stomach still felt achy and knotted. She should have worked harder to convince her parents that Crash wasn't as bad as they thought.

She was lucky to get a parking place close to their apartment. Crash had a nicer car, so it made sense that she got the reserved spot under the canopy. Leaving the books for another trip, Karma grabbed up all the soap and food. She was already wearing the new sweater her dad had knit for her. Glancing down at it, she smiled. Forest-green hues with some deep brown accents. It looked like something a woodland fairy might wear. And it fit her perfectly. Wrapped in homemade warmth from her dad, breathing in the scent of her mother's soap, Karma marveled at how deeply she loved her parents. Growing up, her friends had always complained about their own parents, and Karma used to wonder why she was so lucky. Lately, she had started to wonder if she had exhausted all her good love points on having perfect parents.

Shifting the packages to one hand, Karma let herself into the apartment. Her heart sank when she saw Crash sitting on the couch.

"Hi, honey," Karma said.

Ignoring her, Crash stubbed her cigarette into the ashtray she had propped on the arm of the couch. Trying to calm the anxiety in the pit of her stomach, Karma continued into the apartment and into the kitchen. "I went over to my parents'," she called over her shoulder. "I figured you would be happy that I was able to smooth things over in person."

She put the leftover food in the fridge and dropped her purse and the packages on the counter. Turning around, she gasped. Crash was standing directly behind her.

"I didn't hear you," Karma muttered, laughing nervously.

"I didn't know where you were."

Karma picked at the hem of her new sweater. Crash sounded as if she was trying to control her tone, which was almost scarier than when she yelled.

"I left a note."

"A note that I didn't find until I was already in a panic," Crash said. "You know I hate it when I can't find you."

"I'm sorry. I'm so sorry," Karma said. "I'm so sorry. I just thought since we were cancelling on my parents again that the least I could do was to apologize in person."

"You keep throwing that in my face." Crash's voice was getting louder.

Karma backed up into the counter. Crash advanced, towering over Karma. "I suppose you told them it was my fault we weren't coming over."

"It wasn't like that at all," Karma insisted. "I told them you were sick."

"I am sick," Crash said. "I'm sick of you sneaking around behind my back and lying about me."

"I'm sorry. It wasn't like that. I'm saying it wrong, but it wasn't like that." Karma was desperate, unable to figure out why the conversation was going so badly. She really hadn't meant to hurt Crash's feelings. Why couldn't she ever do anything right?

Crash glared at Karma before looking away, disgusted. "And what's all of this?"

"Birthday presents," Karma said. "My mom made me some soap and my dad knit a sweater."

"And they're so much better than me because they made you presents? I worked hard all week to have the money to give you a nice birthday. You're a fucking ingrate!"

"I'm not," Karma said. "I am grateful. I appreciate just the time we spend together."

"I give you so much more than time and you discount everything I do."

"No, I don't!" Frustrated, Karma heard the yell come out of her before she could stop it.

She felt the slam of Crash's hand into her face, and it took her a second to realize what had happened.

Crash was standing before her, glaring. Karma pressed a hand to her cheek, blinking through tears of shock and pain. Crash lifted her other hand and slapped Karma hard on the other side of her face.

"Don't you ever yell at me again. Do not ever raise your voice to me again."

"I won't," Karma whispered. "I promise I won't."

Crash turned on her heels. "I'm going out. I need to get away from you."

Karma didn't dare ask when Crash would be back or if they were going to have a birthday dinner later tonight. Quiet, she listened to the sounds of her girlfriend gathering her jacket and keys. The front door slammed, and Karma sank into a kitchen chair, sobbing into her hands. She thought about calling her mother, but she knew her parents would insist on coming to get her, and that would make things so much worse with Crash.

Karma reached for her purse and dragged it to the table by the strap. Rummaging around, she found the baggie of pot and a small one-hitter bowl she kept for emergencies. She filled the small bowl and lit the pipe, sucking in deeply. *Happy birthday to me.*

Chapter Two

Jane Edmunds peered furtively around the corner. Looking around to make sure there still wasn't anyone behind her, she slipped into A Woman's Place bookstore. She had never been into the store, though it looked like any other bookstore from the outside. It had a big display window with colorful books that tried to catch her eye every time she scurried by. She had never had a reason to stop in before. After all, what could she possibly want in a feminist bookstore?

A woman approached her. "Can I help you find something?

"No," Jane said. She cleared her throat. "No, I mean I just want to look around." She wanted to find the lesbian section, but she didn't want to ask the woman where it was. The woman smiled and left her alone. Jane looked around the store in wonder. It was bigger than she'd expected, clean and well lit. There were display tables and posters. It wasn't that much different than the small bookstores near campus. She had expected it to look weird, somehow. Walking through the store, she finally spotted a small sign way in the back that said lesbian fiction, and ducked into the row. She dragged her finger along the spines of the paperbacks. They even looked different, she thought, but she couldn't say why. Someone cleared their throat and Jane jumped, looking around. The person wasn't in this row. It was stupid to be so scared to look at lesbian books anyway. She could say she had to find something for a class. She could just not say anything. It wasn't 1950, after all. Still, she would hate to have to explain to her parents what she was doing in a feminist bookstore, let alone in a section for lesbian fiction. Turning back to the shelf, she searched the authors until she found one of the ones on her list. *Curious Wine.* She held it gingerly as if a lesbian was going to suddenly jump out of the book and start yelling, "Gay!" at the top of her lungs. She touched the cover. It was an older book, used. Good. She could buy more if she bought some used. It didn't look like a lesbian book. She'd half-expected naked lounging women all over the cover. *Expected, or wanted*? Laughing to herself, Jane tossed the book into her basket. Jumping again at the throat clearer from the other aisle, Jane quickly looked at the rest of the row. Most of these books looked used. She picked up a book with a plain cover. *Lesbian Images.* She barely glanced at it before throwing it in her basket.

At the counter, Jane quickly unloaded her books without making eye contact with the woman from before. Pushing a bunch of cash across the counter, Jane waited for her change and grabbed the bag. She threw the whole thing into her own oversized shoulder bag in case anyone saw the label on the store bag and wanted to know what was in it. Jane whispered a quick thank you to the clerk before scooting out of the store as fast as she could manage. She felt like a thief, rushing out with the stolen goods before the cops rushed the scene. Just on the other side of the door, she slammed into someone. Rocking back, she reached up to rub her chest, sore from the collision.

"I'm so sorry," the other woman said.

Jane looked at the woman, trying not to blush. She was slightly taller than Jane, but just as skinny. Jane wondered if this woman always had to mend the elbows in her shirts. She forced herself not to check the woman's sleeves. Jane gazed at the woman's clear, pale skin with its smattering of light freckles across the bridge of her nose. The woman had a wild mane of curly brown hair, so unlike Jane's pale blond lifeless hair which was most often pulled back in a bun so the flyaway pieces wouldn't fall in her eyes.

"I'm really sorry," the other woman repeated. "Are you okay?"

Jane nodded, unable to speak. The woman had deep brown eyes with long lashes. Jane thought she might be the most beautiful woman she had ever seen.

"Are you hurt?" The woman looked concerned. "Did I knock the wind out of you?"

"I'm sorry," Jane stammered. "I'm fine. I was just surprised. I didn't mean to bump into you."

"Of course not." The woman laughed. "No one means to bump into people, do they?" She paused, looking into Jane's face. "You have really pretty eyes."

Blushing so hard she could feel it up to the roots of her hair, Jane put her hands to her cheeks. She felt hot. The woman was being nice. Blue eyes just weren't that common, so people thought they were pretty. Besides, with her super-thick glasses distorting her face, she knew she didn't look anything close to pretty. She shook her head, looking down at her own feet.

"I'm Karma," the other woman said.

"Karma?"

"Yes, Karma."

Jane cleared her throat and managed to look up. "That's an unusual name."

"My mother is a total hippie," Karma replied.

Jane could see that Karma was wearing big black boots, lacy tights, and a long, flowered dress with an army green jacket over it all. "I can see where you get it," Jane said, smiling.

Karma smiled, too. "Now you're supposed to tell me your name."

"Jane. Just Jane."

"Jane is a perfectly lovely name."

Shaking her head, Jane looked away. She couldn't think of anything else to say, yet for some reason, she didn't want to go. Chancing a look back at Karma's face, Jane was enchanted by full lips curved into the widest smile Jane had ever seen.

Karma reached out to touch Jane's shoulder. "Do you feel like we've met before?"

Jane shook her head, but she didn't break the eye contact. "It's not possible. I know I would remember you."

"I guess. You just seem so familiar." She glanced around nervously as if she was looking for someone. "But I guess we could have run into each other before," Karma continued loudly as if talking over her nervousness. She laughed loudly, as if she'd said something funny.

Jane cringed a little, knowing Karma's deep and loud laugh was drawing stares from the other people walking by on the sidewalk. She knew she had to get going. Her parents would be mad if she was late for dinner. Still, there was something familiar about Karma.

"I don't go anywhere but school and home," Jane said. "I'm studying at Excelsior Christian College."

"Well, I've definitely never been there," Karma

said. "I'm pretty sure lightning would strike if I tried to walk through the doors."

"Why would you say that?" Jane said. Suddenly defensive, she stood up straight. "It isn't like that."

"Maybe," Karma said. "But I'm a lesbian and we typically aren't welcome in anything with the word Christian in its name."

Shocked, Jane took a step backward. Karma had practically shouted the word lesbian. Jane looked around to see if anyone had noticed. She turned back to see Karma staring at her. Jane blushed again. "It's just…"

"I get it," Karma said. "I'm used to people having a problem with it. It was nice meeting you."

Jane opened her mouth to stop the woman from leaving, but she had already ducked into the bookstore. If Jane went after her, she would be late for her parents. She stared at the door for a moment, hoping Karma would stick her head back out and smile at her. Jane looked at her watch. If she didn't leave now, she'd be in trouble. She cast a look back at the store and trotted toward the bus.

When she got to her parents' house, Jane took one last look at her bag, making sure none of the lesbian books were showing. Not that she thought her parents would recognize a lesbian book if it jumped up and smacked them in the face, but they'd recognize the word if nothing else. Jane didn't know if she would have the courage to read it, but since she hadn't yet mustered up the courage to do anything else, she had to start somewhere.

Homosexuality was a sin; Jane knew that. She'd heard it enough from the pulpit and from her parents. If that wasn't enough to drive it home, there was always her mother's reaction that time she and Cindy Watkins had taken off their shirts to look at each other's barely formed breasts. She was eleven at the time and Cindy was twelve, and Jane's mother had nearly died from the shock. After calling Cindy's parents and grounding Jane from every activity except school and church, Mary Edmunds took to her bed with chest pains and dizzy spells. Her father had sat her down to talk about it since her mother was too sick to move. "I know you didn't mean to do that, Janey. Cindy is wild, and I know she talked you into doing something that you never would have done otherwise." Jane didn't remember it quite like that, but her father looked so pained and earnest that there was nothing she could do but nod in agreement.

After that, her mother got better and started liking Jane again, but Jane had learned a lesson about looking at other women's bodies.

Before Jane could put her key in the door, it was flung open. Her mother grabbed Jane's shoulder and pulled her into the house. "You should have been home an hour ago."

"I'm sorry, Mother," Jane said. "It was a lovely day, and I wanted to walk around downtown before coming home."

A look at her mother's pursed lips was all Jane needed to gauge the reaction to that bit of news. Jane leaned in to kiss her mother on the cheek. "I'm sorry, Mother. I should have called."

"Don't forget to take your shoes off," Mary said.

Twenty-one years of living with her mother meant Jane never forgot to take her shoes off. She slipped out of them in the foyer and neatly arranged them in the storage space. She walked into the kitchen and her mother followed. "It's just that I worry when I don't know where you are."

"I know," Jane said. She grinned at her mother. "And I am twenty-one years old, after all."

Mary smiled. "Since yesterday. Don't go getting ideas above your station. You still live under my roof."

"And as such, must obey your rules," Jane finished.

Her mother turned to the oven. "I hope your young man likes roast," she said.

"It smells delicious," Jane answered. "And he isn't my young man. He's just a good friend."

"Well, you never know what can develop."

Jane stifled a laugh. David worked with Jane in the stockroom of the campus bookstore. The two introverts had worked in silence for weeks, but eventually conversation developed. As the weeks and months passed, Jane had come to truly love David. If she was into men, she could have fallen in love with someone like David. He was tall and a little chubby with curly light brown hair and blue eyes. Jane thought their children would be beautiful. They might get her fine features and David's height. Perhaps they would be destined to have blue eyes. Jane shook her head. Two years of working together had helped them forge a deep and loving friendship based on respect, admiration, and a great number of commonalities. In addition to their shared love of Jane Austen, good coffee, and thrift store shopping, David and Jane were both gay and in the closet.

David's parents were as religious as hers, and, Jane expected, far more aggressive about it. In a whispered conversation late one night at an off-campus movie, David had told her about how his dad had once tried to beat the gay out of him after he had caught David masturbating to a magazine with a half-naked man on the cover. For a week, his father had taken David up to his bedroom, opened the magazine in front of him, and beat him with a belt until his butt and back were bloody. David had said that the beatings did nothing to quell his desires, but that the one time he tried to have sex with a man, David had frozen in terror, and left before anything could happen. David wanted to transfer to Michigan State University, but his parents were paying for Excelsior and they wanted him safe at a Christian college where they felt he would get the best moral education along with the regular one.

Jane's mother was still talking, and Jane looked at her. "I'm sorry, I got lost in thought."

Mary smiled. "Thinking about your young man, I expect. Well, I just told you to go change and do your homework. Dinner will be ready at six. Will David be here by then?"

"Yes, ma'am."

"Make sure your room is clean. I hate when you leave a mess."

Jane shook her head and ran upstairs to her room. She had never left her room a mess in her life. Her mother insisted that the house be spotless at all times, in case anyone from church happened by. Though Jane's room wasn't subjected to the constant redecorating her mother did to the rest of the house, it was still expected to look show-worthy. She looked around. Minus the small wrinkle in the middle of the bedspread, the room was immaculate. Her desk was tidy, the chair pushed in. Her one small bookshelf was neatly arranged. Jane knew better than to leave things a mess. It wasn't that her mother yelled. It was more that she pursed her lips and looked unhappy. Often, she'd clutch her hand over her heart and Jane would be instantly filled with guilt, remembering all the times she had made her mother's heart problem act up.

She pushed her mother out of her mind. She had more important things to do. She took out an oversized American History book and put one of the lesbian books in the middle. Propped up on her bed with the textbook across her legs, Jane would look like the model student if her mother should pop her head in. Drawn almost immediately into the story, Jane couldn't help but feel a little odd. Did women just live normal lives with each other? Jane was stunned. The women in this book simply talked to each other and moved about their lives as if loving other women was a normal part of their lives. She wasn't ignorant; she knew that lesbians existed and that being gay was more accepted in the outside world than it was in her own family. However, it was so far removed from her own reality, she found it hard to imagine. Jane had once tried to look up lesbian in the card catalog at the Capital Area District Library. She thought it would be faster to use those new computers, but she was afraid the machine could keep track of what she looked at. She turned back to the book, intent on learning everything she could about women who loved women.

Deeply engrossed in her book, she didn't hear the door open.

"American History," David said. "Heavy subject for a birthday evening."

Smiling, Jane looked up. "First, it isn't my birthday. We just couldn't celebrate it Sunday because of church. Second, it isn't American History." She held up the book she was reading.

"Oh," David smiled. He sat down in her desk

chair. "*Curious Wine*. Something tells me that has some very interesting subject matter. How is it?"

"Oh, David, it's amazing. There's these women and they just…" She paused, unable to say the word. "They just love each other."

David laughed. "I'm so happy. Finding gay books was life changing for me. It's like, I know there are all sorts of people out there being gay and working and having kids and such. I just didn't realize there were so many people doing it without feeling shitty about themselves. I mean, why can't we live in San Francisco? *Tales of the City* makes it seem so natural."

Jane reached out to pat his leg. "It isn't natural, but maybe it isn't as bad as we thought."

David smiled. "It was a little embarrassing the first time I checked out a gay book from the library. But I figured librarians have probably seen it all. And they wouldn't have the book if there wasn't at least some kind of demand for it."

Laughing, Jane shook her head. "I can't even imagine saying the word, let alone telling someone I want to find books about it."

David reached over and took her hand. "We aren't bad people, Jane. No matter what our parents think, no matter what the church tells us, we are not bad people."

Jane looked at their entwined hands. "David, I wish I could believe it."

Her mother popped her head in the door. She looked from one to the other with a small smile. "It's time for dinner."

Jane released David's hand and swung her legs over the side of the bed, making sure to dump her book onto the floor. She dropped her history text on top of it.

David stood and held out a hand for Jane. Taking his, she smiled. Her mother nodded. "I like to see you two studying together," she said. "Just make sure to keep the door open."

"Yes, ma'am," David said. "I wouldn't dream of disrespecting your hospitality."

Mary Edmunds smiled. "I'll see you downstairs. And don't leave that book lying on the floor like that." She left the room.

Jane looked hopelessly up into David's face. "I'm sorry," she said. "I just don't know how to make it clearer that we aren't dating."

"Don't feel bad," David said. "I flat-out told my parents we're dating."

Jane sighed. She wrapped her arms around David's waist and leaned against him. He was tall and solid and strong, but with a softness that felt good against all her bony angles. She wished again for a moment that she could just become straight. Everyone's life would be so much happier if she and David could fall in love with each other. The woman from the bookstore popped into her mind and suddenly, Jane's face was filled with the memory of big brown eyes and a smile that sent Jane's heart fluttering. Maybe she didn't wish she was straight after all.

Chapter Three

Karma bounced open the door to the Katherine Harding LGBT Center with her hip. With her arms full of bins of chocolate chip cookies, she staggered over to the front desk.

"Ah, help me out here!"

The man behind the front desk jumped up and ran around the desk. "Hey, Karma."

"Hey, Mr. G."

As he took the bins of cookies from her arms, Karma smiled at Henry Gunderson. She always loved seeing him here. At maybe six foot five, Henry towered over Karma. As he lifted the trays of cookies, his biceps flexed under his dress shirt and Karma wondered, not for the first time, where he ever found clothes that fit him.

"Your mom has been at it again, I see."

Karma grinned. "I told her I was leading the new coming out group and she insisted. I think she made about three thousand cookies. I'm relatively sure we won't have more than three people in the group. I'm sure I'll be sending you home with some."

"Fantastic," he said, patting his belly. "Marla's been putting in so many hours at the clinic, I think she's forgotten how to make cookies."

Karma shook a finger at him. "Baking isn't just a woman's job, Henry."

"It isn't because she's a woman, kiddo. It's because

I set off the fire alarm if I even look in the kitchen."

Karma laughed. Henry had wandered into the center a few months ago, looking a little lost and bewildered. Karma had assumed he was coming out late in life, but it turned out that Henry's son had just come out of the closet, and Henry, a retired football player, needed help coming to terms with it. Karma was proud of how far Henry had come. Despite having spent most of his life in a hyper-masculine environment, Henry was open-minded and attentive. It was obvious he loved his son, and he attended every group session meant for allies. He started volunteering at the center after about two months, and he had recently even chaired one of the monthly PFLAG meetings.

"How's Carter?" Karma asked. She perched on the edge of the desk.

"Oh, he's doing so well. He got accepted to Yale med school. Guess he's going to follow in his brilliant mother's footsteps instead of mine."

Karma patted one of his beefy arms. "You're smarter than you give yourself credit for."

She glanced around as two young men came walking through. There were always volunteers in and out of the center. Karma was proud of her involvement in it. She and her dad had been part of the team to help raise money to buy the house where they built the center. They had put in hours of work with the renovation committee, fixing it up and making it into a safe space for anyone in the LGBT community. The front desk was in what used to be the front room. It had been expanded and was lined with books and tables and chairs so people could walk in, pick out some books, and sit down to read.

Karma didn't spend as much time at the center

anymore—not as much as she'd like. Crash wasn't a fan of it. She was afraid Karma was hanging out to meet women, and despite Karma's constant reassurance that she wasn't, Crash still wasn't happy with Karma's continued involvement. It hurt her heart to have to lie to Crash about where she was on Tuesdays, but she didn't want to give up the good work she thought she was doing there.

Karma walked into Meeting Room One, formerly a bedroom. Henry followed, carrying the cookies. The room was still set up from the last group, so Karma didn't have much to do. She walked around the circle of chairs, straightening a couple here and there. Henry put the cookies on a table against the back wall.

"I made coffee for you, too," he said. "Just in case you get a crowd."

"I hope I do," Karma said. "Since it's my first time, I'd hate to sit here talking to myself because no one bothered to show up."

Henry laughed. "Tuesday morning sessions are iffy because there's nothing else going on at the center right now. At least on Thursday, you get the leftovers from Yoga With Zsa Zsa."

"I heard you finally mastered chair pose." Karma laughed.

"Hardly," Henry roared. "My arms just do not want to go up to my ears when my legs are bent like that." He threw his arms over his head, demonstrating the arm portion of the position. "See? It's fine when I'm not pretending to be a chair."

Karma laughed and playfully pushed him out of the room. "Okay, go man the front desk. My victims should be wandering in soon."

Henry left and Karma spent the next few minutes

looking around the room. She fidgeted with the cookie bins, debating about opening one of them or leaving it closed for freshness. If it was closed, maybe no one would eat any. If she left it open, maybe the cookies would get hard. She was confident in her ability to run the meeting, but what if no one showed up? Or what if fifty people showed up? She could handle that, she thought. She wished she could run the Thursday group, too, but she couldn't wrangle taking another day off work during the week. Someday, she'd be rich and she'd volunteer at the center almost every day. Maybe. She walked around the room again, straightening the chairs. It was three minutes past ten. Maybe no one was coming.

Hearing footsteps behind her, Karma turned around.

"Oh, my gosh, it's you!"

Karma had a moment to look at the tiny blonde before she found herself being crushed into the woman's arms. With her own arms pinned against her sides, she laughed at the woman's exuberance. Pulling back just enough to get her arms out, she wrapped them around the woman and they both relaxed into a hug. Karma recognized her from their encounter outside A Woman's Place. What was her name, though? Jenny. Jane. It was Jane. Karma was sure of it. As the hug deepened, Karma pressed her face against Jane's hair. Why did she smell so good? As small as she was, Karma was used to feeling dwarfed when most people hugged her, but Jane was even smaller. Karma had always been attracted to larger women—taller, broader, chubbier— because Karma was so slender, she figured her bones would clank up against anyone who wasn't at least a little padded. Yet Jane seemed to melt into all the right places, and Karma thought her body felt soft and luxurious.

Suddenly aware that she had been hugging Jane for a long time, Karma pulled away.

"Jane, right?"

Blushing, Jane nodded. "Jane Edmunds. I'm sorry for attacking you. It's just…my friend isn't here yet."

Karma smiled. "Are you here to support a friend who's coming out?"

Jane blushed even deeper. The blush looked like a sunburn against her pale blond hair and blue eyes. Karma touched her gently on the shoulder. "It's okay. Whatever reason you're here. This is a safe space."

"I hurt your feelings when we met," Jane whispered, looking at the floor.

"A little," Karma said. "But I'm not carrying a grudge."

"My parents are religious. If they found out that I'm…" She trailed off, still looking at the floor.

"A lesbian?"

Jane nodded.

Karma took her arm. "It's scary sometimes, coming out for the first time." She led Jane to the table in the back. "Why don't you take a cookie, or twenty, and tell me about it."

Jane gestured at the bins of cookies. "You're expecting a crowd, then?"

"No, but my mother got a little excited at the idea of me hosting my first group. She baked enough for three hundred. At least."

Jane laughed but her face furrowed. "I can't imagine what it would be like to have a mother like that."

"Who bakes?'

"No. Who bakes for something like this."

"What's your mother like?" Karma asked as the

two women sat down. She didn't know if this was the way she was supposed to respond. In a group meeting, the facilitator just brought up discussion items and the people in the group carried the meeting. Karma's job was supposed to be to moderate. If no one else showed up, she and Jane would be having an intense, personal conversation.

"She's wonderful in so many ways," Jane said. "She's supported me throughout all of my schooling." She paused, smiling slightly. "I'm going to be an elementary school teacher."

"That sounds lovely. I wouldn't mind being a teacher, but it would have to be older kids. I don't like little kids."

"How can you not like little kids?" Jane appeared shocked and Karma had to laugh.

"They're noisy and self-centered," she answered.

Jane nodded. "Well, older kids can be that way, too." Pausing, she looked up at Karma for the first time. "Some adults, too."

Karma laughed. "I like middle-school kids. They're still young enough to care, but old enough to reason."

"Young kids can reason," Jane said. "And they are generally so filled with hope and love."

"Maybe that's the problem. I've lost my hope and love."

Jane studied Karma's face long enough that Karma began to feel uncomfortable. She got the sensation that Jane actually cared about what she said. In a weird way, it was kind of like talking to her best friend. A best friend who gave the deepest, sexiest hugs Karma had ever felt.

"Have you?" Jane reached out and touched

Karma's hand.

Without thought, Karma wrapped her fingers through Jane's. Her fingers felt warm where her skin touched Jane's. Tempted to give a flippant answer under Jane's scrutiny, Karma shrugged. "Sometimes," she said. "Sometimes I wonder if I'm doing everything wrong."

Jane smiled and Karma's heart pounded. She didn't know what it was about this quiet woman, but there was something appealing about her. Karma repressed an urge to reach out to touch Jane's perfect little nose. Jane blinked, and Karma thought for a second that the other woman knew what she was thinking. Blushing now, she looked away from Jane.

"I'm sorry," Jane said. "I didn't mean to pry."

"You aren't prying. It's just...I don't know. I guess I'm not as put together as everyone thinks I am. I mean, friends and co-workers. Just co-workers. I don't have many friends anymore. My parents know I'm not as happy as I present to the world."

"Well, I don't know you, so I haven't formed any opinions about how put together you are. Besides, I'm a wreck. I don't have any room to judge."

Karma released Jane's hand and grabbed another cookie. It was perfectly done, just crispy enough on the outside with those little bursts of melted chocolate in every bite. "I guess no one else is showing up for the meeting."

Jane looked up at the clock on the wall. "I'm surprised David didn't show. He was supposed to meet me here."

"Who's David?"

"He's my best friend. Well, my only friend. He thinks we should both come out to our parents."

"Sometimes it takes a lot of courage," Karma said.

"It's harder for him. If he comes out, his father will beat him. David wants to tell him in a public place and try to reason with him. But I think he needs to move out of the house first."

"Does he know his father will get violent? Sometimes people surprise us."

"Not Mr. Coyle. He's…" She looked uncertain.

"He's…?"

Jane took a bite of her cookie and chewed it thoughtfully. "It's weird. I was going to say that he's a bad man. And I think he is. He hurt David badly once. Several times, actually."

Karma shifted uncomfortably. The idea of David being beaten by his father for being gay was horrific. But Karma had been hit for yelling at Crash. Was there a difference? Karma thought that the difference was that Karma's own behavior had caused Crash to hit her. Maybe David's father felt the same way about David's behavior. "No one should ever be hit for being gay," Karma said.

"No one should be hit for any reason. Never."

Karma stood abruptly. "Since no one else is coming to the meeting, what do you say we go for a walk? It's a gorgeous day. And I'd rather get Bigby's than drink this coffee."

The two women gathered the bins of cookies and took them out to the lobby. "Hey, Mr. G," Karma said. "This is Jane Edmunds. Jane, this is Mr. Gunderson."

Jane shook hands with Henry Gunderson. Karma smiled at the two. Jane looked like a doll next to Mr. G.

"I met this lovely lady when she came in," Henry said. "I'm sorry you didn't have more customers for your first meeting, but I'm happy you're sending me home with your mom's cookies."

Karma put the bins down on the desk but picked the top one up again. "We're taking these."

Henry smiled. "I'll leave these on the desk until I go home. The kids coming in for Rainbow Story Hour will love them."

Karma suddenly stood on tiptoe to kiss Henry on the cheek.

"What was that for?" Henry said, grinning.

"I wish more gay kids had dads like you."

"I'm not perfect, but I love my son more than my own ego."

Karma took Jane's hand and they walked out of the center. Stepping into the sunshine, they both tilted their faces to the sky. "Another warm day," Karma said. "I think September is my favorite month."

"Mine, too," Jane said. "But maybe because it's my birthday month."

"Mine, too," Karma exclaimed. "When is yours?"

"It was the fifteenth," Jane replied. "I turned twenty-one."

"I turned twenty-one on the fifteenth, too."

The two women stared at each other, still holding hands. Looking into Jane's eyes, Karma had that sensation of familiarity again. Jane felt so natural to her, so right. She knew now that they hadn't met before their encounter outside the bookstore, but something about her felt like coming home. They fit together. Even their entwined hands felt comfortable and secure. Without thinking about it, Karma leaned forward and kissed Jane lightly on the side of her mouth. She lingered for just a moment, smelling the faint hint of Jane's soap.

Jane breathed out in a gasp and Karma felt it on her own cheek. She pulled away and the two women stared at each other. "I'm sorry," Karma said. "It's just that…" She paused, stroking Jane's hand. "It's just that you're so beautiful."

Jane shook her head. "I'm nowhere near beautiful. But you. I've never met anyone as beautiful as you." She leaned toward Karma as if she was going to kiss her on the mouth.

Karma licked her lips and leaned in. When Jane's mouth touched hers, Karma's whole body jolted forward. Shifting the cookie bin to one arm, she wrapped the other around Jane's waist, pulling her closer. For a wild moment, she thought about Crash and the punishment this would require should she find out about it. Then Jane's lips parted just slightly, and Karma slipped her tongue as softly as she could against Jane's mouth. The other woman gasped and pulled away.

"I'm so sorry. I'm so sorry," Jane stammered, looking down. "I can't believe I did that."

"You didn't do anything," Karma said. "You didn't do anything wrong."

"It's a sin," Jane whispered. "It's a sin."

She spun around and took off at a fast walk. Karma started to go after her. She stopped. It was better to let her go. She had no right kissing another woman. Crash would kill her if she found out about this. Karma looked around furtively, but no one appeared to have noticed the earth-shattering kiss Karma had just experienced. She put her fingers to her mouth, half expecting it to feel hot to the touch. Karma looked after Jane's disappearing figure, wondering if she would ever see her again.

Chapter Four

And then what happened?" David had abandoned the box he was unpacking and was staring raptly at Jane. She blushed under his questioning, but in a way, it felt good to talk about it.

"Then she kissed me right here." Jane brought her thumb to the side of her mouth and stroked it softly, remembering. "Her lips just barely caught the side of my mouth, but it felt like she set my body on fire." She leaned back against the stack of boxes, remembering. "It felt like a cold glass of water after dragging my dehydrated body across miles of desert."

"Wow."

"I know. And I don't know what happened. I just lost my head. I kissed her. On the mouth."

"No!" David clasped a hand over his mouth.

Jane looked toward the door of the stockroom as if expecting campus security to come bursting through the door. "Yes," she whispered. "It really was like the romance novels. It felt like fireworks. It felt like coming home."

"Wow," David said again. "I hope I feel like that someday."

"You felt that with Jake."

"No. I felt turned on. I felt excited. I might have even felt love. But it didn't feel like coming home. Maybe that's how you know it's right."

Jane looked away. "If it was right, it doesn't

matter. After we kissed, I ran away. She probably thinks I'm an idiot." She turned back to the books and pulled a few out of the box she had been leaning on. "And I probably am one."

"She probably doesn't. Should we go to the group together next week? I'd like to meet her. I promise to disappear right after."

"Stop it." Jane tossed a piece of cardboard at him. "I can't go back there."

"What?" David looked shocked. "How can you say that after what you felt?"

She glared at him. "How could I say anything else? I made a fool of myself."

"If she's kind, she'll look past it. And if she isn't kind, you don't need her anyway."

Jane walked over and wrapped her arms around David. "There are a billion other reasons to walk away, David."

He returned the hug, kissing her once on the top of the head. "Jane, how can it be wrong when it feels that good?"

"I don't know," she whispered against his shirt. "I just know that whenever I think about it, I get scared. What if my mom finds out? She'll die."

"She won't die," David said. "That's her way of controlling you. She might not hit you, but in her own way, your mom is as abusive as my dad."

Jane tightened her grip on her best friend, willing herself not to cry. "That's not fair. She never meant to hurt me. She just believes that love should be between a man and a woman."

"My dad is a terrible man. It took me a long time to realize that someone as mean and violent as he is can't possibly know what kind of love is good or bad."

Jane sighed. "Maybe. Maybe I could talk to Karma. Just be friends. It would be nice to know another…"

David bent his head to whisper in her ear. "Lesbian?"

Giggling, Jane pulled back. "Stop it!"

David squeezed her hard. "Lansing is a lesbian mecca. There are more of you than there are of me. You should be able to meet women. Hang out at that bookstore, go to that one club."

Mrs. Roman, the head of the campus bookstore, popped her head in the door at that moment. "Now, now, you two. I'm not paying you to canoodle."

"Sorry, ma'am," David said, releasing Jane.

Jane apologized as well, but she noticed Mrs. Roman was smiling affectionately. So many people would be happy if she and David could just fall in love with each other. After Mrs. Roman left, Jane said as much to David.

"Yes, except us," he replied.

Jane didn't know if being with Karma would make her happy, but she knew that pretending to love a man to please her parents would not. "We should get an apartment together."

David smiled. "Do you think we could?"

"Maybe. We'd have to make more money than we do here. But if we were sharing the rent, it would make it easier for us both."

"I could leave my parents' house." David stared at her, blinking. "That would be a miracle."

"Maybe I would be braver about meeting women if I didn't have to worry about coming home to my mother," Jane said.

"Okay, let's do it. But first, let's go to the center and find your friend."

❧❧❧❧

Jane grabbed David's hand and dragged him up the stairs to the center. She was looking forward to seeing Mr. Gunderson again. She thought David would like to talk to a man who loved his son even though he was gay. Mr. G wasn't at the front desk. Instead, a young man was standing behind the desk, a pile of paperwork in his hands. Jane smiled. "I was expecting Mr. Gunderson."

"Well, you technically got Mr. Gunderson," the man replied. "I'm Carter. You're probably looking for my dad."

"Yes. Henry." Jane shook Carter's hand. "He was kind to me last week."

"He's a kind man," Carter answered. "And who is this?" He turned to David.

Jane smiled as the two men shook hands and sized each other up. Carter, not as tall as his giant of a father, was the same height as David. David was smiling in a way Jane had never seen him smile before. She looked back at Carter's face and saw he was smiling, too. The two men were still holding the handshake. Watching them, Jane didn't notice Karma until she was right next to Jane.

"Hey," Karma said, softly. "I can't believe you came back after I did such a horrible job at our last group."

Jane stared at her. Karma's face looked a little paler than the last time she saw her, but otherwise, she looked the same. *I don't know why I expected her to change in a week.* "You look tired," she said without thinking.

"I am tired. You, on the other hand, look beautiful."

Jane shook her head.

"I have a girlfriend," Karma said, suddenly. "I don't know why I kissed you. Well, I do know why. But I shouldn't have, and I'm sorry."

"It's okay." Jane's voice sounded steady, but inside she was shaking. The idea of Karma having a girlfriend hadn't crossed her mind. "Is she nice?"

Karma paused for so long Jane thought she hadn't heard. She opened her mouth to ask again when Karma finally spoke.

"She can be."

Jane didn't have a girlfriend, but she did have a best friend, and even when speaking about him, she sounded more thrilled than Karma sounded right now. Jane didn't know if Karma was sad because having a girlfriend meant she couldn't kiss Jane anymore, or because her girlfriend wasn't a nice person. *It's none of my business anyway.*

"I want to be your friend," Jane said. "We'll just have to be careful not to kiss again."

Karma laughed. "I want to be your friend, too. And I'll try to restrain myself from kissing you."

The two women walked toward the meeting room. Jane called back over her shoulder, "Are you coming, David?"

"Oh, yeah. In a minute."

Jane thought David might be blushing, but it was hard to tell under the week's stubble on his face. He had recently come up with the ridiculous idea that a beard would make him look manlier and, therefore, more palatable to his father.

"What's new in your world?" Karma asked as

they gathered again next to the cookies.

"David and I are thinking of trying to get an apartment together. We both have nine months until we graduate, but neither of us think we can wait that long."

"Having your own place is liberating," Karma said. "Can you afford it?"

"No. But we could if we both got full-time jobs instead of part-time ones."

"How would that affect your schoolwork?"

"I would probably be exhausted until I graduate," Jane answered. "But it would take David out of his parents' house."

"And you out of your situation."

Jane sighed. "They aren't as bad as all that. My dad is sweet. But he just wants to get along with my mother. She can't help it, either. Her chest pains act up when she's upset."

"I don't suppose her chest pains are stress-related," Karma said.

"Probably. But that doesn't make them less real."

They chewed for a few minutes. Finally Jane said, "I guess David isn't coming in."

"Well he and Carter looked rather cozy out there." Karma grinned.

"They just met."

"We just met and we kissed in the street."

"That was an accident," Jane insisted.

"An accident." Karma snickered. "Our faces fell on each other."

"You know what I mean!"

"I know. I didn't mean to kiss you. It's just that you felt so familiar, so…"

Jane answered for her. "So much like home?"

"Yes. When you hugged me for the first time, it felt like a homecoming."

"Maybe we're soulmates."

"What would you know about soulmates?"

"I may be religious, but I read other things than the Bible."

Karma stood and held out a hand to Jane. "Soulmates or not, I have a girlfriend and you have parents who think homosexuality is a sin. Let's go find the guys."

Jane took Karma's hand and stood, facing her. Jane could feel the blush creeping up her face as Karma held the gaze longer. Karma's face was so beautiful, Jane wanted to trace her fingers along the curve of her jaw and over her full lips. Karma's hair, so thick and curly in comparison to Jane's flat, blond hair, looked luscious. Compelled, Jane reached out to touch Karma's hair and the other woman sighed softly. Terrified, Jane told herself to stop, but her body refused to listen. She released Karma's hand and reached her other hand up to Karma's hair. Entwining both hands into the thick curls, Jane pulled Karma lightly toward her and pressed her lips to Karma's sweet mouth. The electricity shot through her again. It wasn't a one-time fluke. The desire that flooded her body was deeper than what she experienced kissing Karma last week. She parted her lips slightly, asking Karma to give her that tongue again. She felt just the tip of Karma's tongue brush her upper lip and she moaned, crushing her lips down against Karma's mouth. Karma's arms snaked around to Jane's hips and to pull her tightly against Karma's own slender body. Jane's body burned from the inside. She felt a tingling that started low in her belly and traveled both up and down. For a wild moment, she thought about pressing her hand to Karma's breast. Suddenly, Karma pulled away, breaking the spell.

Jane stepped back, breathing heavily.

"We better go," she whispered. She turned and half-ran out of the room with Karma following closely behind. When they reached the lobby, David and Carter were sitting behind the desk, laughing. Jane was surprised to see them holding hands on the desk.

A booming voice broke the moment. Henry Gunderson strode through the front door, smiling. Carter stood up and walked around the desk, greeting his father with a hug. "Dad, I'm so glad you're here. I want to take this man out for coffee and I didn't want to leave the desk without supremely responsible coverage."

"Yeah, yeah, yeah," Henry said, waving his hand. "Don't worry about me. I'll just work all day while you all have fun." He held out a hand to David. "I don't think we've met before."

"David Coyle, sir," David said, shaking Henry's hand. "It's a pleasure to meet you. I've heard a lot about you already."

"How long have you known my son?"

"About an hour, sir."

Jane laughed with Henry, who turned and gave her a wink. "If my son has been chatting with you for an hour and all he has talked about is how great his old man is, he needs to work on his game."

Carter laughed. "Dad, David's father is vehemently anti-gay. Of course I had to talk about you. I don't want anyone to ever think that they deserve to be treated like shit because of who they are."

Henry smiled, slinging his arm around his son. "It's not like I was the perfect dad when he came out, though."

"Perfectly imperfect," Carter said. "And you've more than made up for it." He paused, reaching a hand to touch David's shoulder. "And he never hit me."

Jane watched them, marveling at the warmth between Henry and Carter. She loved her parents, but she couldn't say that she liked them. Not like this. She glanced at David, who looked floored. They would have a lot to talk about next time they had a private moment.

Karma took Jane's hand. "Mr. G, there are cookies in the meeting room, so please help yourself. We're going to walk through town and get some coffee."

Carter smiled. "We were going to walk down by the Capitol to that little coffee shop on Washington. May we join you?"

Leaving Henry, they stepped into the sunshine and crossed the street. Cutting across the parking lot to the sidewalk around the state library, Jane saw Carter take David's hand. The two men smiled at each other and Jane thought it looked so natural. She turned to look at Karma, who had noticed her watching the men. Karma was still holding Jane's hand, but Jane didn't feel nearly as comfortable as David looked. As they reached the middle of the park, two men on bicycles went by.

"Faggots," one of them called over his shoulder.

Burning with shame, Jane yanked her hand away from Karma. Shocked, she saw Carter raise his middle finger in the air at the departing cyclists.

"Dicks," Karma yelled after them. Jane cringed. She looked around to see if anyone noticed. Karma touched her hand again, but Jane pulled it away, tucking her hands into her pockets. *That's what happens when people are gay.* And though part of her knew that those men were jerks and that Carter and David and Karma were good people who didn't deserve to be treated like that, another part of her kept saying, *But it's a sin. And you are a sinner.* Sinners didn't deserve happiness. Sinners deserved only death unless they repented and sought forgiveness. Looking at Karma, Jane wondered how she could repent for falling in love with someone so beautiful. Blinking back her tears, she followed the group into the coffee shop.

Chapter Five

Karma dialed into the computer and checked for messages. Jane was just getting used to using the chat function. She was still afraid her mother would somehow be able to see that Jane was using the family computer to talk to a lesbian. Jane had figured out how to attach a picture to the message, but it was the most unflattering picture Karma had ever seen. Jane had taken the picture from chest level, with the camera tilted up at her face. It accentuated the dark circles under her beautiful blue eyes. She looked as if she hadn't been sleeping well. Karma's heart melted. Karma knew she shouldn't stay in contact with Jane, not while she was still involved with Crash, and certainly not while Jane was still terrified of her mother. Yet, she couldn't stay away. And neither, it seemed, could Jane. Her instant message chimed again. This time, it was a picture of David and Jane making faces. Karma laughed out loud before clapping her hand across her face. She didn't want to wake up Crash.

Karma had been surprised when Jane found a full-time job. She didn't think Jane would follow through on her decision to get an apartment with David and leave her fragile mother. Yet, she'd hit the streets shortly after their coffee non-date and had a job lined up as a receptionist within a week. The contact came from a woman in Jane's church, so Karma had to admit there was some good to come out of Jane's association with that community. Of course, moving out meant Jane wouldn't have a computer anymore, unless David was bringing one they could share. Karma was seriously considering getting a mobile phone so she and Jane could talk. She didn't think Crash would let her spend money on something so frivolous, especially not to talk to another woman, even if they were just friends. *Best friends*, Karma thought, smiling.

She got up and rummaged around in the fridge, hoping to find something to eat. If she didn't eat breakfast now, she'd be tempted to shovel pastries into her mouth at work all day. She hated working in an office. People brought candy and cookies and cake in every single day. All she ever did was eat. She poked her belly and watched it ripple. *Even skinny people get jelly bellies if they eat doughnuts all day.*

Her computer chimed again, and she bent over to look at the screen. Another message from Jane. *Do you want to have coffee together after work? I have news.* Crash had band practice tonight, so more likely than not, she'd be gone by the time Karma got home anyway. Karma needed Crash to start making some money with her new band. She was paying the entire rent on her own. Before Crash met Wanda, the guitar player, Crash had at least picked up odd jobs here and there. But now she spent all her time at band practice and hadn't contributed any money to the household in weeks. Karma needed to ask her for some money or she wasn't going to be able to buy groceries this week. She wrote back to Jane. *Can't afford coffee. How about a walk?* Pausing for a moment, she swallowed her pride before sending a quick email to her mother. *Mom, I'm sorry. Can I stop by at lunch and get something to eat?*

Karma figured she could always quit volunteering

at the center and pick up Tuesdays again. She loved working four days a week, but the extra day's pay would help cover some of the slack.

She picked the last banana from the counter and peeled it. Cutting off the worst of the brown spots, she ate it, waiting for a response from Jane. Crash stumbled in, rubbing her eyes.

"Is that the last banana?"

"Yes, I'm sorry."

"Fuck. What am I supposed to eat? There's no food in this house."

Karma held out the other half of the banana. "You can have the rest of this."

"Forget it. I'll figure something else out."

Crash poked through the fridge, slamming jars together, before turning to the cupboard and pawing around in there. Karma jumped as the cupboard door slammed.

"I guess I'll go hungry," Crash muttered. "Are you going shopping after work today?"

Karma shook her head. "I can't afford it. Do you have any money you can give me until my next paycheck?"

Crash slammed her hand down on the counter and Karma jumped so hard she dropped the last piece of banana. Staring at it, she felt tears starting to well up. Her computer beeped and she bent over to look at it. It was an email from her mother. *Of course, love. Want to come over for breakfast and dinner, too?*

Karma laughed. It was so like her mother.

"Who's that?" Crash asked.

"My mom. I asked her if I could come over for lunch today. I can't keep eating doughnuts for every meal."

"At least you get a meal," Crash said. "I thought we had an agreement that you would take care of things around here until I get the band going."

"We never agreed to that," Karma said. "We never talked about it." She couldn't believe she was arguing with Crash, but she was tired of constantly worrying about money. They lived in a crappy dark little apartment and the rent was low, but Karma simply did not make enough money to support two people.

"Are you kidding me?" Crash advanced on her. "I've taken care of you all this time and now you're going to back out right as I'm making it big?"

Karma reached down to pick up the fallen banana. She walked over to the trash and threw it away, putting some distance between herself and Crash.

"I'm not backing out of anything. I just need you to contribute a little. I don't think I'm being unreasonable. I can't afford to support you."

"That's rich," Crash yelled. "How many times have I paid for your pot or your drinks when we've gone out? How many times have I taken us to restaurants? Where would you be if it wasn't for me? Living with your parents?"

Karma straightened her shoulders and stood up to her full height. Even though Crash still towered over her, Karma was tired of being bullied. "When I lived with my parents, I had a savings account. If I hadn't moved in here, I was on track to buy my own house in five years. Where is all that money now? Gone to a new bass. Gone to drugs. Gone to that vacation you simply had to take because you needed artistic motivation."

Crash walked toward her until they were inches apart. She glared at Karma, her hands closing into fists. "Are you telling me you would be better off without me?"

Karma didn't mean that. She never meant that. She was angry, yes, but she didn't want to lose Crash. "Crash, that's not—" Her computer pinged again. Ignoring it, she touched Crash's arm. "I'm sorry. I'm so sorry. That really isn't what I meant. Maybe I can borrow some money from my parents to tide us over until you get your first paying gig."

Karma's computer beeped again and this time, Crash shoved Karma out of the way to look at it. "Someone is obviously desperate to get in touch with you."

She read the message and jabbed her finger at the screen. "Who's Jane?"

Karma glanced at the message that had popped up. *I'll buy. You're worth the price of a cup of coffee.*

"She's a friend of mine from work," Karma said. She could feel a flush creeping up her cheeks.

"A friend. That message sounds friendly, all right."

Karma closed the program and shut down the computer, so no more messages could come through. "Crash, she is just a friend. She's nice and I like her. People have friends."

"Don't take that tone with me."

"I wasn't taking a tone, I promise."

Crash grabbed Karma by the back of her neck, squeezing a handful of hair in her fist. Karma cried out. "Crash, that hurts."

"Have you fucked her?"

"No, I swear it. She's just a friend."

"I don't believe you," Crash whispered. "I bet you've been fucking her while I've been working to make a dream for us."

Suddenly mad, Karma reared back, yanking her hair free. "Just because you think it's okay to fuck any woman you meet, it doesn't mean I do."

Karma's head slammed back against the cupboard as Crash's hand pounded into her mouth. Karma reached out for the refrigerator handle, trying to keep from falling. Crash reared back and slammed her fist into Karma's stomach.

With a loud exhale of breath, Karma moaned and fell forward to the floor. On her knees, she gasped for air, sure she was going to stop breathing. She could taste banana in her throat and it made her want to puke. She retched for a moment but didn't throw up. At the edge of her awareness, she realized that Crash had left the room, but Karma didn't know if she had left the apartment. Still trying to breathe, she managed to pull herself to her feet, grabbing for the phone on the kitchen wall. She squinted at the phone with blurry eyes, trying to will the numbers to stand still so she could call her mom. She wasn't sure if she was losing vision because she couldn't breathe or because she was crying. She finally managed to dial her parents' house. "I need help," she gasped into the phone. "Can you come get me?"

She dropped the phone and lowered herself into a kitchen chair. A few minutes later, Karma felt as if she could take a full breath again. She focused on breathing calmly, her head on the table. She listened intently, but she didn't hear any noises from the apartment. Maybe Crash had left. Karma hoped she did. She couldn't imagine looking at her girlfriend's face because at this moment, Karma hated her.

The urge to throw up had left. She rubbed her stomach. She wondered if it was possible to give someone internal damage from a stomach punch. When she lifted her head up, Karma was surprised to see the tops of her hands were covered with blood. She reached a hand up to her mouth and wiped at it. Looking at the blood on her fingertips, she started crying. She should never have pushed Crash so far. She knew Crash was losing it. She should have just apologized. Karma knew better than to bait her when she was angry. It just infuriated her to think of Jane in the same category of the women she knew Crash was picking up at various parties and bars. Those drug- and alcohol-fueled encounters weren't anything like the sweet kisses Karma and Jane had shared.

Now that the pain in her stomach was subsiding, she was intently aware of the throbbing in her mouth. Too tired to get up and walk to the bathroom, Karma reached behind her for a dish towel and held it to her mouth.

The apartment door slammed open and Karma jumped. She heard her mother's voice calling her name.

"Mom, I'm in here."

Karma's parents appeared in the doorway. "Oh, my baby," Henna said. Sitting down, she pulled Karma into her arms and Karma sobbed against her mother's breasts.

"Mom, she hit me."

"We're going to get you out of here," Karma's dad said. "No arguments. Your mother and I will pack your things."

Karma knew her dad was right. With Crash away, Karma could think clearly, but when they were together, when Crash was being kind, she could always convince Karma that it would never happen again. Wrapped in her mother's arms with her dad standing guard over her, Karma felt at peace. *The way I feel when I'm holding Jane.* She allowed the thought for a moment before banishing it.

With her parents' help, Karma washed her face and got an ice pack. Once Henna determined that Karma didn't need stitches—"She hit me open-handed, at least in the face," Karma had said—the three of them set about packing Karma's stuff. As Karma and her mother packed things into boxes and shoulder bags and purses and plastic grocery bags, her father ran everything down the stairs and into the vehicles. When they were almost finished, Henna picked up a baggie of pot from the bedside table and held it up. "I don't have a problem with this, Karma. Lord knows I've smoked more than my share. But I don't want it in the house."

Karma shrugged. "Leave it for Crash. I'm leaving her in a lurch as it is."

"She abused you, sweetie. You don't owe her anything. If she ends up sleeping on the streets because you aren't paying the rent, I won't shed a tear."

Karma rested her head on her mother's shoulder for a moment. She knew Henna was right, but that didn't stop her from feeling guilty. Crash had had a hard life. Her father had been abusive, and she had lived in the streets when she was a teenager. She couldn't help the way she was.

Henna stroked Karma's hair. "You deserve so much better."

"I hope so," Karma replied.

❧ ❧ ❧ ❧

Karma had to promise her parents repeatedly that she would be fine, that she wouldn't try to see

Crash, and that she would be home before dark before she could leave the house to meet Jane. She couldn't blame them. Karma had played with fire and she got burned. *But*, she had told her mother, *Jane was her safe space.*

Jane was waiting at the coffee shop when Karma walked in. Jane jumped up and immediately pulled Karma into a soft hug. "What happened?" Karma curled into the hug and let Jane's warm breath wash across her neck. "Karma? What happened to your face?"

"It's a long story," Karma said, passing a hand across her visage. Her stomach didn't really hurt anymore, but her mouth still throbbed with her heartbeat.

"Does it hurt?"

"Horribly," Karma replied. "It didn't hurt as much when it first happened, but later I wanted to die from the pain." She shrugged. "It still hurts like hell. I might want an iced coffee instead."

Jane guided Karma to a chair. "Stay here. I'll get us coffee."

Karma watched her walk away. She was so kind and full of genuine compassion. It didn't matter how bad Karma felt, just being close to Jane made her feel better. She watched the straight line of Jane's swinging hair and smiled. She liked when it wasn't pulled back in a tight ponytail or a bun. Jane turned and winked at Karma from the counter. Karma's heart swelled, and she blinked to keep from crying. She was in a bad place. She had just left Crash. She was messed up and she was going to be living with her parents, at least for the near future. She knew she didn't really have a good girlfriend pedigree. She thought of all the things Crash found lacking in her. She didn't communicate well, she was needy, she didn't keep the house clean enough, she didn't know when to shut up. She could work on all those things. And somehow, watching Jane's face as she walked back to the table with their coffee, Karma thought that Jane wouldn't find her so lacking. Maybe all the things she found so bad about herself with Crash wouldn't matter when she was with Jane. If Jane was really her soulmate—and Karma believed that she was—they would be perfect for each other. They would love each other unconditionally. Imperfectly perfect. Karma reached for Jane's hand as she handed over the coffee and the two women sat together, holding hands, and looking at each other.

"Do you want to talk about it?"

Karma took a sip of her coffee. The coldness felt good against her throbbing mouth. She shook her head. "I don't want to talk about it. I want to hear your news." She stared at Jane's face, moving closer in her chair. Jane's eyes were a deeper blue than Karma had realized, and it took her a second to figure out why. "You're not wearing glasses!"

"You don't have to sound so accusatory." Jane was laughing. "I have contacts. I just don't put them in very often because they're a pain in the ass."

"You look beautiful."

"No," Jane said. "But thank you for saying so."

"For believing so," Karma insisted.

"You're my best friend, Karma. You're my safe space. I love David with my whole heart, but being with you is like coming home."

"I feel the same way," Karma whispered. "I knew it from the first moment I met you."

"We're going to be friends forever," Jane said. "I can feel it."

Friends. Karma squeezed Jane's hand. There was

so much more than a friendly connection between them. Karma saw them getting married, adopting children, living happily ever after. She thought Crash had been her lesson in what she didn't want so that she could be open to her soulmate. Squeezing Jane's hand again, Karma leaned in and kissed her on the cheek. Jane closed her eyes and melted toward Karma.

Lost in the warmth of Jane leaning against her, Karma closed her eyes. Suddenly blinking, she sat up straight. "Did I fall asleep?"

"Just for a moment. You must be exhausted."

"It was a long day." Karma smiled. "An incredibly long day."

"You can tell me all about it or we can sit here in silence."

Karma took another sip of her iced coffee. "No, I want to hear your news."

Jane looked down at the table, silent for a moment.

"Jane?" Karma prodded. "What's your news?"

Jane looked up, meeting Karma's eyes. "I have a date," she said. "I met a woman at church who is also… like me."

"Like us," Karma corrected.

"Like us. She's…"

"A lesbian?"

Jane cringed and slumped down in her seat, her eyes looking everywhere in the room but at Karma.

"No one heard me, Jane. Or if they did, no one cares," Karma said.

"Well, she's a lesbian," Jane whispered. "She's in the closet with her parents, too, of course."

"Of course," Karma answered.

Jane touched Karma's hair. "I thought you'd be happy for me."

Karma looked at her incredulously. "Why would I be happy for you? I thought we had a connection."

"We do. We always will. But you have a girlfriend. And I… I'm not ready to be with someone who can yell lesbian in a coffee shop and not care who hears."

Karma glared down at the table. "You're giving up on me because I'm proud of who I am."

"No," Jane said. "I'm giving up on you because I'm not proud of who I am."

Chapter Six

Jane climbed down from the ladder and stepped back to survey the handiwork. She and David had been painting all day. Their new apartment was amazing. It was tiny, and her bedroom had barely enough room for a chest of drawers and a full-size bed, but it was hers. It was all hers and she could do whatever she wanted to it. In this case, that freedom meant painting the room a lovely shade of peach. She had found a perfect quilt at the thrift store with shades of blues and peaches in it, and she had decided at that moment that she was going to base her entire bedroom around that quilt.

"It's gorgeous," David said. "When this dries, we can move your bed back in and start on the living room."

"Yes. I can't wait to show you the color samples I picked up at Home Depot."

"You're becoming a true lesbian," David said. "Shopping at the Depot. Tomorrow I'll come home to find you wearing flannel."

Jane laughed. "It's not my style."

"At any rate," David said. "The homo gene passed me by as far as decorating goes. My room is staying white. And I'm sure whatever color you pick for the living room will be perfect."

"Wait till Karma gets here," Jane said. "She has the best eye for color."

"Yeah, except it will end up looking like a throwback from the sixties," David said.

"Hey. Karma has great style."

"I'm teasing," he said, holding his hands up. "Don't shoot."

"Sorry."

"When are you two going to admit you are in love with each other and get it over with?"

"We aren't in love," Jane said. "At least, she isn't. She's still grieving over Crash, crazy as that is."

"And you?"

"I don't know, David. I've never been in love before. Is that what it feels like? I've never kissed anyone other than Karma. Maybe this is how it feels when you kiss someone. Maybe I need to kiss other women to make sure."

"I don't know." David leaned against the ladder. "I've kissed a few men. I didn't fall in love with most of them."

"Most?" Jane raised an eyebrow.

"How do you know Karma isn't in love with you?"

Jane shrugged. "I just know. She sent me an article the other day about soulmates being best friends."

"Hmm. Well, I'm not your soulmate and you're my best friend." He looked at his phone. "Shit. I'm going to be late for work."

"Go. I'll clean up. Thank you for your help."

David kissed her on the cheek as he headed for the shower. "Don't wait up for me tonight," he called. "I have another date with Carter."

Jane sighed. "I can see you two in a little house with a porch and a yard and a couple of kids."

"You're a romantic." He slammed the bathroom

door.

Jane picked up the paint supplies and went to the kitchen to start a pot of coffee. Karma liked doughnuts on Saturday mornings. Since they both had weekends off now, it seemed they spent most of their Saturday mornings together at the apartment. Jane thought Karma would love the new bedroom color. She didn't know why it was so important that Karma loved it. *I guess because she's my best friend.*

A knock at the door sent Jane running to the living room. She opened the door and threw herself into Karma's arms, knocking the doughnut box askew.

"Whoa, settle down." Karma laughed. She wrapped one arm around Jane, trying to hold on to the box of doughnuts. "Why is your bed in the living room?"

"We painted my room. Can't you smell it?"

"Now that you mention it…"

Jane released Karma and grabbed the box of doughnuts. "Did you bring me a chocolate-cream-filled?"

"Always," Karma said.

They poked their heads into the bedroom so Karma could admire the new color. "It's gorgeous. I love how soft and comforting it feels. It's going to look great with that quilt."

Warm inside, Jane hugged the box of doughnuts closer to her chest. Karma had loved the idea of building the color scheme around the new quilt. Jane was happy it paid off.

They moved into the kitchen and Jane poured them each a cup of coffee. She put one sugar and a dollop of cream into Karma's cup. She liked knowing exactly how Karma took her coffee. It made her feel needed, like there was something special she could always give her best friend. Handing the cup to Karma, Jane smiled.

"Thank you," Karma said. "You always make it exactly right."

"Everyone has to have a talent."

Jane studied Karma's face. The bruise had disappeared, but the sadness hadn't. "Do you miss her?"

Karma sat down in a kitchen chair. "No. Sometimes. I don't so much miss her as think about what was so bad about me that she had to hit me."

Jane sat down, taking both Karma's hands in hers. "You didn't do anything wrong."

Karma shook her head. "I tell myself that. Except, I really did. Right before she hit me, I just had a flash that she was on the edge, and I pushed it. Part of me knew I was pushing her to hit me."

"If that's true, it's because part of you knew you needed to get out and you didn't know if you would be able to make yourself do it without an extreme situation."

"Being smacked in the face and punched in the stomach is definitely extreme."

Jane stared down at the table to hide the flash of anger in her eyes. Karma was so soft, kind, and loving. Jane couldn't imagine anyone wanting to hurt her. She stroked Karma's hands for a moment. When she looked back up, she smiled. "You got out. That's the important thing. God was watching over you."

"No, my parents were watching over me. You should have seen my mom butting chests with Crash when she came over to try to talk to me."

"You should have called the police."

"I don't want to talk about her," Karma said.

"Tell me about your date."

Jane sipped her coffee for a moment, taking time to think about it. The date had been weird and awkward, not at all like the time she spent with Karma. But maybe that's because it was a date. There was an anticipation or an expectation that it would feel romantic. Jane hadn't felt romantic. She had been on edge the whole time, wondering if the other people in the restaurant knew she was on a date or if anyone from their church would walk in. Not that they were doing anything noteworthy. They talked about Jane's schooling and her new job and Carol's work and the church and whether Jane was going to come back to church sometime soon.

"It was nice," she said, finally.

"Nice?" Karma laughed. She reached across the table and dragged the box of doughnuts over. Rummaging around in the box, she pulled out a chocolate-cream-filled and a glazed. She handed Jane a doughnut before biting into hers. "Nice is a crap word for a date," she said around a mouthful of sweet glaze.

"Well it was nice. Just because it wasn't super exciting or anything doesn't mean it wasn't nice."

"I'm sorry, I'm sorry." Karma was still smiling. "I didn't mean anything by it."

"She wants me to come back to church," Jane said. "I told her I couldn't come back to a system that allowed for the oppression of people like us."

"Interesting. What did she say?"

"She said it will change, but only if we continue to be part of the community."

"That makes sense. As more gay people are out in church, more people will have to acknowledge that they are friends and neighbors with gay people." She lowered her voice dramatically. "We are everywhere!"

"It would make sense if she was out at church. She isn't. And anyway, I don't have the strength to be an example. I'm learning that I was born this way and I'm learning that there are gay people who are wonderful, loving people like you and David and Carter…" She trailed off, picking her doughnut apart with her fingers. "It's just—"

"You aren't ready to believe that you're a good person."

Jane shrugged. "I guess." She popped a piece of doughnut into her mouth. "I'm mostly just afraid that coming out will kill my mother."

"Your mother isn't going to die from you living your own life," David said, coming into the kitchen. He leaned over the doughnut box and grabbed two.

He kissed Karma on the top of the head before moving toward the door. "Thanks, I love ya."

The women laughed as the front door slammed. "He's going to work and then another date with Carter," Jane said.

"Mr. G likes David a lot," Karma said. "Carter is a good man, too. What will happen when Carter leaves for Yale?"

"They haven't discussed it that far," Jane said. "David said they're taking it slow and getting to know each other. David hasn't had a serious boyfriend before, and Carter was dumped pretty hard by his last lover. I think it's good that they're trying it out cautiously."

"Is that what you're going to do with Carol?"

Jane thought for a moment. "I guess."

Karma stood up for another cup of coffee.

"You're upset," Jane said.

"No."

Jane pursed her lips. "I can feel you," she said. "Please don't hide from me."

Karma put her cup down and leaned against the sink. Jane stood to face her. "Talk to me, Karma. I can feel you and it's making me feel anxious."

"I feel anxious, too," Karma said. "I feel…" She paused, looking at Jane's face. "I feel like I don't want you to go on another date with Carol."

Jane looked into Karma's face. There were a million reasons she and Karma should remain friends. They were too different. Being in public with Karma made Jane nervous, afraid that her outspokenness would get them killed or worse, seen by someone from the church who could take it back to Jane's mother. And Karma would never go back in the closet, not even for short periods of time. Not that Jane would ask her to hide her true self. Jane loved Karma and she was proud of how open she was. In Jane's heart, she wished she could be more like Karma. But she wasn't, and she thought that trying to make herself into someone she wasn't, even for a woman as amazing as Karma, would just be another form of hiding.

"Of course you don't," Jane said brightly. "You think she's boring and you would never want me to date someone boring." She turned around, grabbing her coffee cup from the table. Avoiding Karma's eyes, she filled both cups and busied herself adding cream and sugar. "But I promise you will like her." She turned to look at Karma. "You're my best friend," she said, softly. "I need you to know that."

Karma wrapped her arms around Jane and the two women held each other. "I know that," Karma said. "I know it."

Chapter Seven

Karma ran around the corner to the back hallway of Sheri's Bar. She had to pee so badly, she wasn't sure she was going to make it. Slamming into the bathroom, she found a line. Bouncing from foot to foot, she prayed it would go fast. The woman in front of her smiled. "You can go ahead of me, kid. I think yours is more of an emergency."

Karma nodded. "Thank you. I don't know why I waited until it was painful."

"Because you've been drinking and we all make stupid decisions when we're drinking. Especially when we're afternoon drinking. Why is that?"

"Not peeing in time is probably the least stupid drunk decision I've ever made," Karma said.

"Same here. Most of mine involve inappropriate men."

"Most of mine involve inappropriate women." Karma smiled.

The woman laughed. "Gay or straight, it doesn't matter. We all still make stupid mistakes in love."

The person in one of the stalls finished and the woman waved Karma ahead. She made it just in time. When she came out of the stall, she headed toward the sink and stopped short. She'd recognize Crash's back anywhere.

Before she had a chance to debate ducking back into the stall, Crash's eyes met hers in the mirror.

Karma took the other sink and started washing her hands.

"Hey, Kars."

"Hey."

Crash leaned against the dryer, blocking access to it. Karma stared at her.

"Would you move, please?"

Crash shrugged, moving just far enough that Karma could put her hands under the vent. Karma held her hands under the air stream, trying to blink herself sober. She needed to be clear-headed to deal with Crash.

"Karma." Crash's voice was low and affectionate and for a second, Karma's heart flip-flopped.

Her hands were dry enough. Wiping the last remaining drops on her jeans, Karma turned to leave the bathroom. Crash grabbed her shoulder.

"I just want to talk to you."

Karma yanked her shoulder away and whirled around to face her ex. "I don't want to talk to you."

"Karma, I know I lost my temper. I shouldn't have been so harsh with you. I'm so sorry, babe." She stroked Karma's hair. Blurred by the alcohol, Karma tried to remind herself why this was a bad idea. She tried to convince herself to stalk away but her legs weren't obeying. Crash's bangs were hanging in her face. Karma reached up and swept it back with her fingers. She pulled back immediately. Crash smiled. "I was harder on you than I should have been, babe. I lost my temper. I was so hurt that you were messaging like that with another woman. I didn't understand why I wasn't enough."

Karma shook her head, confused. She couldn't remember the details of the fight, but she did remember yelling at Crash. She was upset because Crash had been ugly about Jane. Jane, who thought they were soulmates but who was so embarrassed by Karma that she couldn't bear the idea of being her lover. Jane wanted to be friends because she was too ashamed to be Karma's lover. Karma never embarrassed Crash. She lifted her face to Crash's. "You hit me, though."

"I know I did. I was hurt and then you yelled at me and I lost my temper. But then you left me without a word. Just disappeared. That was like a gut punch."

"I know," Karma whispered. "I just had to get out and I was scared because you hit me." She paused, trying to formulate the words. "It wasn't the first time."

"Oh, babe, come on. If you're talking about that playful slap, you're crazy. That couldn't have even hurt."

Karma thought back. Maybe it hadn't hurt as much as she remembered.

Crash leaned closer, twisting her fingers lightly into Karma's hair. "You're such a sweet girl, babe. But I feel like you're always looking for reasons to make me the bad guy. It hurts that you keep looking for reasons to hate me." Crash blinked, and Karma was sure she was about to cry.

Her head tilted against Crash's hands and her scalp tingled at the feel of Crash's fingers in her hair. Karma touched Crash's arm. "I'm sorry. I didn't mean to hurt you."

"Let's head back to our place—my place—and talk about it," Crash said.

One of the stalls slammed open and the woman who had been in line came out. She stalked to the sink, brushing past Crash. Washing her hands, she cleared her throat loud enough to startle Karma into looking up. The woman was staring into the mirror and Karma met her eyes. The woman glared for a moment before turning off the water and turning around.

"Remember we were talking about making stupid mistakes when we've been drinking?"

"Yes, ma'am," Karma said.

"This is one of the moments."

"Hey," Crash interrupted. "Mind your own business."

The woman straightened up and stared into Crash's face. "It is my business when a woman is being abused."

Karma stared from one to the other. Was she an abused woman? Crash didn't mean to lose her temper. Karma knew if she could learn to not trigger Crash's anger, she wouldn't get hit.

Crash grabbed Karma's arm at the elbow and started pulling her toward the door. "Let's go now."

The woman held out a hand to Karma and Karma took it. Holding hands for a moment, they stared at each other silently. Crash tugged on Karma's arm and she yanked it away. "That hurt!"

"I'm sorry. I just think you should listen to me over some busybody in the bathroom."

The woman, still holding Karma's hand, ignored Crash completely. "Listen to me carefully. You have been drinking and you are unable to make rational decisions. You probably feel confused and a little disoriented. You're starting to ask yourself if you were justified in leaving. You might be thinking that she only hit you because you asked for it."

Karma nodded, her eyes filling with tears. "I'm so ashamed."

"My name is Jody," the woman said. She patted

Karma on the shoulder. "There's nothing to be ashamed of. But you need to stay with me right now instead of going with Hair-Trigger over there."

"And you need to get the fuck out of this bathroom and mind your own fucking business," Crash yelled.

Another woman tried to come into the bathroom, slamming the door into Crash.

"Watch where you're fucking going," Crash roared. She slammed the door back into the woman, knocking her down to the floor outside of the bathroom. The woman started screaming.

"This is your fault," Crash yelled. She reached out to grab Karma by the hand Jody wasn't holding. Yanking her away, she opened the door and stepped into the hall, around the woman who was lying on the ground. Two large men in logo T-shirts came up. One of them was Karma's server.

"Mother fucker." Crash pushed past the men and took off, leaving Karma standing in the doorway, rubbing her wrists.

"It was her," the woman on the floor said, pointing after Crash. "She knocked me down." Jody came out of the bathroom behind Karma and reached down to help the woman up. One of the servers took her other hand and together, they pulled her to her feet. "Are you all right?" he asked.

The woman gave him a thumbs-up. "I'm fine."

The man nodded toward Jody and Karma. "You two okay?"

"We're fine," Jody said.

"We're gonna go make sure she leaves the bar," he said, jogging away.

Jody smiled at the other woman before putting her arm around Karma and guiding her back to the main room. "Where are your friends?"

"I'm just here with David and Jane," Karma said. "They're....in the back, I think."

Jody led Karma through the bar until she spotted her friends in the corner. They both jumped up and walked toward her.

"We were starting to get worried," David said, touching her arm. "Are you okay?"

"I'm fine," Karma said. "I crashed into my ex in the bathroom. Get it? Crashed?"

Jane smiled at Jody. "Thank you for taking care of her."

Jody smiled. "Women have to stick together. You take care of this one." She gave Karma a hug. "Did you see what she did to the stranger in the hallway?"

Karma nodded.

Jody touched Karma's shoulder. "That's all on her, kid. That stranger did nothing but walk into a bathroom at the wrong moment and that bad news ex of yours knocked her down hard. You want to tell me that was somehow that woman's fault?"

Karma shook her head, staring down. "I'm sorry."

"You have nothing to apologize for. I promise." She pulled away, digging in her purse. Pulling out a business card, she handed it to Karma. "I've been there, and my ex almost killed me. You ever feel the need to go back or you want to talk, or you just get anxiety in the middle of the night, you call me. Got it?"

"Thank you, Jody." Jody nodded and patted Karma on the shoulder before turning away. Karma watched her walk away, trying to compose her face before turning back to David and Jane. "So," she said, turning around. "That was interesting."

"Oh, Karma." Jane took her hand and led her

back to their table. "I should never have let you go to the bathroom by yourself."

"You being there probably would have made it worse."

"You never should have had a Long Island Iced Tea before lunch."

"David had one." Karma knew she sounded petulant, but she didn't care.

"I outweigh you by about a hundred pounds," David said, grinning. "Don't feel bad, Karma. We just should have waited until after we got our burgers."

They sat down and waited for their food. Karma didn't want to talk about it. She didn't want to tell them how close she had come to leaving with Crash. She looked at Jane and Jane smiled at her. It was incredible how her eyes seemed bluer when she was smiling. Karma wanted to touch Jane's hair, but she stopped herself.

David broke the silence. "Are you okay, Karma?"

"I'm okay. It was just freaky running into her. And she yelled and knocked down a woman trying to come into the bathroom."

Jane gasped. "Is she okay?"

"Yeah. She's fine. And two employees went after Crash to make her leave."

Their server came up with the food. He looked at Karma as he set down her plate. "Are you all right?"

"Yes. Did she leave?"

"She took off before we got to her."

Karma smiled. "Thank you for stepping in."

The man nodded and set down the rest of the plates. Karma concentrated on her plate for a few minutes, enjoying the taste of the perfectly cooked burger. Jane kept reaching out to touch Karma's hand now and then and every time she did, Karma looked into Jane's eyes and smiled. The differences between Jane and Crash were legion. Sitting quietly next to Jane, Karma couldn't believe that she had almost been talked into walking away with Crash. She must have a broken circuit somewhere that made her want to punish herself. "You would never hit anyone." She stroked the back of Jane's hand.

"Never," Jane vowed. "Never ever."

Changing the subject, Karma looked at David. "How's Carter?"

David held up a finger so he could finish chewing. "He's dreamy."

"Dreamy?" Jane and Karma both said and laughed.

"Does anyone use that word anymore?" Karma asked.

"No," David answered. "They don't. But how else to describe him? He's gorgeous. He's brilliant and kind and loving and incredibly good in bed."

The two women were silent for a moment as the news sank in. "Oh, my gosh," Jane said. "You had sex!"

"Shhh!" David looked around. "Yes. We had sex."

Karma giggled. "How was it?"

"It was lovely," David replied.

"Lovely? Are you eighty years old?" Karma laughed.

"In fact, I am," David huffed. "I listen to oldies music, I read old books, and I drink tea."

"He's not only old, he's British," Jane said. "He listens to old British music and he reads British literature. Plus, that whole tea thing."

Karma laughed. She patted David on the hand. "We love you just the way you are," she said.

"Anyway," David continued, "he's just a really

great guy."

"What happens when he leaves for Yale?" Jane asked.

"We haven't talked about that yet," he said. "We're trying to live in the moment."

They finished their meal and David asked for the bill. "One of you can buy next time," he insisted. "Besides, with all the other excitement, I haven't gotten a chance to tell you my most incredible news."

"What's that?" Jane asked.

"I got a new job. I'm going to be running the computer lab at MSU. It's a full-time job, nine-to-five, and I'll be making a ton more than I make at our little Excelsior bookstore."

"Oh, David, that's wonderful." Karma gave him a big hug. "I'm so proud."

"Well," he said, linking one arm through hers and holding the other out to Jane. "Carter got me the job. He knows someone who knows someone."

"It doesn't matter," Jane replied, taking his arm. The trio walked outside into the cool but sunny day. "The important thing is you got the job. You wouldn't have if you weren't qualified."

David smiled and wrapped an arm around each woman. "Let's celebrate with ice cream."

"Ice cream." Karma groaned. "We just ate. And it's cold. Let's go to your apartment and have popcorn."

"That sounds great," Jane said.

"I need to stop at A Woman's Place first," Karma said. "I need some more lesbian books in my life, and my grandmother recommended a couple I might like."

They headed toward the bookstore. "I can't believe your grandma recommends lesbian books to you," Jane said. "You're so lucky."

"I guess I am really lucky. My parents had an easier time accepting my sexuality because of my grandmother."

David laughed. "How can your grandmother be a lesbian? She had kids, or at least one."

"She had one," Karma said. "My mom. And a lot of gay people have kids, David. You need to get out more."

"I guess I do." He looked thoughtful. "I didn't mean to be insensitive."

Karma smiled. "I might even have kids someday."

Jane sighed. "That would be nice, wouldn't it? Is it possible?" She paused, laughing. "I mean, I know it's possible. I just wondered if it was possible for me."

"Why wouldn't it be?" Karma asked.

"My parents," Jane said. "They would drop dead if I had a child with a woman."

"Yes, of course," Karma said. "Well, you could always marry a man."

David glanced at her sideways. "Hey. She's working on it." He stopped in front of the bookstore. "Am I allowed to go in here?"

"Don't be a doofus." Karma laughed. "It's a public place. They might even have something you would be interested in reading."

David veered off toward the science fiction section as Jane and Karma went back into fiction. "This is the first place we met," Jane said.

"I know," Karma replied. "It wasn't that long ago."

"Are you mad at me?"

"I'm not mad. I just hate that you have to hide who you are because of your mother."

Jane scanned the shelves, looking for the R

section. "They have another copy of *Lesbian Images*," she said, handing it to Karma. "It's the second lesbian book I read after *Curious Wine*." They browsed in silence for a while. Karma glanced at her watch. "I better not spend forever here. I need to do laundry for work tomorrow."

Jane took her hand as they walked to the counter. They retrieved David from the science fiction section. He was sitting on the floor with five books next to him. "Are these all lesbians?"

"No," Karma said. "This is a feminist bookstore. Those are some of the all-time greats of female science fiction and fantasy writers." She reached down and picked up *Daughters of a Coral Dawn*. "Okay, this one is a lesbian." She handed it back to him. "Read it, though. I think you'll like it."

They purchased their books and went outside. "You know a lot of lesbian books," Jane said.

"I've pretty much burned through my grandmother's collection," Karma said. "Since I could never afford to buy my own stuff, I ended up reading a lot of oldies." She grinned. "Some of those old lesbian books are hilarious. But it's kind of cool to get a feel for what it was like to be a lesbian in olden times. Though, probably not that different than it is for you."

Jane glared at her. "I wish you would stop mocking me for my upbringing."

"I'm sorry," Karma said. "I'm really sorry. I just hate that your upbringing is what's keeping us from being together."

David started whistling loudly as he strolled away. "I think that ice cream is calling my name after all," he called over his shoulder.

Jane laughed. "He's so gracious."

"I like him a lot."

"He likes you." Jane touched Karma's cheek. "I know I'm scared. I'm sorry I'm weak."

Karma felt a pang in her stomach. She made everyone feel bad. She wished she could just accept people the way they were. Jane was a wonderful person and if all they could be right now was friends, Karma needed to accept that. She closed her eyes, savoring the feeling of skin on skin. Jane's fingers were lightly moving, just barely stroking Karma's cheek, and there was more intimacy in this public caress than Karma had ever felt with Crash in their entire relationship. Opening her eyes, she leaned in and kissed Jane on the lips, lightly, as lightly as Jane's fingers were touching Karma's cheek. Jane breathed hard against Karma's mouth and in an instant, Karma was fully aroused. "Jane," she whispered. "I'm in love with you."

Jane pulled back slightly, opening her eyes. She looked startled but not offended. Karma wondered if she had gone too far. She didn't want to risk losing her best friend. "I shouldn't have said that."

"Oh, Karma," Jane breathed. "I'm in love with you."

They kissed again, and Karma pretended not to notice Jane looking around as they separated, as if making sure no one was paying attention to them. Jane was only just learning to come out of the closet and with Karma by her side, it would be that much easier. Taking Jane's hand, Karma led her toward the ice cream shop to find David. She spied him walking toward them, holding an ice cream cone. He was walking with an older man and woman. They were looking at David, listening to something he was saying. Karma winced as Jane jerked her hand away from Karma's and took a step away from her.

When they reached the group on the sidewalk, Jane ran up to David and threw herself in his arms. "I'm sorry I was so long, my love," she said.

Confused, Karma hung back. Jane reached for the older couple. "Hello, Mother and Dad."

"Hello, darling. David was just telling me that you two finished painting your apartment. You know I don't approve of this living arrangement. If you're going to live together, you need to get married."

Karma took a step up and held out a hand toward Jane's mother. "Hello, I'm Karma Miller."

Jane took David's hand as she motioned toward Karma. "This is a co-worker of mine," she said.

Jane's mother looked down her nose and sniffed. "Oh. Hello."

Jane's father shook her hand. "Nice to meet you, Karma."

"I better be going. Nice running into you two," Karma said, nodding toward Jane and David.

"Karma," Jane said.

Ignoring her, Karma walked away. Just before she turned the corner, she overheard Jane's mother say, "Well, she is certainly dressed colorfully."

"Yes," Jane replied. "Her parents are hippies."

Karma was almost halfway home before she stopped crying.

Chapter Eight

Jane took a deep breath and knocked on the door. Karma's mother threw open the door and swept Jane into a hug. "Darling. We haven't seen you around here in months!"

Jane leaned into the hug, cradling Karma's present in her arm. "I know I've been busy. Between work and school, I feel like I don't have time to breathe anymore."

"I know Karma's been missing you," Henna said. "She'll be happy to see you."

Jane didn't know if that was true. She and Karma hadn't spoken much over the past several months, not since the day they had admitted to being in love with each other. They had fallen into a here-and-there friendship, and she missed Karma more than she cared to admit. She shifted the wrapped gift from one hand to another as she followed Henna into the house. Karma had brought Jane to meet the Millers for the first time a couple of months ago and Jane had been overwhelmed by their acceptance of their lesbian daughter. Jane wondered how different her life would be if she had been raised in a house like this.

Frank stood to hug her as she entered the living room. "Hi, Jane." He smiled. "We've been hoping to see you again!"

"I'm sorry, I'm sorry," Jane said. "I've been so busy."

"Karma's up in her room if you want to go prod her to hurry."

Jane ran lightly up the stairs and tapped on Karma's door.

"Come in," Karma yelled.

Jane poked her head in and laughed. Typical of Karma, the room was in chaos, with clothes hanging off every surface and books open on the bed, the floor, and the chair. Karma was perched on the nightstand putting on eyeliner in the full-length mirror she and Jane had found at a thrift store. Jane lifted a pile of clothes from the footstool and set it on the bed.

"Be careful there," Karma warned. "I have a method to my madness."

Jane stepped around a pile of books and leaned in to kiss Karma on the cheek. "It's been too long."

"Far too long," Karma said, eying Jane in the mirror. "Happy birthday, birthday twin."

"Happy birthday, birthday twin." Jane perched on the footstool to watch Karma apply her eye makeup. "You look fancy."

"Fancy?" Karma met Jane's eyes in the mirror, but Jane couldn't read her expression. "Is that a euphemism for too much makeup?"

Jane laughed, shaking her head. "No. It's just I'm not used to seeing you so dressed up."

Karma continued staring at Jane in the mirror for a long moment before turning her attention back to the makeup. "If I'm going to be a femme, I figured I better start playing the part."

"I don't really get all of that," Jane said. "I'm just me. I don't think butch or femme applies to me."

"It only matters if you date someone who thinks it's important," Karma said. "Since Crash is butch, she likes to date femme women. And she prefers very feminine women, rather than sloppy hippie chicks."

"What does Crash have to do with anything?"

Karma paused. "I'm seeing her tonight after our dinner."

Jane blinked. "I thought you were going to the bar with David and me?"

Karma shrugged. "I'm sorry. It's only fair. You get me for dinner. Crash gets me for dessert."

Jane placed a hand over her heart, trying to steady the jump in her heartbeat. Crash was dangerous. Karma knew that. "Karma, I don't understand how you could consider dating her again. After all these months when you've been doing so well without her."

"She's changed," Karma said without taking her eyes from her own reflection. "These past few months without me have been hell for her."

"I'm sure they have. She's had to try to figure out how to pay rent without living off you."

"It wasn't always like that," Karma said. "And her band is getting regular gigs. She's really changed. She isn't drinking anymore." She paused. "It's the drinking that made her lose her temper."

Jane looked away. She didn't trust Crash not to hurt Karma, but Jane didn't think she had a right to fight about it. After all, Jane herself had been mean to Karma when she pretended to her parents that Karma was just a co-worker. She couldn't imagine how badly that must have hurt. It was a wonder Karma even wanted to be her friend after that. Maybe it was better for Karma not to be with someone like her. Jane was a bad person. She made her mother sick. She upset Karma. She was a hypocrite sitting in church pretending she and Carol didn't know each other as they got to know each other in secret. But that didn't mean Karma should be with Crash.

"She's dangerous," Jane finally said. "She's not nice to you."

"Everyone deserves a second chance," Karma said. Her expression said it was the end of the discussion. "And you went back to the church after all the abuse it's heaped on you."

Stung, Jane stood. "I guess you get to make your own decisions. I just don't understand this one."

"You don't have to understand. Someday, you and Crash will be friends and we can go on double dates."

"Sure." Jane forced a smile. Watching Karma putting on lipliner, Jane remembered the way it felt to kiss her mouth. Kissing Carol didn't feel like that. It felt nice, yes, but it didn't curl her toes. When Jane kissed Karma, she felt as if she was being drawn into a deep pool of dizziness and bliss. Her fingers curled automatically, thinking of the way they felt wrapped in Karma's hair. Jane blinked. Karma was smiling at her in the mirror. "I know what you're thinking. I can still feel you."

Blushing, Jane looked away. Karma stepped around a pile of books and knelt on the floor in front of Jane's stepstool. Without thinking, Jane put her arms around Karma and the two women rested their foreheads together. "I just don't understand why it can't be easier for us," Jane whispered.

"Maybe because we don't deserve it," Karma answered.

Jane swallowed. She wanted to argue. She wanted to convince Karma that they both deserved better. But deep down, Jane knew that Karma deserved better than what Jane could give her. Karma deserved someone who wouldn't deny her and treat her like a stranger. Jane was no better than Peter denying Jesus. If she couldn't love Karma unconditionally, she didn't deserve to love her at all.

She pulled Karma tighter, treasuring the hot spots where bare skin met bare skin. Karma's hair cascaded across Jane's arms and for an instant, the desire to lift her hands into it was almost unbearable. Jane just had to reach out and she could be kissing Karma's mouth, getting lost in that deep ache again. Her fingers twitched, and she hovered on the brink of convincing herself that none of it mattered in the face of their love for each other. Her religion, Karma's self-esteem, Crash, Carol—none of it mattered except their souls, and Jane almost believed that if she kissed Karma right now, somehow, their love would work everything out. Except, it wouldn't. No matter how amazing it felt, Jane knew that Karma deserved better. She patted Karma's shoulder and pulled back, looking away. "We should get downstairs," she said. "Your mother probably has dinner waiting."

Downstairs, Jane was happy to see Karma's grandmother had joined the gathering. She was sitting at the head of the table looking for all the world like an elderly version of Karma. Jane kissed her on the cheek before setting the table. When Karma joined them, Henna and Frank surprised Jane by bringing out two small birthday cakes. "Since you have to share a birthday, you should at least get your own cake," Henna declared.

"I don't mind," Jane said. "My parents aren't really birthday celebrating kind of people, so having any birthday cake, even a shared one, is wonderful."

Karma laughed. "Well, I'm happy to have my own!" She cut a piece and scooped some ice cream onto a plate. Pretending to hog it, she held it close to her face. Jane giggled, and Karma's eyes sparkled. "I'm teasing, I'm teasing," Karma said. She handed the plate to Jane, her fingers brushing across Jane's hand.

Jane suppressed a shudder. Ignoring Henna's knowing smile, Jane shoveled a big bite of cake into her mouth. At that moment, Crash walked into the dining room.

"Hi," she said.

"Crash!" Karma jumped up from the table. "I wasn't expecting you so early."

Crash glanced around the room, her eyes lingering on Jane. Jane stared back at her. She was gorgeous, Jane had to admit. Tall and muscular with dark eyes. She was wearing jeans and a white T-shirt with a leather jacket. It was obviously an affectation, but Jane had to admit the dyke James Dean look worked. She smiled politely at Crash.

"Hello," she said. "You must be—er—Crash."

Crash didn't smile. "Yes. And I guess you're Jane." Without waiting for an answer, Crash turned back to Karma. "You ready to go, babe?"

Stunned, Jane turned to look at Karma's parents. Frank was still eating as if Crash had never come in, but Henna was glaring at her across the table.

"Hello, Crash," she said pointedly.

"Hey, Mrs. M," Crash replied. She turned back to Karma. "So, you want to go?"

Karma sat back down. "We just started dessert. Have a seat and join us."

Crash slumped into the chair next to Karma. Jane rolled her eyes as Karma fed Crash a piece of cake from her fork.

Henna cleared her throat. "If we had known you were coming, we would have set an extra place."

Karma shrugged. "Crash just got here a little earlier than expected."

"I didn't know you were going out with her at all," Henna replied.

"We're just going out for cocktails," Karma said.

"Isn't today your twenty-second birthday?" Crash put her arm around Karma. "I mean, just to clarify, you're twenty-two, not twelve, right?"

"Stop it," Karma said.

"I thought you said Crash quit drinking," Jane interjected.

"Why would you be talking about me to her?" Crash asked.

"She's my best friend," Karma said.

Henna stood. "Perhaps it's time for you to leave, Crash. We were having a nice family dinner before you got here."

Crash stood. "Yeah, I should leave. I'm obviously not welcome here."

Frank raised his hand in the air. "It isn't that you aren't welcome. It's that you're being combative with my family. Simmer down, or leave."

Jane stared at Frank with her mouth open. She wanted to jump up and hug him, but she didn't want to risk making things worse. Instead, she gave him a half-smile when he turned his eyes on her. Crash took Karma by the arm. "Come on, babe. I'm not welcome here."

Jane stood. "She isn't going with you."

"What?" Crash turned to glare at Jane. "Are you talking to me, little girl?"

Henna stood, towering above Jane. She was almost as tall as Crash. Jane watched as they stared each other down. Finally, Crash turned on her heel. "I'll be in the car for five minutes, babe. I'll see you there."

Jane jumped as the front door slammed. "I'm sorry, Karma."

Karma looked at each of them. "I can't believe you were all so rude to her."

"Rude?" Henna reared her head back, frowning down on her daughter. "That woman is a walking time bomb."

"And she walked in without knocking," Jane said. She hated the prim and judgmental tone in her voice, but she was exceptionally angry and scared. She didn't want Karma going with someone like that. Jane didn't want to end up visiting her best friend in the hospital someday because Crash had lost control of her temper yet again.

Karma shook her head. "Crash is my girlfriend. And you are all going to have to get used to it." She glared at Jane. "And she isn't embarrassed to be seen with me."

Karma's grandmother cleared her throat. She had been silent so long, Jane was almost surprised she was still there. Everyone turned to look at her. "Karma," she said, "there are defining moments in everyone's life. Moments they look back on with regret as the moments that changed their lives for the worse. If you walk out of here right now, this will be one of those moments for you."

Karma stared at her grandmother for a few seconds, blinking back tears. She ran out of the room, and Jane jumped again at the slamming of the front door. Henna sighed, and Jane was surprised to see she was trying not to cry. Jane wanted to cry as well. She couldn't hate Karma for being mad at her. Jane loved Karma for her openness and her exuberant personality, but at the same time, it did embarrass her when they were out in public. If only their whole life could be hanging out here with the Millers, or kissing at the apartment, or sitting in bed sharing doughnuts and watching TV. It was only when they went out and Jane had to worry about being seen by someone from the church or her parents' circle of friends that everything changed.

Jane finally smiled at Henna, taking her hand across the table. "I better go," she said. "Would you like help cleaning the dishes before I leave?"

"No, sweetie," Henna replied. "Frank and I will take care of it. Thank you."

The women stood, and Jane hugged Henna. Resting her face against the older woman's shoulder, Jane nearly broke down again. She wanted parents like this. Maybe if she had been raised to like herself, she would have been nicer to Karma. On the other hand, Karma was raised to be accepting of herself and she was with someone who treated her like crap. Jane sighed, and Henna squeezed her tighter. She ran around the table and kissed Karma's grandmother on the cheek. "I love you," she whispered.

Jane let herself out the door with a bag full of leftovers that Frank had pressed on her. "You've gotten skinnier since the last time I saw you," he said. "I don't think you're eating well."

Jane laughed, but he was right. Between work and school, some days she felt as if she barely had time to make a box of macaroni and cheese and shove a few bites into her mouth before crashing into bed.

When she got home, David and Carter were sitting on the couch. "Carter. I'm so happy to see you. It's been too long."

Carter jumped to his feet and wrapped Jane in a bear hug. "I've missed you, too."

David stood to divest her of the leftovers. "Can we have some cake?"

"When we get back," Jane said. "Is Carter going with us?"

"If that's okay," Carter said.

"Of course. Let me hurry and get changed."

Jane ran to her room, delighting in the way it made her feel, as she did every time she came home. She smiled at the thrift store nightstand she and Karma had found. Karma had painted it with pastels and it went perfectly with the quilt. Half-tempted to lie down for five minutes, Jane had to steel herself to just change her clothes and leave. Her room was such an oasis. Someday, when she had her own house, she would create every room to be a sanctuary. She didn't think Karma would be helping her with the next project, though. Crash hated Jane and if Crash was going to be part of Karma's life, Karma would be cutting things off with Jane. Maybe that was for the best. Maybe Crash had changed, and Jane needed to give Karma a chance to have a happy relationship with someone else. She changed into a dress and went back to the living room.

Carter whistled. "Not bad for your first foray into a gay bar."

"Do I look all right? I'm scared."

David put his arm around her. "You look beautiful. Fresh and lovely."

"I don't know if we should do this," Jane said.

Carter took her hand and led them all toward the door. "It's just a gay bar. It's not weird, I promise."

David grinned as they got into Carter's car. "And we won't have to worry about seeing your parents."

Jane laughed. "That's true" She looked out the window as they approached the bar. She had seen Charlie's before. It looked like any regular bar from the outside. They had tables set up on a patio outside but it was chilly tonight, so no one was out there. Jane had often seen people sitting out there having lunch after her Tuesday support group. She hadn't been in a couple of months. Maybe she should go back. "I think I was progressing when I was going to support group," she said.

David turned around to smile at her. "Me, too. Maybe we should make a pact to go back."

"It isn't the same now that Karma isn't leading it." Jane sighed.

"It's still good," Carter said. "Obviously, I can't make it every week, but I do try to stop into the center whenever I'm in town."

David reached over and took Carter's hand. The two of them stared into each other's eyes for a few moments and Jane felt a pang of longing. Carol never stared at her that way. But maybe it was because they had just started dating. She tried to imagine reaching out to hold Carol's hand in the car with other people. Jane might work up to that one day, but it didn't matter. Carol was deeply reserved as well. It was one of the reasons they were perfect for each other.

Carter parked the car on a side street and they walked toward Charlie's. Feeling excited suddenly, Jane walked a few feet ahead. She was going into a gay bar for the first time in her life. She had spent time in the LGBT center, she regularly went to a feminist bookstore, and now she was going to see what it was like in a gay bar. This could change her whole life. Laughing at herself, she turned back to the guys just in time to see David and Carter pausing to kiss in the street. Intrigued and anxious, Jane looked around. No one was paying attention, though there were several people walking on the street. Carter reached his hand up to touch David's face as they kissed, and Jane smiled. She wanted that someday. Maybe it was becoming normal enough that she would be able to break through her fear one day. She shook her head. She couldn't imagine ever taking someone to meet her mother and saying the words aloud. *Mother, this is my partner.*

"Come on," she called. The men stopped kissing and turned to her, smiling. Jane watched David's face, suddenly overjoyed. He looked so happy. As she watched, his face changed from bliss to terror. Staring at a spot over her shoulder, David pulled away from Carter and stepped closer to Jane. She turned around. David's father was coming toward them and he looked livid. When he reached David, he grabbed him by the arm.

"What the fuck is going on?"

David opened his mouth, but nothing came out. Jane put her hand on Mr. Coyle's arm. "Sir. Maybe we could go somewhere and talk about this."

Mr. Coyle shook her off. "The only person I need to talk to is David." He squeezed David's arm tight enough that David winced.

Carter put his hand on Mr. Coyle's shoulder. "Sir, don't hurt your son."

Mr. Coyle reared back, releasing David's arm.

"Do not tell me how to treat my son, faggot."

Shaking, Jane reached out to touch Mr. Coyle again. "Sir. The Christian thing to do is to forgive."

Mr. Coyle turned on her and the look on his face made her cringe backward. He looked close to a heart attack, with veins popping out in his bright red forehead. "Don't you dare lecture me, missy. Do your parents know that you've been lying for my homo son?"

Jane shook her head. Carter put his arm around Jane. "I feel we could have a calm conversation about this later. Why don't we meet for lunch sometime this week and talk about it? I'll ask my father to come along. He went through some of the same struggles and questions you're surely going through now."

Mr. Coyle pushed Carter away and Carter stumbled back. "Keep your filthy hands off me, faggot."

There were tears streaming down David's face and his voice shook when he finally spoke. "Don't you dare talk to him like that," he yelled.

Aware that people were stopping to watch them, Jane grabbed David by the hand. "We need to get out of here and he needs to calm down."

Carter shoved Mr. Coyle out of the way and took David by the other hand. The three of them walked quickly away from Mr. Coyle, who was still shouting behind them.

"Is he coming after us?" David was crying hard as they speed-walked. He was holding tightly to Jane's hand and she just kept pulling him forward. "No, he's not. Just keep walking."

"Don't go into Charlie's," Carter said. "He can still see us. We don't want him following us into a gay bar."

They walked past Charlie's and turned on the

next side street. Still walking fast, they circled the block and ended up back at Carter's car. Carter guided David into the front seat as Jane jumped in the back. She immediately reached up to put her hands on David's shoulders.

Carter turned left on Larch. "I should have stayed and tried to talk to him." He reached over to hold David's hand. "I just didn't want to risk him getting even more violent."

David wiped his face on his sleeve. He patted Jane's hand and she lightly squeezed his shoulder. "I'm sorry you two had to see that."

"We love you," Jane said.

Carter nodded. "I'm so sorry you have to deal with that."

David sighed. "I wish it hadn't happened, but in a way, I'm glad. I've been trying to cut him out of my life for a long time and I've never had the balls to do so. Seeing him like this just made him ugly to me."

"He is ugly," Jane said. "Whether or not being gay is a sin, a true Christian shouldn't treat people like that."

Carter nodded. "I wish I could have gotten him to talk to my dad. My dad was never violent, but he did go through hell when I first came out."

"The difference is that your dad loves you and was willing to work through his own prejudices to prove that love," David said.

Jane rubbed David's hair. "His inability to love you the way you are doesn't mean you aren't lovable."

David turned in his seat so he could look her in the face. "I could say the same thing about your mother."

Jane looked out the window. "It isn't that she

doesn't love me. It's that her health…" Her mother was a master manipulator, but her health struggles were real. "She isn't violent," she whispered, pressing her hand against David's shoulder again.

David turned to look at her. "Just because she isn't violent, doesn't mean she isn't abusive."

Carter pulled up in front of the apartment. Inside, the guys went to David's bedroom and Jane took a leftover piece of cake into her own room. Sitting on the bed, she ate the cake and thought about Karma. Carter loved David enough to put up with being called a faggot in the middle of the street. Did she love Karma enough to deal with something like that? She picked up the phone and punched in Karma's parents' house.

"Hey, Jane."

"You're home! I'm glad."

"Crash had to make it an early night because she's going out with some musicians tonight."

"And she couldn't take you?" Jane asked.

"It's business," Karma said. "Did you call to harass me?"

"No. I called because David's dad caught Carter and David kissing. It was awful."

"That's so bad. Is David okay?"

"Yes," Jane said. "But it was a bad scene. Carter was amazing, though."

"He's a great guy."

Jane paused, trying to figure out how to share her insights with Karma. Jane knew she needed to do her own work and she knew she wasn't good enough for Karma. But she thought that if she could get past the hurdle of telling her parents, things would change quickly. If Karma could be patient, Jane thought she could learn to be more accepting of their relationship.

"Karma…"

"Jane, I hate to do this, but I have to go. Crash is jealous of you and if I'm going to make things work with her, I have to stop talking to you."

Shocked, Jane exhaled. "You mean stop being friends."

"I'm sorry. Crash feels that part of what went wrong in our relationship is that I was dividing my attention. And she's right. I was developing feelings for you."

"Because we're soulmates," Jane cried.

Karma didn't respond.

"Karma? We're soulmates," Jane said again.

"Jane. I don't believe in soulmates." She hung up.

Jane stared at the phone. She didn't blame Karma for hating her. She curled up on the bed and closed her eyes, pulling one of her pillows close to her chest. Crying into it, she allowed the guilt and pain to wash over her. She ruined everything. She deserved to be alone and unhappy forever.

Chapter Nine

Karma stared at the pea-green walls of the emergency room and focused on taking deep breaths. She wished she had someone with her to hold her hand, but she couldn't imagine calling her mother over this. Even if she tried to tell her mother that it had been an accident, Henna Miller would never believe it. She held the icepack to her head and tried to keep from throwing up. Crash hadn't hit her that hard, but Karma had banged her head against the bathroom door frame as a result. Worried that she had a traumatic brain injury, Karma had taken a cab to St. Luke's.

Leaning her head back against the wall, Karma settled in for a long wait. She was half asleep when she heard her name. She opened her eyes and saw David leaning over her.

"Are you okay? You look terrible."

"Thanks," she snorted. Dropping the hand with the ice pack to the chair next to her, she blinked up at him. "I hit my head. I might have a concussion."

David sat carefully on the other side and looked closely at her face. "What are your symptoms?"

"Dizziness, nausea." She paused, staring into space. "I'm a little disoriented." She looked at David's compassionate face and tears formed in her eyes. "And I want to cry." David put his arm around her and Karma rested her head on his shoulder. "And I've been here an hour."

"Want me to go talk to intake?"

"Do you have any pull?"

David laughed. "No. I'm just a nursing student. But I did my resident program here and of course I was wildly popular, so I might be able to find out how much longer it will be."

Karma smiled. She had forgotten how charming David was. "David, has it really been almost two years since we've seen each other?"

David smiled and leaned back, still holding Karma with one arm. She leaned back with him, letting her head rest softly on his shoulder. "Maybe a year and a half. We ran into each other at Charlie's that New Year's Eve."

Karma closed her eyes. She remembered. It was right before she moved back in with Crash. They had gone out for New Year's together and gotten so high. Karma was sure that Crash had laced their pot with something else because she was off that night. Paranoid and shaking, she had ended up in the men's bathroom, crying. David had walked in on her and taken her out to a table. Plying her with coffee, he sat and talked to her until Crash came searching.

Karma pressed her forehead against David's cheek. "You're a natural born hero."

"Nah," he replied. "Just care about my friends."

"I haven't been a very good friend," Karma said.

"Not to Jane," David answered.

Karma sucked in a breath. "How is she?"

"She's fine," David said. He paused. "She and Carol are engaged."

"To be married?" Karma blurted, then blushed. "Well, duh." She pulled back a little so she could look at David. "Are they happy?"

David nodded. "You know. They're both so guarded about their relationship, it's hard to tell. I guess so. They don't fight."

"What about Jane's mom?"

David grinned. "It was bad. My dad found out about me and Carter and lost it. He called Jane's parents and told them all about it."

"Wow."

"Yeah. She decided to tell them the truth after that. It was pretty rocky."

Karma stared at the floor. She hadn't seen Jane since the day Karma cut her off to appease Crash's jealousy. Jane was the most respectful woman Karma knew, so even though a large part of Karma was sure Jane would keep trying, the even bigger part of Karma's mind knew that she wouldn't. Jane had stopped coming to the center, and since Karma wasn't leading group anymore, it didn't make sense to hang around. Besides, Karma had made a decision to make things work with Crash, and that meant giving up the center and working full time.

"Are you still roommates?"

"No," David squeezed her gently. "She's living with Carol and I'm renting the mother-in-law cottage behind the Gundersons' house. They're giving us a break on the rent since Carter and I are both students."

Karma smiled. Carter and David were making things work despite the distance and the long hours they both spent working and going to school. She and Jane could have been like that. It didn't matter. Crash needed her.

The woman behind the desk called Karma's name and David helped her to her feet. "I'm going in with you," he said.

They were ushered into a small room with a curtain around a padded, but hard, table. David helped Karma onto the table before perching on a stool nearby. Throughout the exam, he stayed involved, asking questions. Karma was grateful for his presence because she was so tired and she didn't think she could remember anything the doctor said. She thought the doctor was trying to get her to admit that she hadn't just fallen into the door frame, but she stuck to her story. Finally, they were released, and David guided her to his car.

"I'll drive you home, but I think I should take you to your parents' house," he said. "You need to be closely monitored and you need supportive care."

"It'll be fine," Karma said, staring out the window. "Just take me to my apartment." She gave him the address and a few brief directions. Leaning her head back on the seat, she fell asleep for a few minutes. Aware that David was touching her arm, she opened her eyes.

"Are we there?"

"We're here. Come on, I'm going to walk you up."

Karma wanted to say no, but the dizziness was taking over and she wasn't sure she could make it up the stairs on her own. David put his arm under hers and half-lifted her as they walked up the stairs. Taking her keys, he unlocked the door and herded her inside.

He stopped short just inside the threshold and Karma looked around. Empty beer bottles, whiskey bottles, and overflowing ashtrays had taken over the entire apartment. There was a pizza box that they had been eating from a couple of nights ago. It was still on the floor and half a piece of stale pizza was sticking out from the box. Karma thought she saw a cockroach scurry back inside the box as she looked at it.

David took a deep breath and continued into the room. He sat Karma down on the arm of the couch and lifted plates and clothes and beer bottles from the cushions. Placing these on another surface, he picked up the couch cushions and shook them off. Crumbs and dust flew up into the air. He pounded them together until they were relatively clean. Karma stared at the floor, blinking back tears. "Please don't tell Jane I'm living like this."

David took her arm and helped her onto the couch. "What's going on, Karma?"

She closed her eyes. The room was spinning, and it was hard to think. "Crash lost her job again. I picked up some part-time work to cover the bills. I just work all the time. I don't have time to clean."

"And Crash is unemployed and can't manage to do one single dish?"

"It isn't like that," Karma said. "She has band practice. She's really trying to make a go of it. And they're good. Really good."

David clicked his tongue and Karma tried to sit up. "David, really. She isn't all bad. Everyone thinks she is, but she has been so hurt in her life."

David knelt on the floor in front of her. "We've all been hurt, Karma. It doesn't give us license to abuse others."

Karma looked away. "It was an accident," she insisted.

"I'm going to stay here for a couple of hours. I just need to call Carter and let him know I'll be late."

"You don't have to do that. I know you have limited time together."

"I'm not leaving you alone. If you aren't going to let me take you to your parents' house, I'm going to stay here."

Karma didn't have the strength to argue. She wanted a glass of orange juice and some chicken soup, but there wasn't any food in the house. She wondered if she could get David to go to the grocery store. She spent more than she wanted on the cab to the hospital, but she had about five dollars left in her purse. And she thought there was a twenty in the top drawer of her desk.

The front door slammed open and Crash strode in. As always, Karma was stunned by her presence. She filled the room with her energy, her strength, her dark good looks. David stood and held out his hand.

Crash ignored him and looked at Karma. "What's going on here?"

David answered. "Karma has a concussion from her..." He paused for a second. "From her fall."

Crash approached Karma and knelt beside her. "My poor baby. What do you need?"

"I just need some orange juice and chicken soup," Karma said. "I'm so thirsty and hungry."

"I'll go to the store," Crash said. She grimaced. "Do you have any money?"

Karma nodded. "There's twenty dollars in my top desk drawer."

Crash looked away. "Babe, I had to take that. I was hungry."

Karma stared at the ceiling, trying not to cry. "You used it to buy groceries?"

Crash didn't answer.

"Because if we have groceries, you can just make me something here."

Crash stood up. "I used it to buy dinner while I was out. I didn't realize it would be such a problem."

"It wouldn't be such a problem if it wasn't the only money we have until I get paid in five days," Karma snapped.

"You'll make cash tips tomorrow," Crash said.

"The doctor told me I can't work for at least three days," Karma said. "And I'm supposed to stay calm and rest."

"Doctors don't know everything. Let's see how you feel tomorrow."

David held up his hands. "Karma, if you want, I can check on you tomorrow. However, as your nurse, I'm telling you right now you will not be going to work tomorrow."

Crash turned on him. "Who the hell are you?"

"I'm Karma's friend, and I care about her health," he said.

"And I don't?"

David shrugged. "If my partner had a concussion, I'd be doing everything in my power to ensure he was well rested, well fed, and well cared for. If you can't do that, I think you should take Karma to her parents' house until she's healed."

"Get the fuck out of my house," Crash said.

Karma could barely keep her eyes open. "Please go, David. I'll be fine, I swear."

David looked back and forth between the two women and Karma could tell he wanted to argue. "Please, David."

David stepped forward to kiss Karma lightly on the forehead. "Please take care of yourself. Do you have a phone?"

"No, I had one, but I had to sell it."

"I'll stop by tomorrow morning before class."

"Thanks, David," Karma whispered.

She watched him leave, trying not to cry again. He looked back once, and she managed to smile reassuringly. Once he was gone, she closed her eyes and leaned back on the couch. She was so tired. She could hear Crash padding around her, but she couldn't summon the energy to speak to her. She didn't want another fight. She didn't have the strength to do the eggshell dance, tiptoeing around to keep Crash from exploding.

"Babe, I think it's a good idea to take you to your parents," Crash said.

Karma opened her eyes. "What?"

"I have a gig tonight and we don't have any food in the house and I just can't take care of you right now."

Karma blinked at the ceiling, tears dripping down the side of her face. "Just leave. I'll take care of myself."

"No, you need care. I'm going to take you to your parents'. I'll come get you tomorrow, okay?"

Karma didn't move. "I can't. I'm tired. I need to sleep. If you want, you can call my mom and ask her to come here."

Crash sucked her teeth. "You really want your mom seeing this pigsty?"

Karma didn't answer. Ignoring Crash, she focused on her breath, breathing in through her nose and out through her mouth. The deep breathing kept the panic at bay. Half-asleep, she was vaguely aware of Crash lifting her and carrying her out the door and down the stairs. Too tired to resist, she kept her eyes closed and tried not to cry. Her parents would take care of her, but they would ask a lot of questions when she got better.

She wasn't mad at Crash. She knew her partner was just doing what she thought would be best for Karma. Karma really would get better care at her parents' house than she would trying to manage at home alone. She slept through the drive and woke again when Crash tried to lift her out of the car.

"I can walk," Karma muttered.

Crash carefully took her arm and helped her up the porch stairs. Karma pressed the doorbell.

Henna Miller opened the door. "Baby, what's wrong?"

Crash helped Karma through the door. She really was being so gentle. "Karma hit her head on the bathroom door. She has a concussion. I have a performance I can't miss, and she isn't supposed to be alone."

Karma held her breath, waiting for her mother's response. She hadn't called home in months. The last time she and Crash had come over, Henna and Crash had gotten into a huge argument. Frank tried to intervene, but a lot of hard words were said on both sides. Crash had refused to come back since then. Karma thought Crash was stepping outside her comfort zone to bring Karma here. She was putting her own pride in check to take care of Karma. Near tears again, Karma chastised herself for being so hard on Crash all the time.

She felt herself being lowered to the couch. Had her mother spoken? Karma wasn't sure. She couldn't keep her eyes open any longer. Crash said something to her, but Karma couldn't make her mouth move to respond.

It was dark when Karma woke again. Her mother was sitting in a chair next to the couch. Karma watched her sleeping. When she was a kid, Karma thought her mother was the most beautiful woman in the world. Her soft curves, wide, smiling mouth, and expressive eyes meant safety and warmth to Karma. Small lines were starting to form around the sides of Henna's mouth and eyes, but Karma still thought she was the most beautiful woman she knew. Jane's face popped into Karma's head. Another beautiful woman. Jane, with her blue eyes and her pale, blond hair. Jane, who had such passion hidden underneath the guilt and fear.

"I guess we aren't as different as we think we are," she muttered.

Henna started and immediately came to the side of the couch, kneeling next to Karma. She stroked her daughter's hair softly. "Are you okay, sweetie?"

Karma nodded. "My head hurts."

Karma's mother took her through a series of questions about her birthday, the current president, and some multiplication tables. Finally, Karma held up her hand and laughed. "Mom, I know who I am. I promise."

Henna smiled. "How do you feel?"

"Hungry. Thirsty. Tired."

Henna stood. "Your dad made some chicken noodle soup while you were sleeping. I'll heat it up and bring it in. Can you sit up?"

"I think so."

Henna put her arm under Karma's shoulders and helped her to a sitting position. Karma readjusted herself as Henna pushed pillows behind her. Once Karma was comfortable, Henna left the room. Karma smiled at the thought of her dad making homemade chicken noodle soup while she was sleeping. When her mom came back with the bowl of soup, Karma held it in both hands, savoring the warmth and the smell.

"Dad makes the best soups."

"He turns to food when he's upset," Henna said. "He baked a bunch of apple muffins, too."

Karma smiled. "I might want one for dessert." Looking down into her soup, she tried to ignore the wave of guilt that was washing over her. "Mom, I'm sorry."

Henna touched Karma lightly on the face. "We're just going to focus on you getting better. We can talk after that."

Karma nodded. "I love you."

"I love you, too, sweetie. Your dad and I both love you so much."

A tear dripped into Karma's soup. She took several bites to keep from breaking down. "Is chicken soup magic?"

Henna laughed. "Your dad's might be."

Karma ate half the soup before handing it back to her mother. "I might nap a little more."

Henna put the bowl down before helping Karma rearrange on the couch. "You're the best mommy in the world," Karma murmured.

"You deserve to be treated well, my darling."

Karma didn't respond. If she did, she was afraid her mom would want to start talking about Crash. Sometimes Crash treated her well. Sometimes she treated her so well, Karma thought she would explode from happiness. And she loved Crash. Karma wasn't sure she was in love with Crash. Unbidden, Jane popped into Karma's head again. She tried to suppress the thought, but she kept hearing David telling her that Jane was engaged to be married. She couldn't picture Jane married to Carol. Karma suddenly had a flash of Jane as an old woman, laughing as she leaned forward to kiss Karma. It was sunny, and Karma was filled with a full-body warmth. Karma's hair was short and curly and completely white, and she felt such a swell of happiness she thought her heart was going to burst. Karma opened her eyes.

"Mom, I miss Jane."

"Of course you do," Henna said. "She's a good person."

"I'd like to call her, but I don't know if she'd want to hear from me."

"I miss her," Henna said. "We liked having her come around here."

"Me, too," Karma said.

She closed her eyes, warm from the soup and the vision of Jane in the sun. Karma debated the idea of calling Jane tomorrow and apologizing for pushing her away at Crash's insistence. Karma didn't think there was a chance for them to be a couple, but at least they could be friends again. Karma needed Jane in her life. She missed her face, her laugh, her kiss. Karma banished the thought of Jane's kiss. If she and Jane were going to become friends again, they wouldn't be able to explore that connection. It had been so long since she had seen Jane, Karma wondered if that chemistry had been imagined. She remembered Jane saying they were soulmates. "I don't know if I believe in soulmates," she whispered aloud.

"I do," her mother responded.

Karma opened her eyes again. She smiled at her mother before falling asleep.

Chapter Ten

Jane stifled a yawn as Carol and Jane's mother looked at yet another armchair. She didn't know why Carol thought they needed another chair. The chairs they had were all in perfect working order. But Carol wanted one to match the new carpeting in the living room. They had fought about the new carpeting for weeks. The old carpeting wasn't worn out, but Carol didn't think it looked posh enough. Jane knew this procedure. As soon as they had new carpet, they would need new drapes. Then new artwork. New chairs. New throw pillows. The only part of the argument Jane won was over the couch. She put her foot down and told Carol that they were not buying a new couch. They had spent five thousand dollars on their current couch only a year before, and Jane was not willing to give it away.

The women were still talking to the salesperson. Jane should go over and pretend to pay attention; otherwise, Carol could end up walking away with a two-thousand-dollar chair. Jane hated all the new furniture in the living room. It was uncomfortable and expensive, and it reminded Jane of her mother's sitting room. She had to take her shoes off before entering the room and she wasn't allowed to put her feet up on anything. It didn't matter if Jane was plastered to her side, Carol would still buy whatever she wanted. She didn't need Jane for that. And Mary Edmunds was a consummate shopper. She and Carol were made for each other. *They should marry each other*, Jane thought, suppressing a snicker. Jane figured her mother loved Carol so much because she didn't seem like Mary's idea of a lesbian. The two of them shopped together and redecorated each other's houses together. After nearly four years of marriage to Carol, Jane had a new appreciation for her father, who was always exhaustedly following the to-do lists Mary made for him every time she wanted something changed in the house.

Carol and the salesperson moved to a different section. Jane flopped into a chair and sighed. It didn't matter if she got involved in the conversation. They would end up getting what Carol wanted. They always ended up getting what Carol wanted. Most times, Jane just found it easier to give in, as otherwise Carol would sulk and be angry for days. Jane hated the feeling of tiptoeing around, trying not to upset her wife. At any rate, if Jane's mother and Carol both agreed on something, Jane's opinion would be worthless.

This could take hours. Carol had to have the perfect balance between trendy and classic. The only part Jane would have to play in this whole charade would be to move all the furniture as directed by Carol once the new chair was delivered. An entire Saturday lost to shopping and an entire Sunday lost to rearranging everything to Carol's specifications. Jane looked forward to going back to work on Mondays. The children could be exhausting, but at least they didn't have to-do lists for her.

Glancing at her watch, Jane stood. It was still early enough to get coffee. Carol and her mother were all the way across the store, so Jane sent her a text. *Going to Starbucks. Want anything?*

As Jane watched her, Carol checked her phone

and scanned the room for Jane. When she saw her, she shook her head, frowning. The head shake could mean that she didn't want Jane to go to Starbucks, but since Jane had sent a question in her text, she could always pretend she thought the head shake was the answer.

Jane slipped into the drugstore on her way to Starbucks. She rushed through the aisles picking up spiral notebooks, packs of pencils, erasers, tape, and pens. Carol would be mad that Jane was spending money for supplies the kids' parents should buy, but Jane knew that most of her students couldn't afford simple things like paper. Jane had had a privileged childhood and she would never let a child go without learning because they didn't have the right supplies. The order came to thirty-five dollars. Jane handed over her bank card.

"Declined," the cashier said.

"Dammit," Jane swore. "I'm sorry. Excuse my language. Try this." She gave the clerk her credit card and the sale went through. Jane grabbed her bag and stomped out of the store. They should have plenty of money in the checking account, unless Carol was doing online shopping in the middle of the night again.

She slipped into Starbucks and ordered a venti white chocolate mocha with whipped cream. If she was going to buy expensive coffee, she might as well be decadent about it. She paid with her credit card. Screw it. If Carol was going to waste all their money on expensive clothing and furniture, Jane was damn well going to buy coffee, even if she had to put it on credit. She stepped back in line to wait for her coffee. The barista called her name and Jane grabbed the cup, remembering to thank the woman. It wasn't her fault Jane was having a terrible day. *A terrible life*, she thought, before banishing it from her mind.

She set her coffee down on a table and took off her jacket.

"Jane?"

Looking around, Jane tried to pinpoint who had said her name. Karma. Jane caught her breath. Karma was striding across the Starbucks, coffee in hand, looking for all the world exactly as she had so many years ago outside of A Woman's Place bookstore. Her hair was still long and wavy, and her wide smile lit up her entire face. Jane put a hand over her heart, trying to stop the fluttering. It had been years since she'd seen Karma. Years in which she had come out of the closet, rebuilt her relationship with her mother, and made a life for herself and her wife. One glimpse of Karma's face was enough to turn her into a twenty-one-year-old. She smiled, shaking her head.

Karma reached Jane's side, dropped her coffee on the table, and swept Jane into a bear hug. They held each other tight, faces pressed together. Jane had such vivid memories of the way Karma's face felt against hers. She remembered one morning when they were propped up in Jane's bed eating doughnuts and watching TV. Karma had suddenly thrown her arms around Jane and pressed her face against Jane's cheek. They held that, feeling each other's breath. Jane felt a rush of dizziness as she held Karma. She told herself to let go, to not let the hug linger longer than a friendly hug should, but it was too late. Finally, Karma pulled back, though she didn't let go of Jane. The two women looked at each other. Karma looked as if she was close to tears. Jane tried to formulate words, but she didn't know what to say first. Ten million things popped into her head at once and they all got jammed trying to come out first. Finally, she took a deep breath.

"Karma. It's been far too long."

Karma blinked, and a tear fell, but she appeared to compose herself. "It has. It's been far too long."

"For a while I was keeping up with you through David, but he said he hasn't seen you in a while."

"Yeah, it's been at least a year," Karma said. She shifted from foot to foot, looking around nervously. Jane noticed that Karma had lost weight. Always naturally skinny, she was on the verge of looking sick. Her eyes looked too big in her pale face.

"Are you okay, Karma? You look…" Jane paused, looking for the right word. "Tired."

"I'm tired," Karma admitted.

"Sit down." Jane motioned toward the table.

The two women sat and picked up their coffees.

"You look amazing," Karma said.

Jane blushed. "I look old, I think." She grinned. "At least most days."

Karma laughed. "Me, too. I wake up every morning and ask if I'm really only twenty-six."

"I'm an old married woman," Jane said. "I go to work, and I do projects on the weekends. Somehow, I thought being a lesbian would change that status quo."

"Whoa. You said 'lesbian' out loud in public." Karma laughed.

Jane felt the heat rushing to her face again. "I haven't gotten to the point of painting myself in rainbow body paint and leading the pride parade, but I can say the word in public."

"Though I could see you in rainbow body paint."

Jane laughed. "Maybe only for special occasions."

Karma reached for Jane's hand and Jane curled her fingers into the touch. It felt natural and good to touch her dear friend. Carol didn't like to hold hands in public. Despite being married, Carol still believed in being circumspect about being gay and she still introduced Jane to people as her "friend." Jane laughed.

"What's funny?"

"It's just, I'm kind of in the relationship you would have been in with me," Jane replied.

"Oh? You mean fun and romantic with lots of hot sex and doughnuts in bed every Saturday?"

Jane's blush deepened, and she looked away, laughing. "No. I mean, Carol's embarrassed to be seen with me. Maybe it's my karma to experience how that feels."

Karma shook her head. "You were scared. You would have moved past it."

"I know I would have," Jane said. "I have. Mostly." She took a sip of her coffee and looked out the window. "It was hard when my mom found out. She had hysterics and claimed she was dying. My dad cried. I've never seen him cry before. I figured nothing could be worse than that, right?"

Karma nodded. "I get it. Once you've gotten past your mother convincing you that your sin is so bad it's killing her, some guy giving you a dirty look in a coffee shop becomes inconsequential."

"Exactly." She squeezed Karma's hand. Her fingers felt hot where they were wrapped into Karma's fingers. "I should have given you a chance."

"No, it was me. I didn't give you a chance. I couldn't stand the idea of being with someone who was embarrassed by me."

"The thing is, I wasn't embarrassed by you. I was in awe of you. You were so sure of yourself, so open. I wanted that. I just couldn't make myself do it.

Whenever I tried, I thought of my mom having heart pains. I didn't want to kill my own mother. I know how stupid that sounds."

"It isn't stupid. It was ingrained in you way back when." Karma smiled. "Do you ever see Cindy Watkins?"

Jane laughed. "I can't believe you remember her name."

"Your first lesbian experience?" Karma smiled. "How could I forget? We have something in common. She was your first naked boob sighting and I was your first kiss."

"She left the church a couple years ago," Jane said. "Came out of the closet, shaved her head, got a girlfriend and a couple tattoos."

They both laughed. Karma's face had changed. When she first approached Jane, she looked drawn and tired. The laughter or the coffee had brought a sweet flush to her cheeks. Jane wanted to reach out and touch her face. Instead, she just squeezed Karma's hand again. Karma squeezed back.

"How about you, Karma? Are you still with Crash?"

Karma looked down at their joined hands. "Yeah. I guess. It's kind of on-again, off-again."

"And it's on right now?"

Karma shrugged. "She took off a few days ago. We had a fight. I think she went with the woman from her band. I don't know. Crash has never admitted it, but I'm pretty sure they're having an affair."

Jane's heart broke. She wanted to pull Karma into her arms and hold her. "I'm so sorry. I'm sorry. You don't deserve to be treated like that."

"Anyway, she'll probably come back. She usually

does. And it's not like she pays the bills anyway." She blinked several times and Jane knew she was trying not to cry. "Hey, look at the bright side," Karma finally said, smiling. "At least without having to pay for her booze and drugs, I can afford to buy coffee every now and then."

Jane leaned forward and took Karma's chin in her hand. "Karma, I'm going to say this as your friend. You deserve better than Crash. I think you should move out while she's gone. Stay with your parents until you get on your feet. Get your own place."

Karma looked away. "Easy for you to say from your lofty position as a happily married woman."

"I'm not happy," Jane said. She clamped a hand over her mouth.

"It's okay," Karma replied. "I don't think anyone really is."

Jane lowered her hand. "I can't believe I said that."

"I can't either, to be honest. I thought Carol was the perfect woman."

"In my mom's eyes," Jane laughed.

Karma laughed, too. "Maybe that's what you were looking for. Someone who would be palatable to your mother." She shrugged again. "That's definitely not me."

Karma was right. Karma's free spirit and wild clothes would have horrified Mary Edmunds more than her relationship with Jane. Jane could picture her mother trying to get Karma to go to the beauty salon with her so she could get an upscale haircut and a manicure. She snickered.

"What's funny?"

"My mother and Carol like to get manicures together," Jane said. "They shop together, too. They shop a lot. I finally asked my dad the other day how he could afford to keep my mother in the style she prefers. He admitted that he can't. My parents are hugely in debt."

"Wow. You don't think about your parents as having problems like that." Karma looked thoughtful for a moment. "I've never asked my parents about their finances, but they aren't big spenders and they both make decent money."

"Well, Carol makes good money and I'm a teacher. We aren't rich, but we would be well-off if she didn't spend it all."

"I guess we're not that different," Karma said. "I don't make a lot of money, but if I was living on my own, or living with someone who also had a regular paycheck, I wouldn't always be struggling with my bills."

"Same here," Jane said. "I keep thinking that I want to be saving for retirement or that I'd like to buy school supplies for my students, but any time we have the slightest bit of savings built up, Carol insists she needs something new and expensive like a designer purse or a new couch."

"I'd just like to pay off my bills and not have so much credit debt," Karma said. "I was doing great when I was living with my parents. I could have had my own house by now."

"I have a house, but it really isn't mine. It's Carol's. The whole house is decorated the way she wants. Even our bedroom." She paused, thinking back. "I miss my peach bedroom from the apartment."

Karma smiled. "That was a great bedroom. I loved it. You have such an eye for color."

"*You* do," Jane insisted. "You helped me with all of that."

"We always did have the same taste," Karma said.

"Carol thinks my tastes are low-class," Jane said. "She likes things way posher than I do."

"Crash doesn't have any taste at all," Karma said, laughing. "But then, it's not as if we ever have a spare penny for decorating. Not that we'd want to decorate our ugly little apartment." She sighed, squeezing Jane's hand again. "When did life start sucking so bad?"

"I don't think my life sucks," Jane said. "It's just not what I expected. I've never seen myself as someone who would live in a house where I can't put a glass down on a table. I want coffee rings on the bedside table and books open on the floor. I have never seen piles of notebooks as being a mess. Now I have to keep everything in drawers or closets and I forget they exist."

Karma laughed. "I miss books. Crash doesn't think they're important in the budget so it's rare that I buy new."

Jane frowned. "I hate that you're still with someone so abusive."

"She's gotten better," Karma said. "She doesn't drink as much and her band is doing well."

"She's controlling," Jane said.

"You have room to talk about that."

Jane nodded. "I know, but at least Carol isn't abusive."

Karma shrugged. "I don't want to waste our time arguing. I've missed you so much."

"Me, too." Jane blinked, near tears again. "I miss how easy it was to be with you. I miss laughing until my ribs hurt."

"I miss cuddling and eating doughnuts and drinking way too much coffee."

Jane smiled. "I miss going for drinks with you

and David."

Karma squeezed Jane's hand again. "Let's be in each other's lives again. We were better together."

Jane grimaced, shaking her head. "I would love to, but I doubt Carol would go for it. She doesn't like me having female friends unless they're of her choosing."

"So, what? She sets play dates for you?"

Jane shrugged. "More like she picks our friends and we go out to dinner with them sometimes."

"Who do you talk to when you're sad?"

Jane shifted and took her hand back. "Who do you talk to when you're sad?"

"Are you answering a question with a question?"

Jane laughed. "Are you avoiding my question by asking a question of your own?"

Karma threw her head back and laughed. Watching her, Jane felt a stab of joy and love tear through her chest. Karma's laugh, so loud and uninhibited, was one of the things Jane had missed the most. Maybe she could introduce Carol and Karma and the two of them could be friends. She quickly dismissed the thought. Carol didn't like lesbians. *Other lesbians*, Jane reminded herself. All their friends were straight. Besides, how would Jane be able to hang out with Karma without Carol noticing the connection?

"It's still there, isn't it?" Jane reached for Karma's hand again. "Our connection, I mean."

Karma nodded. "I guess it's wishful thinking that we could be friends."

Jane opened her mouth to respond when she spied her mother and Carol coming through the door of Starbucks. Instantly ripping her hand from Karma's, she lifted it in greeting. The two women beelined for the table. Jane sucked her stomach in as a knot of anxiety started rolling around in it. Carol's face looked livid.

"We've been waiting for you forever," she snapped as soon as she got to the table.

Jane stood. "I'm sorry. I ran into an old friend."

Carol glanced at Karma. "Hello," she said. She turned back to Jane. "Let's go."

"Wait," Jane said. "I'd like to introduce you to my friend." She motioned toward Karma.

"Karma, this is my wife, Carol. Carol, this is—"

"Nice to meet you," Carol snapped again. "We had to make a final decision on the chair without you. If you hate it, you have no one to blame but yourself."

Jane looked at her mother, but Mary Edmunds was staring out the window, her lips pursed in disapproval. She hadn't said a word to Karma or Jane.

Jane turned to Karma. "It was really good seeing you."

Karma stood. "It was great to see you, too."

Knowing she would pay for it later, Jane stepped forward and wrapped her arms around Karma. She felt so fragile in Jane's arms and for a moment, Jane considered grabbing Karma's hand and walking out of the shop, leaving everything behind. She and Karma could stay in Karma's parents' house until they saved up for a deposit on a little house. They would decorate it exactly the way they wanted and they would eat doughnuts in bed on Saturday mornings. Holding Karma felt like coming home, and Jane didn't want to let her go. She heard Carol clear her throat loudly, and pulled away. "Thanks for the coffee and talk," Jane whispered. "It was lovely."

Carol snapped her fingers loudly. "We're leaving now." She turned on one foot and stormed out of the shop, Jane's mother close behind.

Jane half-shrugged and trudged after them.

"Hey, Jane?" Karma called.

Jane turned around. "Yes?"

"Just because you aren't being hit doesn't mean you aren't being abused."

Jane turned back around and left without a word.

Chapter Eleven

Karma stared up at the peeling yellow paint on the ceiling. This wasn't the first time she had ended up in the hospital after a fight with Crash, but it was the first time she had been admitted. At least she'd advanced from that ugly green paint in the ER. The doctor, a young and earnest guy who looked to be about twelve, had insisted that she stay overnight. He was worried about the possibility of internal bleeding. Karma tried to argue with him, but she was so tired she couldn't put much into it.

The morning sun coming through the window felt warm on her face. She wondered if Crash knew she hadn't come home last night. After their fight, Crash had stormed out. Karma wanted to get home before Crash came back. She'd be in trouble if Crash stayed out all night and got home to find Karma wasn't there.

She counted the lines on the ceiling. It had a strange swirled pattern and Karma wondered if all the rooms were like this or if the painters had gotten bored with painting everything the same and had started adding swirls to stave off the ennui. She amused herself for a moment with the idea of rogue painters.

She supposed she should call her mother, but she thought her mother was probably getting sick of coming to her rescue. How many times had she called Henna to come pick her up when she was too drunk to drive, or when Crash had stolen all the money from her purse and she hadn't eaten for two days? Henna always stepped up. She always jumped in and came to Karma's rescue. But she always asked questions and tried to convince Karma that Crash was evil, and Karma knew that wasn't true. Crash lost her temper a lot, but Karma knew that she contributed to that.

She closed her eyes. Jane would be so upset to know that Karma was still with Crash after all this time. How long had it been since she had seen Jane? It was that day in the coffee shop. Karma thought it had been two years already. How did that happen? She kept remembering the way Jane's arms felt around her, so powerful, yet so gentle. Karma pressed a hand to her face. She could almost feel the skin of Jane's cheek. That was how they often hugged, their bodies pressed together, their cheeks touching. Jane was so different from Crash. She was more like Karma. They both loved the same movies and the same activities and they both loved lounging in bed on the weekends eating doughnuts. Crash wouldn't consider lounging anywhere. She always wanted to go out and do something. She was never satisfied with just Karma's company. Feeling guilty, Karma tried to stop herself from thinking about Crash and Jane. It seemed whenever she thought of the two of them, Crash always looked worse. That wasn't fair. Maybe that's why Crash still lost her temper so much. Maybe she could somehow sense that Karma still thought about Jane in inappropriate ways, even after all these years. Karma wasn't committed enough, and Crash could sense it.

Karma tried to turn over on her side, but the pain in her ribs screamed. She couldn't remember if Crash had punched her in the ribs. Maybe they got bruised when Crash slammed her into the wall. It was all kind of a blur.

Giving up, she flopped back onto her back, gritting her teeth through the pain. She heard someone come through the door and kept her eyes closed, hoping they would go away. She was tired of people coming in and asking her questions about her fall.

"Karma," a voice said. "I know you're awake, so you might as well open your eyes."

Karma opened her eyes to see David leaning over her bed, smiling. His face was so lovely and warm, and Karma found herself smiling back involuntarily until she remembered she was cranky and forced a frown back onto her face. "I'm not accepting visitors right now," she said.

"I'm a nurse, not a visitor, so you have no choice but to accept me."

Karma snorted. "Am I getting out of here soon?"

"Yes, as soon as the doc releases you."

"How did you know I was here?"

"Carter was working in the ER last night when you were admitted. He was with another patient so he couldn't attend you, but he knew you were there."

Karma closed her eyes. David and Carter. She remembered when they started dating. She was there when they met. That was the life she would have had if she had only been patient with Jane. She and Jane would have fallen in love and gotten married. They would have volunteered together at the center. David and Carter would be their best friends and they would have big combined parties where Karma's parents could hang out with the Gundersons.

She heard David pulling up a chair and sitting down. "I guess you aren't planning on leaving anytime soon," she said without opening her eyes.

"Nope. Not until you talk to me. And if you aren't able to do that right now, I'll just sit here until you are."

"Don't you have a shift?"

"I just finished."

"Don't you have to go home and go to bed?"

David chuckled. "I can sleep upright in a hospital chair. I've done it before."

Karma huffed. "Fine." She opened her eyes and glared at him. "What do you want to talk about?"

"You can tell me about your fall if you want."

Karma rolled her eyes. "I've told twenty people about it."

"Make it twenty-one."

"Forget it," Karma said. "Let's talk about something else."

"Okay, you go first."

Karma turned her head to look at him. "How's Jane?"

David shook his head. "I don't see her much anymore. Carter and I had dinner with them a few months ago. Carter spilled a glass of wine on the carpet and Carol about freaked out."

Karma laughed. "From the little I know of her, I can see that."

David laughed. "It sounds funny, but I think that's why we haven't been invited back. It was an accident, of course."

"Obviously." Karma clucked her tongue.

"Anyway, I miss her."

"Me, too."

"I guess it's safe to say you're still with Crash," David said.

Ignoring the jab, Karma changed the subject.

"You and Carter are still together?"

David smiled. "Yes, almost eight years, going strong."

Karma couldn't help but smile back at him. He looked so happy and proud. "That's amazing. Are you happy?"

"He's my life," David said. "I can't imagine being without him. It's so much better now that he's here doing his residency and we get to live together."

"Are you still living in his parents' guest house?"

"Yes. I love it there. Carter wants to move out, but I want to wait until he's through with his residency. With all the medical school bills and my nursing school bills, it makes sense to keep living in a rent-controlled place where we get fed Sunday dinner every week."

"Carter's mom must be so lovely." Karma sighed.

"She is, but don't be so sexist. It's Mr. G cooking Sunday dinner every week." He laughed. "Though, Mrs. G does still make the best chocolate chip cookies—I mean after your mom."

"Does Mr. G still volunteer at the center?"

"Several times a week." David smiled. "And Jane's parents have come to dinner a couple times."

Shocked, Karma tried to sit up. The pain made her flop back in bed. "I can't believe it."

"Yeah, well, we aren't going to find them at gay pride, but hanging out with us palatable gays is a step in the right direction."

"Mary would probably still disapprove of me," Karma said.

"Maybe. She's still a stick in the mud. But she's trying. That's more than I can say for my dad. I think Carter's parents have been a good influence on Jane's parents."

"I always assumed since they were so homophobic, they'd be racists, too."

David touched her hand. "How are you, Karma? How are you really?"

Karma stared at the ceiling, trying not to cry. She remembered the moment she told Jane to get out of her life. That was the moment that ruined Karma's life. If only she had said yes to Jane, even to being her friend. Everything would be different right now. She might have left Crash years ago. Jane's gentle love would have remained steady, and eventually Karma would have realized that she deserved better than to be with someone who used her fists to show anger. Karma hadn't talked to Jane in two years, but she knew beyond a doubt that if she asked, Jane would tell her that Karma deserved to be treated with respect and compassion. Thinking about it made her feel guilty, but she wondered how much of that guilt came from Crash herself.

Karma turned her head to look at David. He was patiently watching her, his lovely face as open and loving as always. Karma remembered how nice he was to her the last time he found her in a hospital. She moved her hand toward him and he responded by taking it in his.

"David," she finally whispered. "I'm in an abusive relationship."

"I know," he said. "What can I do to get you out of it?"

"I'd like to go back to my apartment and get my stuff. I need to call my parents and make sure it's okay for me to move in with them. I…" She paused, struck by the enormity of her decision. "I need to find a counselor who has dealt with domestic partner violence."

David squeezed her hand. "Would you like me to go move your stuff while you stay here?"

"No. I want to go. And I think we should ask my parents to help."

"And I'll call Carter."

Karma gritted her teeth. "I feel bad. He worked all night. And so did you."

"We'll go to your place, pack up your stuff, and take it to your parents'. With their help, it shouldn't take too long. Carter and I could be sleeping by noon."

Karma blinked back a tear again. "Will you call my mom?" She told him the number and he walked out to make the call. The doctor came in while he was gone. The young, earnest guy had obviously gone home, and this old, cranky guy had taken his place. He gave her a cursory check and signed off on the papers. Karma supposed she should count her blessings. The other guy would have insisted on having a talk or processing their feelings about her injuries.

David walked back in followed by a nurse with a wheelchair. "We have your discharge papers, baby. You're home free."

Karma laughed. She struggled to get up. David ran over and propped her up with his arms. "Come on, little one." He half-lifted her out of bed and lowered her into the chair.

"I'd really feel better if we left you at your parents'," David said. "We can prop you up in bed with cartoons and candy."

"Delightful as that sounds, I need to be there to direct the move. I promise not to try to lift anything myself."

"Fair enough." He wheeled her to the front desk.

"I'm going to run for my car and bring it around to the turn-out. I'll be back in a few minutes."

He ran off and Karma watched him. David was so good to her and she didn't deserve it. She hadn't been a good friend to him. She hadn't been good to her mother, either, yet Henna kept showing up for her. She was so lucky to have these loving people in her life, even if she didn't deserve them.

A nurse wheeled her to the curb and David pulled up. Loading her into the car, he kissed her on the forehead. "You're doing the right thing, I promise."

"I hope so," Karma whispered.

She closed her eyes as he drove. When she opened them, they were parked in front of the apartment. Carter was waiting outside. Karma looked around and saw her parents' SUV. She smiled. Most of her stuff would fit in the trunk of her own little Honda; this was definitely overkill.

Her parents got out of their vehicle and approached David and Karma. David got out to greet them. Karma watched them all shaking hands and smiling. She opened the door and started pulling herself out of the car. Her dad ran around and helped her stand before pulling her into a gentle hug. "You're doing the right thing, my sweetest girl."

"Daddy," Karma whispered into his shoulder. "I'm sorry."

Frank cleared his throat and Karma could tell he was crying. "You don't ever have to apologize to me. You're my baby."

Karma cried into his shoulder until her mother came and wrapped herself around the pair. Luxuriating in the smell of her mother's soap, Karma stopped crying. She felt hopeful for the first time in years. She leaned away from her father, so she could press her face against her mother's cheek. "I love you, Mom."

"I love you now and forever," her mother answered.

David came around to help Karma up the stairs while Henna pulled a bunch of cloth grocery bags from the backseat of her vehicle. "I figured they would be easier to load and carry than boxes."

As they entered the apartment, Karma looked around frantically. It wasn't as bad as she thought. She had given the place a thorough cleaning on her last evening off after she and Crash had yet another fight about Karma's housekeeping skills. The clutter of two people who spent a lot of time drinking had started to work its way back through the apartment, but it still didn't look that bad. They traipsed into the living room. Karma listened carefully but she didn't hear Crash.

"Crash?"

No answer. Maybe she had stayed out all night.

Carter held out a cardboard box he had brought with him. "Where should we start?"

Karma pointed at two bookshelves she had found in a thrift store and refinished herself. "All of those are mine. Crash doesn't own any books. The shelves are mine, too."

"I'm on it." Carter knelt in front of the first case and started packing it up.

"What should I do?" David asked.

"All of the kitchen stuff can stay. It's either hers or came from a thrift store. The only things I want from there are the pizza stone, the loaf pans, and the food processor. I bought all of those things new and I don't want to give them up."

"I'll find them." David headed toward the kitchen.

"You two can help me pack my clothes, if you want," Karma said to her parents.

"We'll pack," Frank said. "You can sit on the bed and direct us."

They moved into the bedroom. Karma sat on the bed and pointed out which clothes were hers, not that there would have been much difficulty in figuring it out. Karma watched Frank and Henna working together, folding clothes, occasionally smiling at each other. She dragged herself out of bed.

"I'll grab my bathroom stuff. There isn't much."

In the bathroom, she looked in the mirror. The dark circles under her eyes looked deep purple in this light. Her hair, which was usually her best feature, was stringy and unwashed. She grimaced at her sunken cheekbones and pallid complexion. She had lost far too much weight. Sometimes, she wondered how she didn't just disappear. Pinching her stomach, she sighed. Skinny as she was, she had a soft, flabby belly from all the drinking. Crash had poked it the other day and told Karma it was time to start hitting the gym. "Hit the gym," she muttered under her breath. "Fuck her."

Karma gathered her soaps, shampoos, toothbrush, and toothpaste and piled them all in the sink. She carefully bent down to retrieve her hair ties from under the sink. On impulse, she grabbed the box of Q-tips as well. Crash cleaned her ears obsessively, but since Karma had paid for these, she was going to take them. She felt guilty almost instantly, but she left them on the pile in the sink.

Henna popped her head in the door waving a grocery bag. "You got everything, sweetie?"

Karma motioned toward the sink and Henna

tossed everything into the bag. "Is this it?"

Karma nodded. "Years of living boiled down to a few grocery bags and a box of books."

Henna shifted the bag so she could wrap an arm around her daughter. "It's better to escape with your life and your health than with a bunch of stuff."

Karma kissed her mother's cheek. "I know. Let's get out of here."

They walked back to the living room holding hands. Carter was just walking back in the door. "We got everything into your parents' car," he said. "David and I are going to follow you all over there to help load the stuff into the house. And your dad had us take your whole desk from the bedroom. It looked like everything in it was yours."

Karma nodded. "I forgot about that old desk. I'm glad we have it."

Henna touched Carter's shoulder. "You are wonderful men."

Carter shook his head, but Karma could tell he was pleased. "We're just glad we were there at the right time."

David and Frank came through the door, laughing. "It was totally your fault," Frank was saying.

"What was whose fault?" Henna asked.

"We might have put a small scratch on the side of the car while we were loading the desk," Frank said.

Henna shrugged. "I was just telling your daughter that health and happiness is more important than possessions. Guess I can't prove myself a liar now."

Karma laughed. "Hey, I need to drive my car home."

"No." Henna frowned. "Your dad can take our car home and I'll drive yours."

"You're on lockdown, missy," Frank said, wagging a finger at her.

"I'm grounded?" Karma was dumbfounded.

Frank laughed. "No, you're just not doing anything until we have a chance to go through your medical paperwork. We're not taking any chances."

Henna agreed. "You're on bed rest until we say otherwise. Nothing but reading, eating, and listening to music."

Carter raised his hand. "Can I get in on some of that action?"

Everyone laughed.

"Come on, everyone. Let's head over to the house and get this stuff unloaded."

"We'll be right behind you," Henna said.

The guys headed out and Henna put her arm around Karma. "Do you have your keys, sweetie?"

"Yep. They're in my pocket."

Henna pulled her head back to look seriously at Karma. "This is it, kid. I'm not going to let you go back to this one again. She will kill you. She will continue to escalate until she kills you."

Karma nodded. She wanted to cry but she didn't have anything left. "I know. I know. I don't know why I keep letting her talk me into coming back. I guess there's a big part of me that thinks I deserve to be treated like this."

"That's because abusers carefully tear down your self-esteem piece by piece, abuse by abuse, until one day, you think there's no point in leaving them because you'll never be good enough to be with anyone else."

Shocked, Karma looked at her mom. "That sounds like the voice of experience."

"Sweetie, you can't live life as a woman without

seeing abuse, whether on a personal level or through the eyes of someone you love. Come on. Let's get out of here."

Karma grinned. "I figured if we gave them enough time, they'd have everything unloaded by the time we got home, and we could sit on the couch and eat chocolate chip cookies."

"Cookies. Damn." Henna smacked herself on the forehead. "I haven't made cookies in weeks. I think I have everything I need. I just have to stop for chocolate chips."

"There's a package in the kitchen," Karma said. "In the cupboard to the left of the stove."

"I'll be right back." Henna walked to the kitchen.

Karma turned to watch her go. Out of the corner of her eye, she saw a flash of movement. One of the guys must have been worried about them. She turned. Crash was standing in the doorway.

"What's going on, Kars?"

Karma shrugged and looked down at the floor.

"Babe, I'm sorry for losing my temper last night. You know how it is when I'm so exhausted from work and practice."

Karma nodded without saying anything.

Crash took a step forward. "Anyway, I saw you flirting with that woman at the party and I lost control."

"I wasn't flirting," Karma said automatically.

"Babe, I'm trying to apologize and you're arguing again."

"I'm sorry," Karma said. "I just wanted you to know I wasn't flirting. I was just talking to her."

"It's the way you were talking to her," Crash said. "The way you tilted your head and laughed. I could tell there was something going on and it felt really disrespectful to me."

"I'm sorry," Karma said again. "I promise I wasn't flirting with her."

"You can say that all you want, but I know what my eyes saw." She paused and took a deep breath. "But I forgive you, babe. I should have been paying more attention to you."

Karma finally looked up. Crash was smiling. "I know you didn't mean it," she said. "It isn't your fault that women try to steal you from me. I'm a threat and they want to take me down a notch."

Karma shook her head. "I don't think it was anything like that."

"You're arguing with me again, babe." Crash's voice was starting to get louder. She looked around the room for the first time. "Where are the bookshelves?"

"She's moving out," Henna said, striding into the room. She had the bag full of bathroom supplies over her shoulder and the bag of chocolate chips in her hand. As she walked toward Karma and Crash, she waved the bag of chocolate chips. "And we're taking these."

Karma bit her lip to keep from laughing. Crash glared at Henna. "I'd like to finish my conversation with my partner."

Henna stepped between them. "This conversation is over."

Crash took a step closer and leaned toward Henna. "I don't think so."

Henna dropped the chocolate chips and the grocery bag and slammed both fists into Crash's chest, knocking her back against the wall. Rushing forward, Henna threw her full body weight into Crash, pinning her to the wall. She pressed her forearm into Crash's throat. Karma tried to speak, but the only noise she could make was a shocked gurgle. She had never seen her mother so angry. Karma couldn't remember Henna ever raising a hand to anyone in her life.

"Listen to me like you've never listened to anyone in your life," Henna said. She leaned closer until her face was almost touching Crash's. Karma had a wild moment of thinking they were going to kiss and she clamped her hand over her mouth to keep from bursting into hysterical laughter. "Go to AA, go to narcotics anonymous, do whatever you need to do. Get clean, get counseling. Deal with your unresolved issues so you stop taking them out on defenseless women. And after you've done all that and you're clean and sober and you've had all the counseling you need, go fuck yourself because you're still not coming near my daughter."

Karma gasped, but neither Crash nor Henna turned to look at her. Crash's face was turning red and she struggled to get away. Henna pushed harder with her body and her arm. "Look into my eyes right now and know that I am telling you the truth. If you ever come near my daughter, if you call her, if you write to her, if you show up at her work, if you come to our house, if you so much as glance at her on the street, I will kill you. I am not afraid of going to jail to save my daughter."

Henna released Crash and Crash shoved her away. "You're a fucking psycho," she screamed, rubbing her neck. "You're a goddamn, fucking psycho." Her voice broke and she started crying. Karma's heart pounded with guilt and compassion. Before she could move toward Crash, Henna grabbed her arm. "Come on, sweetie. We're going home." She picked up the bag and the chocolate chips. Karma let her mother guide her toward the door.

"If you leave now, you can forget about ever coming back," Crash screamed.

Karma stopped. She could feel Crash's pain and fear and anger radiating off her and the force of it nearly brought her to her knees. Holding tightly to her mother's arm, Karma lifted her chin and gritted her teeth. She fished her keychain out of her pocket and wiggled the apartment key off the hook. Without turning around, she tossed the key over her shoulder and walked away.

Chapter Twelve

Jane let herself into her parents' house and marveled at the new living room décor. Everything was beige or cream with deep browns thrown in. It looked amazing with the darkly stained hardwood floors. She picked up a throw pillow and cradled it to her chest, luxuriating in the softness. She had always been a tactile person and things that felt soft drew her without fail. She sat down in an ivory armchair, still holding the pillow.

Mary came in clicking her tongue against her teeth. "Jane, get up. I have company coming today and you've already put things in disarray."

Jane stood, still holding the pillow. "Mother, I just picked up a pillow."

Her mother snatched it from her hands and took it back to the couch, fluffing it the entire time. She came back to the chair and squeezed between it and Jane, brushing her hands over the seat to make sure there weren't any impressions left on the chair. Jane scoffed. "Are you really wiping my butt prints out of the chair?"

Mary Edmunds raised one perfectly arched eyebrow at her daughter. Jane's guilt reared up for just a moment and she felt herself falling back in time to her childhood when the living room was absolutely off limits and only bad girls made messes and got dirty. She curled one of her hands into a fist at her side and dug into her palms with her fingernails, breathing deeply to keep from saying something rude to her mother.

"You know the living room is for company," Mary said. She paused and smiled. "What do you think of my new décor?"

Jane shrugged. "I like it a lot. But I thought it looked great before, too. I didn't think it needed to be updated."

Mary let out an exasperated sigh. "You sound just like your father. You have no idea what it's like to be a committee head at the church. Of course, you wouldn't know since you dropped out of church again."

Jane walked away from her mother and into the kitchen. It smelled like her mother had been baking. Before she could poke around under the foil-covered plates on the counter, she heard the angry click of Mary's sensible heels on the tile floor. "Keep your hands out of those. They're for the ladies."

"I'm a lady," Jane quipped.

Mary ignored her. "What brings you here this morning anyway?"

"Carol's out shopping with a friend so I decided to drive into town and go to a bookstore. You and Dad live close enough I thought I would come see you."

"Carol told me she was going out today. I would have gone with her if I didn't have this important meeting."

"Okay, okay. I can take a hint. Where's Dad, anyway?"

Mary pursed her lips. "He's out playing golf with Bob Weatherby again."

Jane laughed. "What's wrong with that?"

"Golf is expensive, and your father has played every weekend this past month."

"Well, we've had beautiful weather all month. He probably wants to take advantage before winter rolls around."

Mary sniffed again, and Jane had to bite her lip to keep from laughing. She could bet that her father's golf habit didn't amount to even a fraction of what her mother spent on redecorating the house. Come to think of it, it probably didn't amount to a fraction of what Carol spent redecorating their own house. She'd have to put her foot down fast. Obviously, Jane's mother hadn't changed as she got older.

"Maybe I'll call him later. Is he coming back for your meeting?"

"No," Mary said. "This is for women only."

"Even lesbians? I noticed Carol wasn't invited."

"Don't bait me, Jane," her mother said. "Carol isn't on the women's mission committee."

"Okay, okay." Jane held up her hands. "Truce."

Mary sighed. "I'm doing the best I can, Jane. The women at the church ask me questions constantly and I never know what to say."

"Well if they ask which one is the man, tell them neither. That's the point."

"Jane!" Visibly flustered, her mother pressed a hand to her heart. "I don't know when you got so saucy."

"On my thirtieth birthday," Jane said. "Which was last week."

"Oh, dear," her mother said. "I've been so busy with the church. How about I have you and Carol over for a birthday dinner sometime this week? Maybe next weekend? Let me check my calendar first."

"Yep. Just send me a text."

"I'm trying," Mary said. "I've come a long way since I found out you were... Since I found out you were other."

Other. Jane was other. No matter what else happened, for the rest of her life, she would always be other. Jane wondered why Mary had so little trouble accepting Carol over her own daughter. Maybe it was because Carol was always perfectly made up and perfectly dressed up. Maybe it was because of their shared love of shopping. Jane didn't know.

"I know you're trying," Jane said. "You've come a long way."

She leaned forward and kissed her mother on the cheek. "I'm going to head out and leave you to your party."

Her phone rang, and she took it out of her pocket. "It's Carter," she told her mother.

Jane pressed the accept button. "Carter?"

She looked at her mother as she said hello to Carter. Her mother stepped closer and touched her arm.

"Carter, what happened?" She grasped the edge of the counter to steady herself. It had to be David. Why else would Carter be calling?

Jane shook her head, staring down at the counter.

"David's in the hospital, Jane," Carter said.

She shook her head. "What? Why?"

She could barely wrap her mind around the thought of her beloved David in the hospital. She got through the conversation with Carter and glanced up at her mother. Mary's face was lined with worry and Jane suddenly thought she looked old for the first time in Jane's life. She swallowed the panic in her throat. "Mom," she said, reaching for her mother's hand. "David's been shot."

Jane drove to the hospital, while her mother

made phone calls to let the church ladies know the meeting had to be moved. "Lena's going to come get the cookies," Mary said. "She'll probably try to pass them off as her own."

Jane texted Carter as soon as they hit the parking lot and he was waiting for them when they came through the door. He threw his arms around Jane, holding her tightly. "He's okay. He was already out of surgery by the time I called you. He's going to live."

Jane heard Mary exhale sharply, but Jane wasn't ready to let down her guard. "Can I see him?"

"He's still out. I'll take you back there so you can see that he's alive, but you can't stick around. As I said on the phone, there was no point in coming over immediately."

"There's no way I would have not come over," Jane said.

Carter directed Mary to a lounge where his dad was having coffee and took Jane back through the hospital. As they entered David's room, Carter took her hand. She managed to stop herself from gasping, but she couldn't help the shudder that ran through her body. David was hooked up to wires and tubes full of fluid. It looked like he was breathing on a machine. Jane glared at Carter sideways without turning away from David.

"It isn't as bad as it looks," Carter whispered.

"He looks so fragile," Jane whispered. She approached the bedside, looking down at David's beautiful face. "I love you, David," she whispered. She looked at Carter. "Do you think he can hear me?"

"Probably not. He's heavily sedated. Come on, I'll take you back to your mom."

They left the room and Jane took Carter's hand

again. "He was shot in the heart?"

Carter shook his head. "The chest. Some guys in a pickup truck." He swallowed and Jane thought he was trying not to cry. In a moment, his professional expression was back. "They yelled something, David yelled something back, and then he was down. I heard the noise and he was down."

Jane squeezed his hand. "That's terrifying."

"There were other people on the street. Someone got the license plate. Others called the ambulance. He never stopped breathing and his blood pressure stayed relatively high. The bullet missed his heart. We were able to prevent tension pneumothorax." He paused again, swallowing hard. "His lungs didn't collapse."

Jane realized she was crying. David was her lifelong friend and she had let him drift away because Carol didn't like hanging around with gays. She swore to spend more time with them both in the future.

Carter continued. "We were lucky, in a way. They were driving away so there was a lot of distance between us by then. I was able to staunch the blood flow quickly."

"Carter," Jane whispered. "I'm so sorry."

"The police have already been here. They caught the guys. The one who fired the gun will be prosecuted. Not that it will change anything. Hate keeps growing in this country." He pulled her into a conference room and finally let the tears come. "The thing is, I don't even know if they hate us so much because we're gay or because we're an interracial couple. With those types of people, you never know."

Jane wrapped her arms around him. "It doesn't matter."

"It does matter." Carter raised his voice before

composing himself. "It matters."

They held each other, crying. Jane wondered if she should call Karma. She might not even have the same number. But she cared about David and she would want to know.

Carter sniffed loudly and pulled away. "I need to get you back to the lounge, so I can get back to David."

"How long will he be out?"

"At least another few hours, and he'll be woozy and in and out of sleep for hours after that. I recommend going home and coming back tomorrow morning. I'll be with him nonstop until then, I promise."

Jane wanted to stay, too, but she knew better than to argue with Carter. She stood on tiptoes and kissed him on the cheek. "Okay, I'm coming back at six o'clock and I'm bringing you a breakfast burrito."

Carter smiled. "Between you and my parents, I'm going to gain ten pounds by tomorrow night."

They walked back to the lounge. Henry Gunderson jumped up to hug Carter. The two men held each other tightly for a few minutes before Carter turned to greet Mary.

"Thank you for being here," he said.

Mary nodded. "David has been part of my life longer than he's been in yours."

Carter turned to give Jane a kiss on the cheek. "Go home and rest," he whispered. "I'll see you tomorrow."

"David's in good hands," Mary said as Carter left.

Jane patted her mother's shoulder. "Carter loves him so much."

Mary shrugged, looking uncomfortable. "I meant because Carter is a doctor."

Henry put an arm around each woman. "Carter chastised me not to sit here and wait all day. He said he didn't want to feel he had to keep checking on me when he could be with David."

Jane nodded. "We're heading out, too. I'm going to come back tomorrow morning." She looked around the lounge. "Where's Mrs. G?"

"Marla was one of the surgeons working on David all night," Henry said. "She went home to sleep. I'm going to go home and prepare a fine breakfast for her." He grinned. "I've become quite the housewife since Marla went on overnights."

Jane laughed. "If only you could learn how to bake."

"Hey, my last batch of cookies made the neighbors swoon. If you came over more often, you'd have tasted my baking already."

Jane looked down, feeling guilty. She had abandoned everyone. She couldn't even remember the last time she had been to the Gunderson house. She was pretty sure she hadn't seen Mrs. G in years. Henry reached out and held her chin. She looked up at him.

"I know life happens, kid," Henry said. "But you have to make time for the people who love you."

"I will," Jane vowed. "I promise I will."

Jane took her mother's arm as they walked back to the car. She helped her into the passenger seat. As she started the car, she glanced at her mother. Mary looked sad and thoughtful.

Jane pulled out of the parking lot. "This is what happens when people learn that being gay is a sin."

"I highly doubt the men who shot at David were good Christians." Mary sniffed.

"It's the whole culture. Religion has given people sanction to hate. You let people believe that being gay is so terrible that there is nothing worse in the world.

David was beaten by his father for being gay. Now he's been shot. That could just as easily have been me."

Mary shook her head. "You don't know that. Those men were looking for a fight. They yelled, and David yelled back. You don't even know if it had anything to do with being gay."

"Are you fucking kidding me?"

Mary gasped. "Watch your language."

"I can't even believe this. Carter and David were targeted because they are a couple. That could happen to me and Carol."

"It wouldn't happen to you and Carol because you don't flaunt your homosexuality in public."

Jane turned down her mother's street. "We don't flaunt it?" She gripped the steering wheel hard. "We don't flaunt it. You think David and Carter were somehow flaunting their homosexuality. Like, they were practically naked in rainbow loin cloths prancing down the street."

Mary shook her head, staring out the window.

"I can't believe what I'm hearing. Somehow it is David's fault that he got shot because he's gay. You're telling me that he deserves to die because he's gay."

"That's not what I mean at all," Mary whispered, tears streaming down her face.

"Go ahead and cry," Jane snapped. Filled with rage, she yanked the wheel and slammed to a stop in her mother's driveway. "Cry all you want. Cry me a fucking river."

Mary's head bent, and she sobbed.

Jane's rage didn't lessen. "You are a bigot, Mother. You are a fucking bigot. You put up with Carol and me because we're palatable gays. You can deal with us because we don't act gay, look gay, or sound gay. You need to take a good look at yourself and your own sins and shut the fuck up about mine."

Mary turned to her daughter. Her face was covered with tears and she could barely speak through the sobs. "I love you. I have always loved you even when I couldn't understand you."

Jane glanced at her mother and looked away. "Get out of my car," she said.

From the corner of her vision, Jane could see her mother's mouth open, but she didn't say anything. Instead, Mary got out of the car. Jane didn't wait to see her get into the house. As soon as the passenger door closed, she took off.

Driving home, Jane's anger didn't dissipate. Instead, it grew and filled her body. Her vision blurred, and she started to shake. She wanted to punch someone. She wanted to kill everyone who had ever violated another person's right to safety. Crash popped into her head and Jane wished for a second that the woman was standing in front of her so she could slam a fist into that abuser. David had told her that he and Carter helped move Karma out of Crash's place, but Jane knew that was no guarantee that she hadn't gone back. If Jane wasn't such a coward, she would have agreed to be friends with Karma again that day in Starbucks. She would have convinced Karma to leave Crash. They would be close again and that bond between them would have come back instantly. Jane would have had to leave Carol because why would she stay in a loveless relationship when she could be with her soulmate?

She made it home without an accident. Carol was in the kitchen.

"I'm glad you're home. What's for dinner?"

Jane stared at her, trying to remember why she

had married this woman. There must have been good times, there must have been something. Right now, Jane couldn't remember any. All she could remember were the times Carol had made her feel guilty. Guilty for making messes, guilty for wanting to go out with friends, guilty for disagreeing with Carol about anything.

"David was shot," Jane said shortly. "I'm going back to the hospital first thing in the morning with breakfast for Carter."

"Oh, no," Carol said. "Is he okay?"

"He's going to live."

"What time are you going to the hospital? Don't forget we're having brunch with Sue and Larry at eleven."

Jane slammed both hands down on the kitchen island. The pain radiated up to her shoulders. She raised her voice to hear over a sudden roaring in her ears. "Fuck Sue and Larry. Fuck brunch. Fuck your straight friends, and fuck you."

Carol's mouth dropped open and it took all of Jane's willpower not to laugh at the shocked look on her wife's face. She stormed out of the kitchen and into the office. Slamming the door as hard as she could, she stomped to her desk and sat down. The anger drained from her body and the guilt crept back in. She had never yelled at Carol in all the years they had been together. She had always gone along with what Carol wanted, not just because it was easier to get along, but because Jane didn't have a lot of strong opinions about the things Carol cared about. If she wanted to paint the bedroom gray because that was the trend that year, Jane didn't argue because ultimately, she didn't care enough about the bedroom color to make it worth a fight.

Jane turned on her computer and opened a browser window. She searched for Karma Miller and found a Facebook page. Staring at Karma's profile picture, Jane smiled. She didn't know if this was a recent picture, but Karma looked beautiful. Her face was rounder and her smile went all the way to her eyes. She looked rested and happy. Jane touched the computer screen. Karma's brown eyes were directed at the camera and Jane almost felt as if Karma was looking into her soul. "I miss you," Jane whispered. "I miss you so much."

She touched the screen one more time before closing the program. She had a lot of work to do before she could consider being there for Karma again. Jane didn't want to be married to Carol, but she couldn't imagine how she could divorce her. They owed so much money on the house and they were deep in credit card debt. Carol made good money, but she wouldn't be able to keep the house on her own. Jane sighed. This was her purgatory. She was destined to spend her life with someone she didn't really love, not because she was gay, but because she had wasted her chance to be with the one person who ever truly saw her. "I did this to myself," Jane muttered. "I did it to myself."

She put her head down on her desk and sobbed.

Chapter Thirteen

Karma locked the door of A Woman's Place and breathed deeply. She never got tired of the smell of books and coffee. *And women,* she thought, grinning to herself. She walked through the empty store, running her finger over the spines of the books she passed. Other than expanding the lesbian section, she hadn't made many changes since buying the store from Jenna.

She had sent Lauren, her only employee, home half an hour early today. They were slow sometimes in the evenings, and Lauren was young and raring to go out and party. Karma rarely partied—in any sense of the word—these days. Most evenings, she closed the store and went home to play cards with her parents. She supposed most women in their thirties would be embarrassed to admit they lived with their parents, but Karma knew a good thing when she saw it. Her savings had seemed to increase daily once she was living at home. It helped that she wasn't buying drugs and takeout for Crash. To be fair, it also helped that Karma herself had quit drinking and smoking pot. Since she spent all her time working or hanging out at home, she didn't have anything to spend her money on except the occasional groceries her parents would let her buy.

Karma smiled, thinking about her parents. She was so lucky to have them. They refused rent. They just kept telling her to save her money so she could make smart decisions about her life. Henna had sat her down shortly after the last time Karma broke up with Crash and told her unequivocally that there was to be no going back. No arguing, no conditions. Karma could live in their house and Henna would do everything in her power to nurse her back to health, with the caveat that Karma go to counseling. She and Frank offered to go to family therapy with her, but Karma didn't feel her family dynamic was in question. She had just gotten sucked into a role where she felt she wasn't good enough for anything else.

Karma confirmed all the doors were locked and the coffee pot was off. She gave the fridge a kick. It tended to not seal properly, and Karma didn't want to risk her favorite creamer going to waste.

When she got back to the register to close out, she noticed a book sitting on the back counter with a note on top. Karma picked up the note.

Dear Karma,

I can't believe how much I liked this book. I didn't think I would. I mean, what do I care about old lesbians from the eighties? Anyway, it was so good. I even got my mom to read it. She's middle-age like you so I figured it was more her style anyway. You're the best. I love you.

Love forever,
Lauren

Karma laughed, holding the note. Lauren was only ten years younger than Karma, but it felt like a lifetime sometimes. Karma usually thought that she looked younger than thirty, but she felt like she was sixty. She picked up the book. It was Karma's own copy of *Curious Wine* by Katherine V. Forrest. An oldie, but goodie. Karma held it to her chest. This was the first lesbian book Jane had ever read. Karma remembered discussing it with her over doughnuts. Karma had gotten a chocolate fingerprint on one of the pages and she had panicked, sure that Jane was going to be pissed, but Jane had laughed. *Books are meant to be loved and covered with chocolate*, Jane had said. Karma had offered to trade copies with Jane, but Jane refused, insisting the chocolate fingerprint gave it more character than a new book. The memory made her smile. Lesbian literature had changed so much in the past decade. Back then, the lesbian section had been one small shelf in the back of the bookstore. Karma smiled again before slipping the book into her shoulder bag and shutting off the rest of the lights.

It was a beautiful October evening, and Karma was glad she parked down by the bakery. She had closed just early enough to pop in and buy some bread at half-off. It was almost as good as fresh, especially when watered down and put in the oven for a few minutes. Smiling, swinging her shoulder bag, Karma strode down the street. A couple of men turned to look at her as she went by, but they didn't feel predatory, just admiring. Karma gave one of them a smile and kept going. If either of them tried to talk to her, she'd tell them that they had the wrong tree. For now, it felt good that people were smiling at her. Karma went into the bakery and, tempted by the smells and the last-minute prices, bought a few loaves of bread and an oversized chocolate chip cookie. Karma remembered how Crash used to tell her that her metabolism was going to catch up with her in a few years, but Karma had yet to see it. After she quit drinking, she lost her Pooh Bear belly, and though she had gained weight since the Crash days, she felt she had just filled out in all the right places.

She walked out of the bakery with the bag of bread tucked into her shoulder bag and the cookie in her hand. Taking a bite as she pushed open the door, she reveled in the melting goodness of the chocolate on her tongue. Henna still made the world's best cookies, but these could rival even her mother's. Besides, Henna had them all eating healthy now. Her dad was coming up on sixty, and at his last physical his doctor had recommended he eat less fat and fewer carbs. Good for Dad, bad for Karma. She probably shouldn't bring bread into the house, but she figured she would pop it into the freezer and bake it when her parents went on their semi-regular date nights.

She turned the corner toward her car and shoved the rest of the chocolate chip cookie in her mouth.

"Karma?"

Recognizing Crash's voice, Karma froze. She tried chewing the cookie as fast as possible, so she wouldn't turn around with her cheeks wadded out like a chipmunk. Scolding herself silently, she firmly reminded herself that she didn't care what Crash thought of her. She whipped around, wiping cookie crumbs from her mouth.

"Karma, how you doin'?"

Karma, still chewing, shrugged. She made a point of slowly finishing the food in her mouth and swallowing it. "I'm fine, Crash. How are you?"

Crash didn't have to answer for Karma to guess. No longer streamlined and muscled, Crash was thin and drawn. The lines around her eyes and mouth were thrown into sharp relief under the streetlights. Red blotches covered her nose and she had dark circles under her eyes. Karma felt a rush of pity and almost reached for her before she remembered that Crash wasn't her responsibility.

"You know, not so good, babe. Not so good. The band split up and I lost my last job."

"I'm sorry to hear that," Karma said. She started glancing around to see if anyone else was in the area. With most of the businesses now closed for the night, there wasn't much foot traffic, though cars went by regularly.

Crash stepped closer. "Look, Karma. It really wasn't right of you to take off like that."

Karma squared her shoulders. "Crash, it was the best thing I could do for myself."

"I tried to kill myself after you left."

Karma put her hand over her mouth for a second. "I'm so sorry." Karma was vaguely aware that her phone was ringing and for an instant, she had a desire to grab it and shout to whomever it was that she needed help. Instead, she folded her arms across her chest. "That must have been a difficult time."

Crash nodded, looking down. "Nothing really made sense after you left. I didn't have a reason to go on."

Karma blinked back tears. Crash, once so vibrant and full of life and promise, was drooling as she talked. "Crash, are you high right now?"

"Don't judge me," Crash suddenly screamed in Karma's face.

Karma thought of Jody, the woman who had helped Karma find a domestic violence therapist. Karma had called her in the middle of the night more than once, crying over her guilt. Karma had been so sure Crash would die without her. Crash didn't know how to take care of herself without Karma. Karma was the only thing holding Crash afloat. Jody had talked her down every time. *Abusers abuse*, she had said. *Nothing you do will stop it, just as nothing you did caused it.*

Karma noticed a couple walking toward them. "Excuse me," she said.

The couple turned toward her, smiling. The woman looked at Crash, her nose wrinkled. "Is something wrong?" the woman asked.

Karma nodded. "I need to get to my car safely, and I think this woman wants to hurt me."

"Fuck you, Karma." Crash reached out to grab Karma's collar and the couple both jumped in front of her.

"Step away or I'll call the cops," the man said.

Crash spit on the sidewalk. "You're a cunt, Karma," she said, pointing a finger in Karma's face. "You're a vile, fucking cunt."

Don't engage, Jody's voice was whispering in her ear. *Don't engage.* Karma kept her eyes on the couple in front of her. The man took a step closer to Crash. "Ma'am, you are going to have to go now."

The women whipped her cell phone out of a pocket and started dialing. "I'm calling the police right now."

"Fuck," Crash snapped. She turned on her heel and took off down the street. "I deserve better than you, Karma!"

Karma bit her lip to keep from shouting after her. Guilt stabbed her in the gut. She managed to keep from crying as the couple walked her to her car and waited until she had locked the doors and started the engine. As soon as she was on the road, she pulled her cell out of her purse and called Jody.

"Jody, I saw Crash," she shouted over her sobs.

Jody exhaled. "What happened?"

Karma told her the story. "Girl, you did great," Jody said. "I'm so proud of you."

"I feel like such shit," Karma said. "She looks horrible."

"She did that to herself, honey. There is nothing you could have done to stop that."

"I wonder. Maybe I could have convinced her to get counseling with me."

"And risked your life as she tried to get better?" Jody scoffed. "The only thing that would have happened is that you would have been dragged along on her ride. Karma, you did the very best thing for yourself. Look at you now. You'd still be drowning in debt and taking extra dinner rolls from the restaurant just to have something to eat."

"That's Crash's life now," Karma said.

"And that's her choice," Jody said. "You are choosing you."

Karma smiled through her tears. "Thanks, Jody. You're the best. I owe you dinner."

"At least that," Jody said, laughing.

"Come over Sunday. My mom invited our friends David and Carter. Bring your hubby and we'll make a party of it."

"I would love it. Now go home and eat something and watch some aliens blow things up."

"I love you, Jody," Karma said.

"Back at you."

Karma hung up and drove the rest of the way home. When she pulled up to the house, she checked her face in the mirror. She looked a little puffy, but her eyes weren't red. She didn't know if she should tell her mom about running into Crash. On the other hand, what did she have to hide? *I stood up for myself*, Karma thought. She smiled. She had been tested by Crash and her manipulations, and she had managed to pull herself out of it. Two years of therapy wasn't wasted money. She grabbed her bag and went into the house.

"Mom, Dad, I'm home!"

In the kitchen, Karma stashed her loaves of bread in the freezer and checked the fridge for leftovers. Pulling out a Tupperware of what looked like chicken curry, Karma leaned against the counter. She pulled open the lid and grabbed a fork from the drawer. Deciding not to heat up the food, she ate it out of the container. She knew she had to get better about bringing dinner to the store. The house was strangely quiet. Her parents must have gone to bed early. Dad had been going to sleep earlier lately, but her mother usually stayed up to see Karma in from the store. All of Karma's savings had gone into purchasing the bookstore, but even if she wasn't back to zero, Karma wasn't sure she wanted to move out. *I may be destined to be single forever, but at least I have my parents*, she thought, smiling. Sometimes she missed sex, but not enough to send her out seeking a girlfriend. A couple of bad dates after her breakup with Crash had reminded her that she wasn't ready to try again.

After two years of therapy, Karma still wasn't completely sure that it hadn't been something in her that had caused Crash to become abusive. On the surface, she knew. She had studied narcissistic personalities and the steps abusers take to bring down the self-esteem of their victims. She had spent enough time talking about it with Jody and Henna. She had faithfully gone to therapy every week. And she had helped counsel other women out of abusive relationships. Karma knew without a doubt that those women didn't deserve to be hit. So why did she still have the small voice in her head that told her Crash wouldn't have hit her if Karma had behaved better? Until Karma had that resolved, she knew it was better to not even consider dating. If she ran into another abuser, she didn't know if she would be able to extricate herself quickly enough.

She shoveled the last couple of bites into her mouth and put the dish in the sink. Thinking about dating inevitably led her to thinking about Jane. Karma had never known a gentler or lovelier soul. She had fucked things up with Jane and lost her to a marriage to someone who could never appreciate Jane the way Karma could.

She should call Jane one of these days just to see how she was doing. Jane had told her that the wife wouldn't let her hang out with other women, but that was years ago. Maybe things had changed. She reached for her phone and noticed she had voicemail. Someone had tried to call her while she was dealing with Crash. Smiling, she tapped the notification. Maybe Jane had read her thoughts and reached out already.

Hi, sweetie. It's mom. Dad had a heart attack and we're at St. Luke's. He's alive and going to be fine, we think. But maybe you should come over when you get this. I love you with all my heart.

Karma hung up the phone, stunned. Frank was the healthiest man she knew. Sure, he ate a little too much, but he exercised every day, he didn't smoke, and he had never done drugs, not even pot. And he was skinny, almost as thin as Karma. Karma shook her head. If she had been told someone in her family was going to have a heart attack, she would have guessed it would be Henna.

Driving to the hospital, Karma called Lauren.

"Hi, boss," Lauren said.

"Lauren, you're going to kill me. Can you open the store tomorrow?"

"I can do it. I'll be hungover, but I can do it."

"You have my permission to wear sunglasses all day," Karma said.

Lauren laughed. "Is everything okay?"

"My dad just had a heart attack. I'm headed to the hospital. I don't know how long I'll be there."

"I'm sorry, Karma. Is there anything else I can do?"

"Don't drink and drive," Karma laughed.

"I promise. Love you, sister."

"Back at you."

Karma hung up. She may not have a lover, but she was rich in friendships. She felt sorry for Jane living with just her wife and their occasional dinners out with the straight couples what's-her-name deemed acceptable. Karma had lost all her friends during her years with Crash, but some had filtered back, and she had gained some new ones. There was nothing quite like the love of a group of women.

She parked in visitor parking and ran into the hospital. She knew this hospital almost as well as her own home. Between her own experiences being here after fights with Crash, and the times she had come to visit David after he was shot, she figured they would give her an honorary cot. Getting a pass from the front desk, she speed-walked to her dad's room. Henna was sitting at Frank's bedside, holding his hand. Frank was sleeping. Karma rushed in as quietly as she could. Henna stood to hug her before pulling her out of the room. Karma looked back on her father's sleeping face. He looked peaceful and healthy, other than the machines hooked up to his slender body.

She followed her mother out of the room. "Mom, what happened?"

Henna put her arms around Karma. "It was just a normal night," she said. "We didn't do anything out of the ordinary. We had chicken curry for lunch and a little later, your dad had heartburn. Sometimes spicy stuff gives him heartburn, so I didn't think anything of it. I should have paid more attention." She sniffed and started crying.

"Mom, it's okay," Karma said. "Dad is the heartburn king. I wouldn't have thought anything of it, either."

Henna nodded. "We've been trying to eat our bigger meal for lunch and a light snack for dinner. I thought that was healthier."

Karma squeezed her hand.

Henna went on. "He was getting ready to go out for a walk. He sat down on the couch to put on his socks and he said he felt sick to his stomach. He went to stand up and he just collapsed."

Karma put a hand over her mouth. "Oh. That must have been terrifying."

"I didn't know what was going on, but at Frank's age, you can't be too sure. And his doctor was worried about his cholesterol and blood pressure last visit, remember."

Karma nodded.

"So, I just called the ambulance. They brought him in and a cardiologist was waiting. They say he's going to be fine but we're going to have to make some drastic changes to our lifestyle."

Karma sighed. "I haven't been helping with all of the sweets and bread I bring into the house."

"Oh, baby," Henna said. "Your dad is a grown man and makes his own choices about what to eat." She paused, looking stern. "That is, he used to make his own choices. From now on, he will be eating what the doctor advises. I will, too. And so will you when you eat at home."

"All for one and one for all," Karma said.

She and Henna laughed, holding each other. "He woke up a while ago. The doctor said it was a good heart attack, whatever the hell that can mean."

"Did he have surgery?'

"No. It was something called non-segment myo-something. Oh, Karma. I don't remember. They gave him an EKG and hooked him up to an IV. I think they said they gave him a beta blocker. There was a lot of medical talk. Carter talked to his doctor, so he'll be able to tell you more. They think it can be controlled with medication and lifestyle change."

"Mom, we will do whatever it takes," Karma vowed.

"I know," Henna said. "Besides, it's not like I can't stand to get a little healthier." She patted her stomach.

"You are perfect the way you are," Karma said, snuggling against her mother. "The most beautiful woman ever."

"I love you, sweetie."

"I love you, Mom."

Henna pulled away. "Now that you're here, would you sit with your dad for a little bit? I want to get some coffee and use the bathroom. And I'm going to call your grandma and let her know what's going on."

"Of course. Take your time."

Henna touched Karma's face. "I don't know what I'd do without you."

Karma kissed her mother on the cheek and slipped back into her father's room. Sitting beside his bed, she held his hand gently. On closer look, he looked pale. She swallowed the lump in her throat and focused on breathing, trying to keep the knot of anxiety in her stomach at bay.

Frank stirred, opening his eyes. "Wa—"

"Dad?"

He swallowed. "Water."

Karma didn't know if she should give him water. She glanced around the room. There was a pitcher on the side table. *I guess they wouldn't provide it if he wasn't supposed to drink it.* Pouring half a glass, she held it so her father could take a sip.

"Love you," Frank whispered.

"Oh, Daddy." Karma took his hand again. "I love you."

He smiled slightly, and Karma's heart broke. "Daddy, are you okay?"

"I'm the picture of health," he whispered.

Karma shook her head. "What can I do for you?"

"Find true love."

She leaned back in her chair. "What?"

"Your mom thinks you are still pining over Jane. You need to call her. Set it to rest. Life's too short to spend it pining over what could have been."

Karma patted his hand. "Just focus on getting well. Just concentrate on you. Go back to sleep for now, Dad."

He closed his eyes and Karma watched his chest moving up and down. A few minutes later, he opened his eyes again.

"More water, please."

Karma got up and held the glass for him and he drank a little more this time.

"Now a cheeseburger?" Frank quipped.

"Forget it," Karma laughed. "There's gonna be some changes in this town from here on out."

Frank chuckled. "Karma, I meant what I said. You are a beautiful, loving woman. I love having you at home, your mom and I both do. We never want you to leave. But we want you to be happy."

"I am happy," Karma said. "Besides, I blew it with Jane. Long ago. I hated that I embarrassed her. It made me feel ashamed of who I was." She paused, looking down at her father's hand. "I mean, if that sweet, accepting, and kind woman didn't want to be seen with me in public, what did that say about me? I was ridiculous. No wonder I ended up with someone like Crash."

Frank shook his head. "Crash has nothing to do with this. She's out of your life forever."

Karma decided not to tell him about her run-in with her ex this evening. "Still."

Frank cleared his throat and Karma gave him a little more water. Karma resumed her position next to the bed, holding his hand.

Frank smiled. "You're a good daughter, Karma, and a good woman. Your mom and I are so proud of you."

"Thanks, Dad. That means a lot."

"I don't know if this will change anything, but

when I first started dating your mother, I was often embarrassed by her."

Karma stared at her dad. Frank and Henna were the most perfect couple she had ever known.

"It's true," Frank continued. "She was loud and vivacious, and she had this laugh—well, you know her laugh. She just throws her head back and roars and everyone in the room turns to look at her."

Karma nodded, smiling. She loved her mother's unabashed laughter. It sounded like pure joy to Karma's ears.

"She was a big woman and she wore outrageous clothes. And she was so opinionated. She was never afraid to call out someone who was being sexist or racist, no matter where we were."

Karma smiled. "It sounds like she never changed."

"She didn't." Frank smiled, squeezing Karma's hand. "I did. I became more confident in myself. I became less interested in what other people thought about me. And I realized that if I was going to hold on to my soulmate, I was going to have to love her unconditionally, loud laugh and all. And I have, Karma. I have never regretted my marriage to your mother in the entire time we've been together. She is my light and my soul, and she brought you to my life. The two of you are the best things that have ever happened to me." His voice broke and he started crying. Karma instantly stood and started rubbing his head.

"Dad, don't get upset. It's okay."

Frank cleared his throat. "I'm all right. I just don't want you to miss your soulmate because you're still harboring some resentment that she wasn't able to move past her entire religious upbringing the instant she met you."

Karma patted his hand. "Thanks, Dad. Now rest, please."

Frank smiled at her and closed his eyes. Watching him, Karma tried to match her breath to his. She held his hand softly, praying to God or Goddess or whatever might be out there that Frank would make it through this and live forever.

Maybe he was right about Jane. She knew Jane wasn't in love with the wife. And she and Karma had been so connected. Karma didn't know if she believed in soulmates, but if there was such a thing, Jane was hers. She thought about calling but decided against it. The wife might be around, and her presence would keep Jane from feeling free to talk. Karma decided to write a letter. She didn't have Jane's address, but she could get it from David and Carter. She could send it to Jane's parents' house. Jane's mother may be a bitch, but she was a well-mannered bitch. She would certainly think that etiquette dictated passing on a letter that was addressed to her daughter.

She composed the letter in her head.

Dear Jane,

I think of you daily and I miss you deeply. The times I spent with you were the best in my life. I know it's been years and everything has changed, but I still feel that connection in my soul. You were the one who once called us soulmates. If that's true, how can we possibly be so out of touch with each other. Please call me, write me, or come see me at A Woman's Place. (I own the bookstore now! Long story, I'll tell you in person.) I love you forever.

Warmly,
Karma

Smiling to herself, Karma leaned back in the chair and closed her eyes, still holding her father's hand. She'd write the letter as soon as she got home and send it from the store.

Chapter Fourteen

Jane threw her purse across the counter, scattering mail everywhere. She scrambled around, picking up the letters, swearing at herself under her breath. The entire stack of mail was nothing but bills and late notices. She tore open the shut-off notice from the electric company. How could two people who made as much money as she and Carol be so broke? She ripped into the credit card statement. The balance had jumped by over three thousand dollars since last month. She skimmed the purchases. Six hundred dollars at Nordstrom. Three hundred dollars at Harbor Antiques. This was all Carol. Jane sat down on a stool, near tears. She and Carol fought about money more than anything else. She just couldn't get it into Carol's head that having a credit card wasn't a license to spend money. She glanced at the rest of the bills on the counter. Carol's direct deposit would go in tonight, so Jane could pay the electric and the minimum on the credit card after paying the mortgage. She looked at the dates on the statement. These purchases had been made after the last big blowout they had over money when Jane had told Carol that they simply could not buy any more luxury purchases until they paid down their credit card and paid off the home improvement loan. Jane often woke up with chest pain in the night, wondering how they would ever get out from under this massive debt. She wanted to sell the house and use it to pay off the loan and the credit cards, but Carol wouldn't even consider it.

Looking around the kitchen, Jane sighed. She was partly to blame. She liked the house and she enjoyed living in a place that looked luxurious. She knew the other teachers were impressed on those rare occasions Jane was permitted to bring someone home. But she didn't need all of this. She didn't need to spend thousands of dollars on the latest fashion trends in bathroom curtains to be happy.

She decided to make herself a snack while she thought about it. Not wanting to make any rash judgments, she took her time, fixing herself a peanut butter and jelly sandwich on toast. Jane had a couple of hours grading to do after going through the bills, and Carol would be home in an hour demanding to know what was for dinner. Jane decided they were having leftovers tonight and Carol could heat up her own. Carol was useless in the kitchen, refusing to make even her own breakfast or lunch to take to work. Jane wondered what would happen if she went on strike and just refused to do it anymore. After all, Jane worked as many hours as Carol. More, if grading and teacher conferences and going to the store for supplies for the classroom counted. It counted, Jane decided.

It was a pattern. She felt as if she had been Carol's servant for years. Taking care of the house, taking care of the meals, and contributing to the money so Carol could do nothing but work and shop. Jane knew she couldn't just pull everything out from under Carol. It wouldn't be fair. She was in a pattern, too. It just seemed to be more beneficial to Carol than to Jane.

She finished her snack and put the plate in the sink. Carol would be angry if she came home and there were dishes in the sink, but for today, at least, Jane didn't care. She picked up her phone and dialed the credit card company.

"I need to cancel this card."

After the call, she felt better. Carol was going to be angry, but they needed to do something drastic. From now on, if it couldn't come out of the checking account, they didn't need it. Carol didn't even carry her debit card with her. She had been so embarrassed the few times she tried to use it for major purchases and it had been declined that she stopped carrying it, even for small purchases. She just whipped out the credit card for everything. Not anymore. Jane went into the office and dug out Carol's debit card. She took it to her own desk and hid it in a drawer, behind a stack of paperwork. She buried the checkbook and the extra checks as well. Since Jane paid all the bills, did all the grocery shopping, and dealt with any repairs or services, Carol didn't need access to money. From now on, Jane was giving her an allowance for coffee and snacks during the work day. In cash. If she needed more, she would need to justify why she wanted it.

Jane played around with the figures. If she stuck to her plan, she might actually be able to buy some new clothes in a month. She had been sewing holes in her work clothes for a year, trying to get by without getting any new ones, but she needed a new wardrobe. She shook her head. It wasn't fair that Carol bought whatever she wanted, whenever she wanted, and Jane had to make do with clothes that were literally falling apart. Not anymore. It was time to stand up for herself.

Jane busied herself grading papers. When it started getting dark in the office, she reached to turn on the lamp and noticed that it was almost seven. Carol should be home by now. Jane finished the last paper and stuck everything back in her briefcase.

She headed to the kitchen to grab her phone, figuring Carol might have texted to say she was late. Carol was sitting at the kitchen counter. Jane flipped on the light. "What are you doing sitting here in the dark?"

Carol didn't answer. Jane glanced at her. She looked livid. Jane's stomach knotted instantly. She opened the fridge and pulled out some leftover pot roast. "I didn't have time to cook today. I just finished work five minutes ago."

"You've been home for hours," Carol finally said.

Jane sighed. "And as I've said a billion times, a teacher is not finished working when she gets home from school."

Carol glared at her. "Do you want to guess what happened to me today?"

Jane could guess but she thought better of saying so. She put the leftover pot roast in the microwave and turned to face Carol.

"I went to the store to pick up something I need," Carol said. "And when I got there, my card was declined. I knew it wasn't possible we were at the limit, so I argued with the clerk."

Jane swallowed. The knot in her stomach was getting heavier, but she couldn't let Carol scare her. They were in danger of losing everything. She straightened her shoulders. "I canceled the card today."

"Yes," Carol hissed. "I realized that after I called the credit card company to raise hell. How are you even allowed to cancel a joint credit card?"

Jane shrugged. "Maybe because I'm the primary user and you were an additional."

"Not that it matters how," Carol said. "What matters is why. Why you felt the need to humiliate me. Why you made a major decision about our money without talking to me."

Jane picked up the pile of bills from earlier and sat down, holding them in her hands. "Here is our credit card statement. Please read it. All of this happened after the last fight we had when I told you we could not afford any more luxury purchases."

Carol barely glanced at it. "I know what I spent. I also know what I can afford."

"Except you can't," Jane said. "We just got a shut off notice for the electric because there isn't enough money in the account to pay the whole thing. Do you know why? Because our minimum payment on the credit card has gotten so huge, I can no longer afford to pay it. And do you know why it's gotten so huge?" She pointed to the bill. "Look at your purchases. Look at them."

Carol glanced at the bill again. "I make way more money than you. I don't think you have a right to tell me what I can and can't spend."

Jane threw up her hands. "Are you kidding me? Are you even listening to me at all?"

Carol hit the counter with her palm. "You humiliated me. I stood there and argued with the clerk in front of people. Do you know how small I felt?"

"Carol, this is not about what other people think. This is about our life and we're going to lose all of it if you don't curb your spending."

Carol stood. "And I'm telling you that you are going to reinstate that card immediately. I will not be told what to do when I bring home the bulk of the money in this house."

Jane's rage vanished. Carol made way more money than Jane, so she would always feel entitled to spend what she wanted, no matter how much Jane begged her to stick to a budget. "No. I won't reopen it."

Carol's face got red. "Are you telling me no?" She leaned forward on the counter, her face contorted with rage. Jane's hands were shaking, but she knew this was the only solution.

"I'm not going to do it," Jane said. "You can open a new credit card that's only in your name and you can pay the bill every month."

"Fine," Carol said.

"I'm not finished," Jane said. "We are going to pay off the canceled card out of the home loan. Once it's paid off, we don't have to worry about it anymore because it won't exist. We are going to close our checking account and open separate accounts. We will each pay half of the mortgage and we will pay seventy-thirty on the home line because the bulk of that went to your wardrobe, your purses, your shoes, your need for new curtains and faucets. You will pay your car payment and I'll pay mine. I will give you a receipt for the groceries and you'll pay me half. I'll do the same for all of the utilities."

Carol was staring at her, open-mouthed, and Jane felt the guilt stabbing into her stomach again.

"This is ridiculous," Carol shouted. "What the hell is wrong with you?"

Jane managed to keep her voice soft and calm. "It's what is wrong with us, Carol. We are drowning in debt and I have tried over and over to get you to see it and work with me on it. Since you have no interest in doing so, I'm going to have to divide our finances." She stood. "Look at it this way. You should be better off since you make so much more money than I do."

Jane strode out of the kitchen and back into her office, slamming and locking the door behind her. Drained, but relieved, she pulled a throw from the closet and stretched out on the love seat. Her little office was a safe space, the only room that Jane had been allowed to decorate and furnish herself. Unlike the rest of the rooms in the house, this one had not undergone any redecoration over the years. Jane had painted it all white. She had found a big, ugly table at a thrift store for her desk. Over the years, she had added file cabinets and the top half of a dresser she had gotten out of someone's trash. It was her favorite piece, her handmade desk. Big, beautiful, and eclectic. The whole room was lovely, clean, and white. Adding color with prints and pillows gave it a splash and hanging a big seascape behind the small sofa made it feel sunny and warm.

Jane rested on the sofa, staring up at the painting. She would just spend the night here and deal with Carol tomorrow after work. She pressed the guilt down as she thought of not making lunch and breakfast for Carol tomorrow. Carol didn't even know how to work the coffee maker. *Tough shit*, Jane thought.

Carol knocked on the door. Jane debated for a second about not answering, but she figured it would be worse later. She heaved herself off the love seat and opened the door.

Carol put her foot in the door and pushed her way in. "I'm going to need money for tomorrow. I'm supposed to be going to lunch with the other VPs and I need to be able to pay for it."

"Okay," Jane said. "I'll make sure there's fifty dollars on the counter in the morning."

"Get it now," Carol said.

Jane's stomach started flip-flopping again. Jane had two hundred dollars hidden in the desk and if she took fifty dollars in front of Carol, Carol would insist on all of it.

"It'll be there in the morning," Jane repeated.

"What the hell is wrong with you?" Carol snapped. "What's happened to the woman I married? You used to be so sweet, now you're nothing but a nag."

"Maybe I'm a nag because this relationship is so one-sided. I do everything around here. I cook, I clean, I pay the damn bills. You work and shop. That's it."

"It's the golden rule," Carol said. "She who makes the gold makes the rules."

"Are you kidding me?" Jane's mouth dropped open. "I somehow thought your abuse of me was inadvertent. I didn't realize you do it on purpose because you think you're better than me."

"That isn't what I meant."

"I think it is," Jane said. "I think you finally said exactly what you meant. You think you're the lord of the manor because you make so much more money. I can't believe you value wealth so much that you think it's the only thing you need to contribute to this marriage."

"That's bullshit," Carol said. "Just because you're habitually unsatisfied."

"Unsatisfied. Maybe if I wasn't in a completely one-sided relationship, I would be a little more satisfied. We are in debt, we aren't in love with each other, and our sex life sucks." Aware that she was yelling, Jane attempted to control her voice. "I don't know why we're even still married," she said softly.

Carol rocked back. "You're always complaining.

Nothing I do is good enough. And we have sex all the time."

"Yeah," Jane said. "Why don't you think back and try to remember when the last time was that our sex life was about anything other than you having an orgasm."

Carol opened her mouth to respond but stopped when the doorbell rang. "Who the hell is that?"

Jane pushed past her and went to the living room. Unsolicited visitors were rare. She sent up a small prayer to thank God for the interruption. Pulling open the door, Jane froze.

"Mom?"

Her mother came into the house. Her hair was disheveled, and her eyes were red and puffy. Jane had never seen her mother looking so terrible. She closed the door and ushered her mother into the house. Mary went through the house to the kitchen and sat down at the kitchen table. "Could you get me a cup of coffee, please?" she said to Jane.

Jane started the cappuccino maker, glad for a distraction. She felt her anger at Carol dissipating in carrying out the small task. She could hear her in Jane's office opening drawers and resisted the urge to run in and stop her. When she finished making the cappuccinos, she put one in front of her mother and sat down at the table.

"Mom, what's wrong?"

Mary picked up her coffee and held it in both hands, breathing in the scent. Jane did the same. She loved to savor the smell of her coffee before she drank it. She must have learned the behavior from her mother. They did have one thing in common, Jane supposed.

Jane watched her mother smelling the coffee

before taking a small sip. She didn't press her to respond. She knew her mother would talk as soon as she was ready.

"We're losing the house," Mary said.

Carol walked in and sat down next to Mary. "What?"

"We're behind on the payments. Way behind. Paul says we have to sell if we can before it's foreclosed."

"Maybe we can help," Carol said. "We have a line of credit."

"We cannot," Jane said. "We are already in debt."

Carol clicked her tongue. "But your parents are losing their house."

"They aren't losing it to be out on the street," Jane said. "They're going to sell and buy something cheaper." Jane looked at her mother. "I know it seems upsetting right now, but if you downsize, you can sell a lot of that expensive furniture. You might break even, or even come out ahead."

Mary shook her head, staring down into her coffee. "How can you be so blasé about it? That's your childhood home and we're losing it because your father couldn't pay the bills."

"My father couldn't pay the bills because you have never worked, and you spend his paycheck faster than he can make it."

"Jane!" Carol glared at her. "How dare you talk to your mother like that in her time of need?"

"Someone needs to talk to her like that." Jane pushed away from the table and stood up. She pointed a finger at her mother. "You spend and spend with impunity. You compulsively redecorate the house when there is nothing wrong with the way it looks. You buy the most expensive shoes, the most expensive purses, the most expensive jewelry. You are still hurt that Dad hasn't gotten you a bigger diamond than the monstrosity he gave you for your twentieth wedding anniversary. Dad has been working himself into the grave just trying to stay afloat and you keep spending like you're lottery winners. Something has got to break. A person can't keep fighting and fighting to pay the bills when their partner keeps digging them deeper and deeper into debt. I know you and Dad have had this fight before and you've refused to listen to him. Well you need to listen to me now because if you don't find a way to curb your behavior, Dad is going to come to his senses and put you on an allowance where the only thing you can afford to buy is generic toilet paper." Aware that she was screaming, Jane paced away. Her heart was pounding wildly, and she was near hysterical laughter. Generic toilet paper. She was losing it. She shook her head. She didn't want her parents to lose their home, but if their only option was to sell, that's what they needed to do.

Jane turned back to look at her mother who was staring back, tears streaming down her face. "I'm sorry for yelling at you, Mom," Jane said gently. "But I don't want to see you lose everything."

"It's too late," her mother whispered.

"What do you mean?"

"We're not just selling the house. Your father is leaving me. He's getting an apartment and he wants a divorce."

Jane sucked in her breath. She glanced at Carol out of the corner of her eye. She was glaring at Jane as if Jane was a monster. Jane felt like a monster. She knelt in front of her mother and held her. "I'm sorry, Mother. I'm so sorry."

Mary took a deep breath. "It's a good thing you and Carol have a spare bedroom," she said.

Jane looked at Carol who shrugged. "Are you planning on moving in here?" Jane asked her mother.

"Well, I don't have anywhere else to go," Mary said.

Carol reached out for Mary's hand. "You can stay here as long as you need."

Jane glared across the table. "That's something we need to discuss together."

Carol ignored her, patting Mary's hand.

Mary smiled at Carol. "Thank you, Carol. I'll stay in the house until it sells and then I'll need to move in."

Carol nodded. "We'll help you when the time comes."

Mary sniffed loudly. "I just can't believe he wants a divorce. Divorce is a sin. And we've been so happy."

Jane hugged her mother tightly. "Don't worry, Mom." She stood up and grabbed the box of tissues from the counter. Handing them to her mom, she forced a smile. "Don't worry. I'm going to talk to Dad. I'm sure he'll change his mind."

He better change his mind, she thought.

Chapter Fifteen

Karma stretched thoroughly, smiling at the woman next to her. Eve murmured and turned away, exposing a long stretch of creamy back. Karma moved her hands over the soft skin, enjoying the feel of Eve's body. She moved up behind the woman, pressing her body against Eve's ass, reaching over to cup one of her full breasts in her hand. Kissing Eve's shoulder, Karma's hand massaged the soft breast, pulling the nipple into sweet firmness again.

"Karma, we just did it," Eve said. Karma could hear the pout in her voice. "Why can't we just cuddle?"

Karma flopped her head down and sighed. When Eve said they just did it, what she really meant was that Karma had just given Eve a couple of orgasms and Eve had barely touched Karma at all. Not that it always had to be one for one, but it seemed as if Eve only reciprocated once every four or five times they were together.

Crash had been the opposite way. She rarely wanted to be touched and when Karma reached for her, most of the time Crash would push her away. As Eve fell asleep, Karma turned over and stared at the ceiling. It would be nice if sex was just equal sometimes. It wasn't as if Eve and Crash were the only two women with whom she'd ever had sex, but Crash had been her only real girlfriend until Eve came along. *Unless you count Jane*, she thought before pushing it out of her mind.

Karma was drawn to Eve's full hips, her big breasts, and her soft mouth. Eve was soft everywhere Karma was hard, and it felt so good to press into her body and feel enveloped by the sensation. After only a few months of dating, Karma was starting to wonder if maybe they weren't right for each other. Eve pouted more than she smiled, and half the time Karma couldn't figure out what she had done wrong to upset her so much.

Still, they did have fun together. It wasn't like with Crash where Karma had to walk on eggshells to keep from provoking Crash's outbursts—at least not constantly. She turned back over and put her arm around Eve again. Eve took Karma's hand in her sleep and Karma's heart did a flip. She still wasn't sure if she was in love with Eve, but she was happy enough.

Eve sometimes came to the bookstore with lunch for Karma and Lauren. She would keep them all laughing with her bawdy stories of the years she worked as an exotic dancer. In private, Eve told her it was the worst time of her life and she would kill herself before going back there. She hated men after her time in the strip club. Every single man that came into the place was depraved and entitled and thought that women's bodies belonged to them. Eve's private stories were haunting, and it hurt Karma's heart to think of her suffering through that.

Eve started to snore softly, and Karma squeezed into her tightly. She didn't want Eve to ever have to go through anything like that again. Maybe if they moved in together, Eve could go back to school, do something she really wanted to do. Right now, she was working as a server at one of the chain burger places. It wasn't horrible money, but it didn't afford her a nice lifestyle. Karma grinned. Not that she had room to talk. Karma still lived with her parents. She nudged her forehead against Eve's back and closed her eyes.

When her alarm went off, she threw on the extra clothes she had brought over the night before and stepped into her shoes. She didn't have much time to get to the bookstore and open it for the day. Even though Lauren was coming in at ten, Karma had promised to get there early to open. Once dressed, she headed to the kitchen and more importantly, the coffee maker. Karma knew she was addicted to coffee, but she wasn't ready to give it up. Dad had switched to decaf at home, but Henna and Karma still indulged in the good stuff after Frank left for his morning walks.

Karma reached for the organic coffee she had gotten at the farmer's market. Eve liked coffee as much as Karma, so bringing her expensive coffee was never a bad idea. She filled the reservoir and sat down to listen to the coffee dripping through the machine. Karma's mother liked to use a French press and while Karma admitted Henna's coffee was delicious, she enjoyed the few moments of peaceful meditation she spent waiting for the pot to brew. The coffee smells started to fill the kitchen. Karma heard Eve's bare feet slapping against the kitchen floor.

"Hi, gorgeous," Karma said.

Eve rubbed her eyes and smiled. Karma loved the way she looked in the morning with her hair all tangled and her eyes still sleepy and half-closed. She jumped up to give Eve a kiss.

"Coffee should be done in a second," Karma said, stroking Eve's face. "Would you like a cup?"

Eve kissed Karma on the nose. "When do I ever

not want a cup?" She grinned, and Karma laughed. Eve was probably more addicted to coffee than Karma. On the rare mornings when neither of them had to leave for work they would share two pots, and sometimes Eve would make just a little more after that.

Karma lingered for a moment in Eve's arms, tasting her mouth, before turning back to the coffee pot. She had already pulled two mugs from the cupboard and put in just the right amount of flavored creamer for each of them. She pulled the carafe from the pot but as she started to pour, her elbow knocked into the side of the fridge. Karma paused for a second in horrified fascination as the entire carafe of coffee fell to the kitchen floor. It shattered at her feet, splashing hot coffee across her feet and ankles.

Eve screamed, making Karma jump again.

"It's okay, it's okay," Karma said. "You need to stay away since you're barefoot."

Karma made a giant step over the pile of glass and coffee. She didn't feel burned, but her feet were soaked, and the bottom of her jeans were splattered with coffee. She grabbed a roll of paper towels and a broom.

"You are an idiot," Eve yelled.

Karma jumped and turned around. "What?"

"You are a fucking idiot. How could you have been so careless?"

"It was an accident," Karma said.

Karma dropped a bunch of paper towels on the floor and let them absorb coffee before sweeping the entire wad into the dustpan. When she was sure she had all the glass cleaned up, she sprayed the floor with surface cleaner and got on her hands and knees with more paper towels to wipe up the floor. She was shaking and angry at Eve's response. Aware that Eve was glaring at her as she worked, she fought hard not to cry. She wasn't an idiot. She just made a mistake.

"It's not like I'm made of money," Eve said. "It's not like I can afford to just buy a new coffee pot every time you get careless."

"I'll buy a new carafe," Karma replied from the floor.

"Damn right you'll buy a new one," Eve yelled. "And what am I supposed to do about coffee this morning?"

Karma didn't look up from the floor. She found a few more pieces of glass with the paper towel in her hand and carefully put them in the garbage. "You'll have to stop for coffee on your way to work," Karma said. "I'll leave you some money."

She got up from the floor and did one more sweep of the kitchen with the broom.

"I'm pretty sure I got all the glass," she said. "I have to go change."

Eve, still glaring at Karma, didn't answer. Karma looked at her for a few moments, trying to think of something to say to diffuse the situation. Finally, she decided not to even bother trying.

Back in the bedroom, Karma changed into her dress from last night. She wadded up her wet jeans and shoes and tossed them into her overnight bag. She would have to do laundry when she got home later. She grinned at the thought of what Lauren would say when she came in to find Karma in a low-cut dress and heels at 10 a.m. Fortunately, her button-front shirt hadn't sustained any damage from the coffee assault, so she buttoned it over her dress. Wearing an Oxford over a silky dress looked a little odd, but at least her breasts weren't hanging out. Somehow, she didn't think the early morning bookstore crowd would be impressed with last night's date outfit.

She finished packing everything up and went back to the kitchen. Eve was still sitting at the table, staring into space. Karma touched her shoulder. "Eve, I'm really sorry."

Eve shook her head without looking at Karma. "The only apology I want is a new coffee pot on my counter."

Stung, Karma left. Driving to the bookstore, she cried for a few minutes before wiping her tears. When Eve lost her temper, Karma felt that she was waiting for the rest of the explosion. If it had been Crash, the next thing would have been a slap in the face, maybe more.

As she stepped into the bookstore, Karma breathed in, relishing the familiar smells of her second home. As she walked around flipping on lights, straightening books, and rearranging merchandise, Karma decided she was going to have to have a talk with Eve. It wasn't the first time Eve had gotten mad and called Karma a name and in Karma's opinion, it wasn't right. *Maybe it's just me,* Karma thought. *Maybe I bring this mean streak out in people. Still, it isn't as bad as it was with Crash.* Karma made a fresh pot of coffee and waited while it brewed. When she had a cup of coffee in her hands, she breathed it in, delighting in the smell before taking her first sip.

She wandered into the used books section of the store and ran her fingers along the spines. It was only recently that they had started a book exchange, and it was doing well. The coffee bar had expanded as well. Lauren had made arrangements with a local bakery to bring in pastries and they had gotten a couple of cappuccino machines. They hired a young woman to run the coffee bar on the weekends and they had been getting quite a bit of foot traffic. Karma smiled. She had three employees now. If things kept going the way they were, she could afford to hire another couple of clerks and make Lauren the manager of the store. Then Karma could cut back her own hours and take the weekends off. She laughed. Weekends off were a dream and not for small business owners.

She opened the register and finished setting up for the day. She flipped the sign over at nine o'clock and welcomed her first customers.

"Let me know if you need anything," Karma said to the two women who came through the door.

The women smiled and went to browse. Karma watched them from behind the register. One of the women leaned heavily on a cane. The other helped her move through the store. As she watched, the one with the cane reached out to touch the second woman's face and they both smiled at each other. Karma's heart skipped. The two women were old, maybe in their nineties, and Karma had a flashback of the vision she had once had of her and Jane as old women, curled together on the couch, basking in each other's love. She put a hand over her heart and closed her eyes.

When the two women moved into the lesbian fiction section, Karma grinned. That was what she wanted. That's what she had always wanted. She wanted to be in love. She wanted someone who reached for her as much as she reached for them. She wanted to feel cherished.

A few more customers wandered in and Karma spent some time helping them find specific books. The elderly women finally came back to the counter. They had a pile of books, but Karma was fixated on one. *Curious Wine.* She blinked, willing herself not to cry as she rang up the purchases. *Curious Wine* had come from the used section. Karma remembered when she had taken it in. It wasn't in great condition. Obviously, the previous owner had read it several times. But Karma gave her store credit anyway.

"Are you okay, dear?" The two women were looking at her, concerned.

Karma smiled. "Yes." She picked up the book. "This is the very first lesbian book a friend of mine read when she was trying to come out. It just made me think of her for a moment."

The woman with the cane smiled. "Are you still friends?"

Karma shook her head as she finished scanning the books and collected money from the women. "No. I gave her up for stupid reasons."

The two elderly women looked at each other. The one with the cane patted Karma's hand. "I gave up this one once, as well. Fortunately for me, she's a stubborn old mule and she wouldn't let me walk away."

Karma glanced around the store. There were a couple other customers, but they all looked occupied. "Would you like me to carry your books to your car?"

The women shook their heads. "We may look decrepit," one said, "but we are tough old biddies."

They took their bag and shuffled out of the store. Karma watched them go, smiling.

Lauren came in a few minutes before ten. She looked Karma up and down. "Nice outfit."

Karma laughed. "It's my walk of shame outfit."

"I might have been tempted to leave the dress and

just wear the button-front as a dress in this situation," Lauren quipped.

"In my defense, I broke an entire pot of coffee at my feet this morning. I was at Eve's so I had to change back into last night's date outfit."

Lauren wrinkled her nose. "You wore that on a date?"

Karma smacked her on the arm and they both laughed.

Karma stuck around for another hour, taking the time to set up some displays with Lauren's help. As she headed out the door, she gave Lauren a hug. "I'll be back before six." Their new clerk, Katie, was coming in at five so there would be an hour overlap before Lauren left at six. Katie was still new enough that Karma didn't want to leave her alone in the store. Besides, the evening crowd was often heavy enough that it required two people on duty.

"I'll be here," Lauren said. She gave Karma a salute. Karma waved back and stepped out in the midmorning sun. She walked to her car and jumped in, rolling the windows down. Winter would be coming soon, but for now, Karma would take every sunny fall day she could.

When she got home, she greeted her father and ran upstairs to take a shower. She put her button-front back on and added jeans and a crew-neck sweater. Back in the kitchen, she put her arms around her father and kissed the top of his head. "You're starting to go bald," she said.

Her father smiled. "It's all of the electricity from my brain working so hard. It zaps the hair."

"Let's go for a walk," Karma said.

They took light jackets from the closet and

walked outside. Karma laughed as she and her father both lifted their faces to the sky. "Like father, like daughter," Karma said.

Frank held out his arm and Karma linked hers through his. They walked together in companionable silence for a while. "Let's head to the park," Karma said.

They left the neighborhood and turned onto Grand River, heading for the riverfront park. Karma smiled as they reached the greenspace. Her parent's neighborhood was lovely, and she loved walking the tree-lined streets past the big old house, but she was most comfortable walking here, where there was no traffic and they knew the faces of many of the other people. Karma and her dad had walked this park so many times since his heart attack that they had become known fixtures. Her dad knew the names of most of the dogs they passed, even if he didn't know the owners. In the evenings, while Karma was at work or out on a date with Eve, Frank and Henna walked together. Oddly, her father had actually gained weight in the last few years, but he was solid and healthy. Henna had taken her husband's heart attack seriously, and the whole family had started eating a whole food omnivore diet. Karma thought her father had never looked better. She leaned her head against his arm for a moment.

"What's up, little one?" Frank asked.

"Just thinking about how lucky we are to have you," Karma said.

"I'm the lucky one," Frank answered. "I am truly blessed. I have the best daughter in the world and I'm married to the love of my life. What else could I ask for?"

Karma grinned. "A billion dollars?"

Frank laughed. "I enjoy my work and I get to do it from home. If I won the lottery, I'd be tempted to quit and then I'd be bored."

"Well, then Mom would be retired, too, so you could travel."

"We do travel," Frank said.

"You could travel more," Karma insisted.

"We don't want to travel more." Frank was laughing. "Little one, your mother and I have always been comfortable and lately, we've been more than comfortable. We don't want to be rich. We just want to be able to take care of you and each other."

"I know I should move out, Dad. But I was hoping to buy a house someday and I don't think I can do that yet."

Her father squeezed her hand. "Don't rush it. Buying the bookstore was a big commitment. You need to focus on that for a while."

"I've been paying more than the loan every month, just like you advised," Karma said. "If I keep going like this, I'll have it paid off in five more years."

Frank stopped and turned to face her. "Your mother and I both feel the same about this, Karma. You are welcome to stay with us the rest of your life. I know you want your privacy and independence and I don't blame you. But I think a five-year plan for buying a house is a great idea."

Karma hugged him. "How did I end up with the best parents? I don't deserve you."

Frank frowned. "You do. Don't ever think that you don't deserve to be treated as if you are valuable."

"Hey, you two!"

Karma looked up to see David and Carter striding toward them, hand in hand. Karma and Frank stepped forward to meet them. Throwing her arms around David, Karma laughed. "You two look more gorgeous every time I see you. How is that even possible?"

She released David and hugged Carter while her father greeted David.

"It's love," Carter said as he hugged Karma tightly. "We just get more beautiful every day."

Karma laughed. "It's so true."

Karma held David's hand as they caught up on their lives. She hadn't seen them in several months. After David was shot, Karma spent a lot of time at their house, bringing pre-made meals and reading to David when Carter had to go to work. Later, after Frank's heart attack, the guys reciprocated by coming over in their spare time and helping to clean the house or prepare healthy meals. Carter would often show up at odd hours between shifts at the hospital with fresh produce, and David sometimes took Henna out just to give her an escape from caretaking.

"I hate that life gets in the way of us seeing each other more," Karma said.

Carter nodded. "We miss you, too. All of you. David was just pining about needing a pedicure date with Henna."

"She would love that," Frank stated. "She hasn't had one in months. I know she misses it."

"I'll call her this week," David said. "I promise."

"How are you doing, David?" Frank asked.

Karma, still holding David's hand, suddenly realized she was feeling a thick ring against her fingers. She picked up David's hand and looked at his fingers before reaching for Carter's hand and doing the same. "Are those wedding rings?"

Carter laughed. "You don't have to sound so

accusatory. Yes, they are wedding rings, no we didn't have a ceremony, yes, you definitely would have been invited if we had."

"Congratulations," Frank said. "I'm happy for you both."

"I can't believe you didn't have a wedding," Karma said.

David laughed. "We didn't want to worry about becoming bridezillas. We decided the only two people who would be affected by this marriage would be the two of us. So we planned a weekend trip, we hired a photographer, and we asked the officiant to provide a couple of witnesses."

Carter smiled, taking David's hand. "It was magical. We spent the whole weekend giving each other the best present in the world."

"Us time," David said. "It always seems to be in short supply."

Karma smiled. "I'm so happy for you both."

Frank nodded. "It's the world's greatest blessing to find your soulmate."

Karma looked away. If she and Jane had gotten together, her life would have been radically different. They would have been together twelve years by now. Karma tried to imagine what her life would look like, but she couldn't do it. Karma didn't really believe that Jane was her soulmate anymore. Maybe some people really did have soulmates. More likely, there were just great relationships and not-so-great relationships.

Karma didn't need a soulmate anyway. After the years of therapy and focusing on self-care, Karma felt relatively well equipped to handle life on her own terms. Yet, here she was, again dating someone who made her feel like an idiot. Eve wasn't as bad as Crash, was she? Karma remembered telling Jane a long time ago that the absence of physical violence didn't mean it wasn't abuse.

Carter was talking, and Karma missed what he said. "I'm sorry, what?"

"I said I was diagnosed with MS a couple months ago which was one of the reasons we decided to go ahead and get married when we did."

David nodded. "We didn't want our wedding to be postponed over medical concerns. We had already put it off for so long because of school and then work."

Karma wrapped her arms around Carter. "I'm so sorry."

"Don't be," Carter replied. "I'm in good health. I'm married to my soulmate. And I'm incredibly good-looking."

Frank laughed, and Karma smiled. "It just seems like you two have to deal with so much."

David touched her face. "It's just life, my friend. It's what happens when two people decide they cherish each other enough to make a life together. Life still happens but you get a partner to share the load."

Cherish. That was the common denominator in these happy relationships. Her parents cherished each other, as did David and Carter. Jane had cherished Karma, too, back in the day. Karma hadn't felt worthy of being cherished back then, and she thought Jane probably didn't, either.

As Karma and Frank said goodbye to the guys, Karma thought about regret. Her grandmother had once told her that she would regret going back to Crash, but in the end, Karma didn't really regret it. She hated that she had been so badly hurt, but in a way, the abuse from Crash had left her strong enough to know that she needed to break up with Eve. Without her past, Karma might not have recognized that she deserved better than this. She deserved to be cherished. Karma needed to focus on her own self-esteem before she could date someone else. The best thing to do was to put Jane out of her mind. After all, Jane was married, for better or for worse, and Karma wasn't part of that life. It was time to close that chapter and take care of herself. The right woman would come along when Karma was ready.

Walking home with her father, Karma linked her arm through his and smiled at him. "We all deserve to be cherished," she said.

"We sure do, sweetie. We sure do."

Chapter Sixteen

Jane strolled through the house picking up her mother's magazines, coffee cups, and discarded sweaters. Mary Edmunds had been living with them ever since the divorce was finalized and her parents were forced to sell their house. Because of the ridiculous amount of debt Jane's father had to take on after the divorce, he hadn't had to pay much in spousal support. Jane was proud of the way he had fastidiously worked down his share of the debt, paying the high-interest cards off first. Mary and Paul had come out ahead from selling their house, despite the late payments, and they had each walked away with a small stipend of about five-thousand dollars. Of course, Paul had used his to pay off some of the debt and Mary had spent hers within the first two months.

Two years later, Mary was still living with Jane and Carol. Paul, almost completely debt-free, had a tiny little house on the shores of Lake Michigan. When Jane had called him last week, a woman answered the phone. Jane couldn't blame him for moving on, but up until the moment her father admitted he was dating someone, Jane had harbored the slightest bit of hope that her parents would get back together, and Mary would move out.

She took everything that belonged to her mother and dumped it on the bed in the spare bedroom. Jane had grown up in an immaculate house where the act of leaving her shoes anywhere other than the rack next to the door was practically a mortal sin. Apparently, with the divorce and the loss of the house, Mary had also lost her will to pick up after herself. The spare room, which Jane still refused to call "Mary's room," was a mess. She sighed and closed the door.

Jane was jealous of her dad with his tiny house and his debt-free life and his new girlfriend. Sometimes she would lie in bed at night, staring at the ceiling, fantasizing about having her own little place. Sometimes, Karma was there with her, but lately, Jane had been forcing Karma out of the picture. It was long past time to stop pining over her old friend, a woman with whom Jane had never even been in a real relationship. When Karma popped into Jane's mind, she always looked the way Jane thought she must look now, with laugh lines around her eyes and maybe a stray silver hair creeping in here and there. Jane decided that Karma was probably going to let herself go gray naturally. Carol had recently started coloring her hair and suggesting that Jane consider doing so as well.

Jane stepped into the master bathroom and stared in the mirror. She might have a couple gray hairs, but with the natural blond, it was so hard to tell. Still, Carol thought Jane's blond was fading and looking dingy, and that a dye job would lighten it up. Jane squinted at her reflection. She couldn't tell if she was pretty or not, and she was unconvinced that dying her hair would change anything. Sometimes the little girls in her class would say, "You're so pretty, Ms. Edmunds. I wish I was pretty like you." And Jane would always tell them that they were beautiful the way they were and that girls didn't need to compare themselves to others to be happy. It was a small dig at a society bent on damaging the fragile egos of such young kids. Still, Jane thought as she made a face at herself in the mirror, it would be nice if Carol would tell her she was beautiful now and then.

She went back to the kitchen and finished putting the dishes away. David and Carter would be here soon, and Carol and Mary weren't even home yet. She glanced at the clock. Twenty minutes until dinner. Carol had promised to help her make something. Jane opened the fridge. She didn't even have a clue what to make.

Finally, she grabbed spinach, romaine, and kale from the fridge and chopped it into bite-sized pieces. Dumping a can of artichokes in a bowl, she started a salad bar buffet on the kitchen island. She rummaged in the fridge and the cupboards, pulling out a variety of potential salad toppings. Finally, she placed a few dressings on the counter and piled plates and forks next to the spread. Stepping back, she smiled. Easy prep and easy cleanup. Carol would be horrified that it wasn't fancy enough, but since she didn't bother to get home in time to help, she didn't really have room to talk.

At the sound of the doorbell, Jane ran to the front hall. David and Carter came in, hugging her. Jane smiled at the young woman half-hiding behind David. "Hi, Suri," Jane said. "Your uncle has told me all about you."

Suri stepped forward to shake Jane's hand. "Hello, ma'am."

Jane fought the urge to laugh. She didn't know when she hit the magic age when teenagers saw her as a "ma'am," but it made her want to giggle every time. Jane put an arm around Suri and ushered her into the house. David, carrying a bottle of wine, took Carter's arm with his other hand. Jane noticed Carter was walking with a cane, but he looked healthy and as handsome as always.

In the kitchen, Jane urged everyone to sit at the big table. If Carol had been here, she would have insisted that they set the dining room table and eat in there, but Jane preferred the hominess of eating in the kitchen.

David opened the wine and poured a glass for Jane. She hugged him again. "It's so good to see you."

Wrapping his arms around her, David kissed the top of Jane's head. "Where are the others?"

"I have no idea." Jane had sent a text to each of them but hadn't heard back. "If they're not back in about fifteen minutes, we'll go ahead and eat."

She heard the front door opening. "Well, someone's home."

Mary rushed into the kitchen carrying two big shopping bags. "I'm so sorry I'm late. There was a huge sale on linens at Macy's and our towels have gotten so threadbare lately."

David and Jane exchanged a look behind Mary's back. Jane sighed. "It's fine. Go wash up and we're going to eat."

Mary greeted the men and was introduced to Suri. Glancing at the counter, she pursed her lips. "We're having salad for dinner?"

Carter cleared his throat. "I think it all looks amazing. I love salad for dinner."

"Me, too," Suri said. "Almost as much as breakfast for dinner. Do you have that fake crab meat stuff?"

Jane smiled. "As a matter of fact, I do." She

looked in the fridge and pulled it out. "Want to open this and cut some into a bowl for me?"

Suri jumped up and grabbed a bowl.

Jane turned to look at her mother. "Now, please, Mother. We've all been waiting."

Mary rushed out of the room and returned a few minutes later. "I'll take care of putting out the new towels after dinner." She looked around. "Where's Carol?"

"She texted me after work and said she was going to be a little late. I haven't heard from her since then."

Mary took her phone out. "That's not like her. I hope she's okay."

"It is very like her," Jane countered. "And I'm sure she is fine."

Jane directed her guests to help themselves to salad. She was pleased to see Suri heaping her plate with vegetables and toppings. She thought Suri might be even skinnier than she and Karma had been when they met.

"So, Suri," Mary said, once they were all seated around the table. "How long are you going to be living with your uncles?"

Suri shrugged. "I don't know. Maybe until I graduate from high school."

Carter put his hand over Suri's. "She is welcome to stay with us as long as she wants."

"But what about your own parents?" Mary asked.

"My dad took off and my mom doesn't like me," Suri said. "So there's no point in going home."

"It isn't that she doesn't like you," David said. "Your mom was raised under the same damaging belief system I was. It's hard to escape that."

"It isn't fair to call it a damaging belief system,"

Mary said.

Jane pressed her lips together to keep from entering the conversation. She had spent most of her life trying to overcome the effects of her religious upbringing and her relationship with her mother was still strained because of it. Suri was lucky to be able to live with David and Carter while she came to terms with her own feelings, whether she turned out to be gay, straight, or something in between. Jane smiled at David. Suri wasn't really his niece. She was the daughter of one of his cousins, but it didn't matter to him and Carter. They loved the girl.

"Anyway," Carter said. "Suri has just started volunteering at the center. She and my dad go over together some days."

"I love Mr. G," Suri said, grinning. "He's funny and weird."

"Funny and weird are two of the best adjectives for my father," Carter said, laughing.

"I still think a child belongs with her mother," Mary insisted. "I don't think living with two men is healthy for a young girl."

David turned to her, his eyebrow shooting up. "Are you kidding me? You think living with two gay men is unhealthier than living with a mother who hits her with a wooden spoon for being queer?"

Mary shook her head. "I'm not saying that. I don't think it's right to hit a child. But the first step would be to have family counseling to repair their relationship."

"Bullshit," Jane said.

"Jane, language!" Mary placed a hand over her heart.

"Mother, stop. You're insisting that living with an abusive mom is better than living with two gay men.

That's an ignorant and bigoted attitude."

"That's so typical," Mary said. "If I disagree with you, you call me a bigot."

Carter patted Mary's hand. "Just because you have a lesbian daughter doesn't mean you aren't homophobic. Believing that two gay men are somehow unhealthy role models for a child is homophobic."

"You're modeling gay behavior for her," Mary said.

"We're showing her what a loving, long-term relationship looks like," David said. His voice was still calm, but Jane could tell he was getting upset.

Suri held up her hands. "It doesn't matter anyway," she said. "My mom hates me because I'm queer."

Mary scoffed. "You're only fourteen. You can't possibly know that yet."

Suri glared across the table. "I'm almost fifteen."

Carter smiled. "Mary, are you saying that when you were fourteen, it was still up in the air whether you were going to end up with a woman or a man?"

"Don't be ridiculous," Mary said. She stabbed salad greens with her fork, taking a bite so big her cheeks bulged out.

Suri scowled down at her own plate. She picked up a piece of imitation crab meat with her fingers. "I know I'm young, but I'm not too young to know that I like girls."

Jane smiled at her. "There's nothing wrong with that. You just need to follow your heart."

Suri nodded. "I want what David and Carter have and what you and Carol have. I want to fall in love with my soulmate and get married and live happily ever after, totally in love, until I'm old."

David took Carter's hand and the two of them looked into each other's eyes. Watching them, Jane felt a stab of self-pity. She touched Suri on the arm. "Suri, just because someone gets married doesn't mean they are as happy as David and Carter. Always follow your heart. And if you meet your soulmate, you just make sure you say yes to being with her. The price of saying no is being unhappy for the rest of your life."

Carol walked into the kitchen, glaring at Jane. "Sorry I'm late," she said. "Had some issues at work. Glad I didn't miss Jane's words of wisdom, though."

Jane stared at Carol. She seemed to be swaying a little. As she walked past the table, Jane inhaled. She thought she smelled alcohol. "Carol, are you drunk?"

Ignoring her, Carol fixed a plate of salad from the counter. "Salad bar in the kitchen," she said. "Very classy." She grabbed a bottle of dressing and a fork and left the room. Jane heard the bedroom door slam a few moments later.

David patted Jane's hand and turned the conversation to some work he and Carter were doing at the Gundersons'. "We keep saying we're going to move out," Carter said, "but it always seems there is more work to do. It's just more convenient to do it from there."

"Plus, now that we have a child, it's good to have grandparents around to watch her when we go to work," David said.

Suri flushed and smiled. "I don't need a babysitter." She popped an olive in her mouth. "But I have to admit that I love hanging out with the Gundersons."

Jane laughed. "I wish I could be back in school and spending my spare time with Carter's parents."

Mary made a clucking sound under her breath but didn't say anything. Jane chose to ignore her.

Carter grinned. "I guess I got pretty lucky in the parent department. I think I'm beat out only by Karma's parents."

Jane caught her breath. "How is Karma?"

"She's doing well," David said. "Still owns the bookstore. They have a little café in there now." He patted his stomach. "I stop in far more than I should."

Carter reached over to rub David's stomach. "I happen to love your belly just the way it is."

Suri smiled at them. "I hope someday I find someone who loves me exactly as I am."

Me, too, Jane thought. *Me, too.*

"You should stop in and see her sometime," David said.

"Maybe," Jane replied.

She got up to clear the plates and Carter stood to help. "Carter, you don't have to."

"I'm not useless," Carter said.

"I know you're not," Jane replied. "I'm sorry."

They cleared the table and stacked the plates in the sink. "Don't worry about the dishes," Jane said. "I'll throw them in the dishwasher later." She touched Carter's shoulder. "Are you okay? How's your health?"

"I'm doing great. We've determined I have relapsing-remitting MS. I'm currently asymptomatic."

Jane frowned. "And the cane?"

Carter grinned. "Touch football injury."

"Oh, you!" She smacked him on the arm.

Carter shook the remaining lettuce into a bag. "Are things bad between you and Carol?"

Jane shrugged. "I can't say they were ever that great." She threw the leftovers into the fridge. "I mean,

I honestly don't know that I was ever in love with her. But if I was, I haven't been for years."

"I'm sorry, Jane. You know, getting divorced is not a failure, but staying where you're miserable is."

Jane looked up at him. "I wish that I had gotten together with Karma back when we all first met."

Carter smiled and touched her arm. "Everything that has happened in your life to date has made you who you are."

"I'm not sure that's a good thing," Jane said.

"It's a wonderful thing. You are a caring, compassionate, intelligent, and loving person. But it's time for you to think about turning some of that compassion onto yourself."

He kissed her on the cheek. David and Suri said goodbye to Mary, and Jane walked them all to the door.

"David, my mother didn't really mean—"

David held up his hand to stop her. "We both know what she really means, Jane."

Jane sighed. Her mother had become more accepting over the years. It was hard not to when you were counting on your lesbian daughter to provide your bread and butter. She still had a long way to go. Jane hugged David and Suri and watched the family as they walked down the front steps. As they reached the car, Carter said something and David and Suri both laughed. Carter threw an arm around Suri and smiled at David. Jane closed her eyes. She was transported into a vision of her and Karma, laughing together, holding hands outside in the sunlight. They were older but not old. Jane bit her lip. She needed to make some changes. She had to fix her life, and then she needed to seek out Karma and find out of there was a chance for them to rekindle what they once had.

She stalked into the spare room. Her mother was sitting at the small vanity applying face cream.

"Mother, we need to have a talk."

"We certainly do," Mary said, her eyes meeting Jane's in the mirror. "You behaved abysmally tonight. How dare you attack me in front of company?"

Guilt stabbed into Jane's gut, but she squelched it down. She wasn't going to let her mother's manipulation stop her this time.

"Mother, you have six months from today."

Mary blinked. "What are you talking about?"

"I'm marking it on the calendar. You have six months from today. By that time, you need to be working and in your own place. If you can't find a job and a place to live by then, I will help you find a low-income senior retirement home."

Mary gasped, pressing her hand to her heart. The blood drained from her face and she leaned back in her chair, gasping. "My heart."

"Don't," Jane snapped. She pressed down the wave of guilt that was rocking her stomach and making her dizzy. "Just don't. This is non-negotiable. You were supposed to be here for a year. You've been here two years and you haven't even tried to contribute to this household. You do nothing but make messes and spend money and it's over." She paused, confused. "Where are you even getting the money?"

Mary averted her eyes. "You give me an allowance."

Jane glared at her mother. "Not that much of one. Tell me where you are getting the money."

Mary's eyes darted toward her purse and Jane grabbed for it. She took out Mary's wallet and flipped it open. Her mother had three credit cards. Three. "How did you get credit cards?"

Mary looked down at the vanity, tears dripping down her face. "Carol applied for those and she added me as a secondary user."

"And how is Carol paying the bills?" Jane was aware that she was screaming, but she couldn't rein it in.

Mary tilted her head. "I guess from her paycheck."

Jane looked at the ceiling, counting to ten, willing herself not to lunge forward and strangle her mother. She focused on her breathing until she thought she could speak again without screaming. "I'm taking these cards. Your allowance is over. You have food and a roof over your head. From now on, if you need anything, you will justify it to me, and I will decide if you can have it."

She took the credit cards and threw her mother's purse back on the dresser. "And that six months is firm."

She slammed the door shut behind her and stalked to the bedroom.

She paused outside the door, trying to calm down. She had been working overtime lately, taking every tutoring opportunity, signing up for every summer class. She taught two evening courses, and she still had to come home every night and pick up after the two women in her house. She couldn't do it anymore. She was exhausted. Dragging herself out of bed every morning had become a chore. She didn't remember when she stopped packing lunches for Carol, but Carol had not stopped complaining about it yet. Jane took a deep breath and opened the bedroom door.

Carol was sitting on the bed watching television. Her dinner plate was on the nightstand. She glared up at Jane.

"I hope you had a lovely meal with your friends."

Jane focused on keeping her voice steady. "We need to talk."

Carol nodded. "Yes, we do. That was humiliating to walk in on you telling everyone how unhappy you've been with me."

Jane swallowed the guilt. She was getting good at that. Her anger was burning hot in the pit of her stomach and she kept fueling it with thoughts of the credit cards. "Tell me the truth about the credit cards you and my mother are using."

Carol frowned, and Jane thought a shadow of fear crossed her face for a moment before her features settled back into anger. Staring at her wife, Jane had the passing thought that she had never been truly attracted to Carol. Carol had perfectly arched eyebrows and professionally cut hair and the loveliest dye job that kept her hair shiny and soft. Her figure was still as trim and fit as it had been when they met. And her skin had barely a wrinkle. It shouldn't, with the amount of money Carol spent on face creams and makeup. Jane leaned back against the wall, stunned. As mad as she was right now, she had to accept that a great deal of the blame lay on Jane herself. She was not attracted to her wife. She didn't love her. She had felt trapped in this relationship for as long as she could remember. Even now, Jane couldn't muster up the smallest bit of feeling for Carol. The resentment between them had gone on too long.

Carol opened her mouth, but Jane held up a hand to silence her.

"You know what? Never mind. It doesn't matter."

"What are you talking about?"

Jane gritted her teeth for a moment and took a

big breath through her nose. "I want a divorce. I'm calling a lawyer tomorrow. All of our financial shit will be laid out after that."

Carol stared at her. "Just like that? You can't just decide to get a divorce. We can go to counseling."

Jane nodded. "I am going to go to counseling. By myself. And I highly recommend you do the same. You have a compulsion to spend money, even to the point of ruining your own life. You need help."

"No," Carol said. "I won't do it. I refuse to consider divorce until you agree to go to counseling with me."

Jane shook her head. "I'm not in love with you."

Carol looked away. "I lost my job today."

Jane closed her eyes, leaning her head back against the doorframe. Visions of supporting her mother and Carol for the rest of her life flashed through her mind.

Opening her eyes, she nodded at Carol. "Then tomorrow you can start organizing the stuff to be sold from this house."

Carol stood. "That's it? I lost my job and you tell me to have a yard sale?"

Jane pressed her lips together and squared her shoulders. She stared at Carol until Carol looked away. "I haven't been the best wife, but you have treated me like a servant. A servant who still has to pay for your out-of-control shopping. I'm done. I'm not in love with you, I don't want to be married to you, and I'm not going to support you for the rest of my life. Starting now, I'm no longer taking on any new night classes or tutoring jobs."

Carol stepped closer, looming over Jane. "You can't just stop being married to someone. You can't turn your back on me. What am I supposed to do? Go to a homeless shelter?"

Jane stared back at Carol without taking a step back. "I don't care what you end up doing. We're going to sell this house, but I doubt we'll end up with any profit after paying off your debts. We're going to sell everything in this house and again, we are going to use the money to pay off debts. We are going to sell both of our vehicles and use the money to pay off our debts. Then I am going to rent a tiny apartment within walking distance to my school and live the life I would have lived if I hadn't married you."

Carol slumped. Tears filled her eyes and Jane clenched her fists to her sides, determined to keep her resolve. Carol turned back to the bed and stumbled before sitting down heavily. "What about your mother?"

"She has six months from today to find a job and a place to live."

Carol burst into tears and it took every ounce of Jane's willpower not to take it all back and agree to go to counseling. It would be so much easier than the road facing them now. The thought of lawyers and realtors and yard sales and paying off loans and credit cards was exhausting. Jane watched Carol crying. She realized the only thing she felt was guilt. *I can't build a marriage on guilt.* She grabbed her pajamas and a pillow and turned to leave the room.

Carol grabbed her hand as she was passing. "Please, Jane. Let's at least talk about this."

Jane looked down at the woman who had treated her as an unwanted guest throughout their entire married life. She thought of the insults and the anger and the times Carol had spent money mere hours after Jane had told her they were in too much debt. She remembered a time she was standing in the bedroom, naked, and Carol walked in. Jane had turned to reach for her, and Carol pulled away. "You have snot on your nose," Carol had said before pushing past Jane to grab the remote. Staring at Carol, Jane felt the bubble of anger dissipating. She touched Carol's shoulder. "Don't leave that dirty plate for me to find in the morning," she said before slipping out of the room.

Back in her office, Jane stretched out on the love seat, pulling the quilt over her body. She supposed she should be upset, but the only sensation she could muster right now was relief. Reaching over her head for the paper calendar on the desk, Jane opened it and made a note. The countdown had started.

Chapter Seventeen

Karma perched on the stool behind the counter, smiling at Lauren and Callie. The two younger women were rearranging the main display table. Their laughter and gentle teasing sounded like music to Karma. She loved watching the two of them move through the store together, cleaning, straightening the books, discussing their favorites, and their least favorites. Callie was unfailingly good with all customers, even the difficult ones. Lauren had an eye for displays that would grab attention as soon as a customer walked through the door. Between the two of them, Karma felt confident leaving the store for a few hours. She still loved being here and would often stop in even when there was enough coverage. She sometimes brought food to the women, freshly baked cookies or warm banana bread. Happy employees were loyal employees.

Grabbing her purse from behind the counter, Karma checked her phone for a text message from Angie. Nothing yet, but there was a message from Suri. Karma smiled. David and Carter's foster daughter was anticipating her sixteenth birthday and wanted to work in the bookstore. David and Carter had promised to buy her a car if she worked for the insurance money. Karma had been impressed when Suri figured out the bus system to get herself to the bookstore and filled out an application.

Karma thought about it. It would be nice to have more time with Angie. It seemed like they hadn't had a moment together since Karma moved in a few weeks previously. She could use some vacation time. Another part-time employee in the bookstore would ease some of the overtime from Lauren as well.

She texted Suri back. *I'll have Lauren give you some training hours in the week after your birthday.*

Before she put the phone away, a text came in from Angie. *Missing your gorgeous face already.*

Karma smiled, holding the phone to her chest. Karma delighted in Angie's sweet laughter, her sharp wit, and her fierce defense of social justice. Karma had gone on a few dates before she met Angie, but no one had engaged her the way Angie did.

Karma texted Angie back. *Missing your face and the rest of you. Want me to pick up dinner tonight?*

Angie responded with a yes and Karma smiled. It was their Friday tradition, even if they both had to work on Saturday. Takeout food and sex. She laughed to herself. She would pick up some takeout and they would spend the evening flirting. Grinning, Karma tried to turn her attention back to the bookstore, but she was still remembering the sensation of Angie's soft skin rubbing against hers as they woke up this morning. Waking up to easy sex with Angie was better than waking up in her childhood bedroom at her parents' house. She thought of the substantial chunk of money she had saved over the years of not paying rent. Karma had dreams of putting it down on a small house of her own. After a lifetime of living with her parents and sometimes Crash, Karma had been ready for some alone time. Yet, Angie was so sweet and loving that Karma couldn't think of a reason to keep holding out.

Sighing, Karma dragged herself off the stool and headed to the café to grab another coffee. She talked to a few customers on her way through the store. The café was almost full and the women behind the counter were busy. Karma jumped in to take a few orders before making her own coffee and going back to the main part of the store. She smiled as she walked through her store. She had bought the adjoining office this year and Lauren had overseen turning it into a children's section with books and games meant to empower girls. She brought in guest speakers to do activities and to highlight the many career options available to women. It was a beautiful space, and Karma was proud of it.

Lauren appeared at her shoulder, looking into the children's space. "It's lovely, isn't it?"

Karma nodded. "I was thinking we could put Suri to work in there. David says she babysits a lot and is good with kids."

Lauren smiled. "I'll gladly give up some of my hours in there. I got peed on last week. When is she coming in?"

Karma laughed. "End of the month. She has to turn sixteen first."

"Let me know the exact dates and I'll put her on the schedule."

Karma agreed. She went back to the counter and took care of the customer who had come up to the register. Working through the day, Karma's thoughts kept turning back to Angie. Angie was sexy and loving and even if Karma wasn't necessarily head over heels in love, it didn't mean she wouldn't eventually get there.

At five, Karma waved goodbye to the other women and walked to the pad thai place across the street. This neighborhood had seen a lot of changes in the past few years and Karma never regretted her decision to buy the bookstore. The first two years were hard, but as more businesses moved into the area, the foot traffic at the bookstore increased as well. Adding the café, the girls' room, and a section for local female artists had helped, too. Karma's mother was addicted to the handmade paper and had suddenly taken to writing paper letters again.

Food in hand, Karma walked up the street to Angie's apartment. *Our apartment,* she corrected herself. It was convenient that her commute had dwindled to a mere ten minutes by foot. Not that the drive from her parents' house was unreasonable. Karma found herself stopping in at home on a regular basis. She missed them now that she was gone. Not that she was completely gone. Her father liked to joke that half of her wardrobe still lived there.

Karma let herself into the apartment and walked through to the kitchen. Angie was elbow-deep in dish water. She leaned her head back, smiling. "Come kiss me and I'll hug you when the dishes are done."

Laughing, Karma stepped behind Angie and kissed her on the cheek. She lingered, letting her lips open against Angie's skin. Angie turned her face to brush her lips against Karma's and for a second, they stood still, breathing each other in.

"Do you want me to serve while you finish the dishes?" Karma asked.

"Yes, please."

Karma got a couple of plates and scooped out the noodles. Watching Angie from behind, she smiled. Angie was a big woman and Karma loved the way it felt to get lost in her soft body. Karma loved watching the round curves of Angie's butt as she shifted from foot to foot at the sink.

"You're beautiful," Karma said.

Angie looked over her shoulder, smiling. "So are you."

Karma scoffed. After years of self-work, Karma didn't think she had low self-esteem, but one thing she couldn't get behind was the idea of herself as beautiful. She was still short and skinny with almost non-existent breasts. A couple of weeks earlier, she had decided to finally give in to her boyish looks and chopped all her hair off. She thought she looked kind of cute and dykey, but hardly beautiful. She stuck her tongue out and crossed her eyes. "How about now?"

Angie rolled her eyes and turned back to the dishes. She rinsed the final piece and turned off the water, shaking her hands over the sink. "Come eat," Karma said.

"First kiss me properly," Angie replied.

Karma jumped up and curled into Angie, pressing herself against her lover's body. She pressed her lips against Angie's mouth, thoroughly exploring it with her tongue.

"Lovely," Angie whispered as they broke apart.

They sat together at the table, talking quietly about their respective days. Angie worked for a non-profit environmental protection group, and she had spent her day arguing with representatives from various government agencies regarding their funding.

"Talking to a bunch of bureaucrats sounds like a shitty way to spend your day," Karma said. "What if I gave you a massage?"

Angie smiled. "Being on your feet all day can also be tiring. What if I gave you a massage?"

Karma shoved the last bite of food into her

mouth and stood up. Still chewing, she tried to speak. "Wass woo woo wah bedwoom."

Angie burst out laughing. "Try swallowing first."

Karma gulped. "That's what she said."

"Stop it now." Angie said, laughing. She got up to clear the table. "What exactly did you say before?"

Karma grinned. "I said, race you to the bedroom."

Angie leaned forward to kiss her on the mouth. "Let's put the leftovers away first."

They cleaned up the kitchen together and went into the bedroom. As they got undressed, Karma insisted Angie get a massage first. Liberally dripping massage oil onto Angie's back, Karma kneaded the soft skin under her hands. Sighing, she luxuriated in the feel of Angie's body, the thickness of her thighs between Karma's legs, the way her back arched and released under the pressure of the massage. Angie's dark skin glistened under the massage oil. Karma wanted to rub her face against the smooth span of the round shoulders. She moved down Angie's back and let her hands trail over the deep curve of Angie's butt. Leaning down, Karma kissed the indent where it met her spine. "Beautiful," Karma whispered.

Angie rolled over and pulled Karma into her arms. "My turn to rub you," she said.

Karma feigned offense. "I wasn't even close to being done with you."

Angie laughed as she grabbed more massage oil and squirted it across Karma's breasts. Laughing, Karma tried to grab the bottle. Reaching for it, she squeezed the middle of the bottle and massage oil gushed out of the top. "Mount St. Helens," Karma yelled.

"Oh, dear," Angie answered. She sounded so

much like a prim schoolmarm that Karma lost it again and rolled over onto her back, laughing until she couldn't breathe.

"It's good, isn't it?" Karma said when she had regained control of her breathing.

"It's good," Angie replied, though Karma thought she looked sad.

"I love living here," Karma said. "I don't know why I held out so long."

"Maybe because your heart isn't fully in it," Angie said, quietly.

Karma pulled back to look at her. "What are you talking about? We have an amazing relationship."

"It is amazing," Angie said. "But your heart isn't fully here. You're still living in the past, pining for a love that never was."

"Jane," Karma said. She had told Angie all about Jane when they were first dating. She had told her everything, everything that was important in her life. Yes, Karma spent too long pining for Jane, but she had put that part of her away long ago. Jane was a fantasy from her youth. Angie was right. It was a love that never existed. A few stolen kisses, some doughnuts in bed on a weekend morning. Jane didn't even exist in Karma's world except through their mutual friendship with David. Maybe that was it. She needed to call David and get Jane's number. See her. Make sure there was nothing there. But how could anything be there? She hadn't even seen Jane in years. She had an image in her head of how it felt to be with Jane, but it had no basis in reality. This was what her former therapist would call cognitive bias. She wasn't remembering her relationship with Jane as it was, but as she had wished it could be. It wasn't real. She looked at Angie, who was patiently waiting for Karma to reply. This was real. This beautiful woman covered with massage oil was real. She held Angie's hand, thinking.

"Angie?" she finally said.

"Yes, Karma?"

"You're right. I haven't been present. But I will be. I promise."

Angie blinked, and a tear rolled down her face. Karma's stomach clenched. Why couldn't she be grateful for what she had? She was about to ruin the only kind and loving women she had dated in her adult life because of a ghost. Karma pulled Angie into her arms and held her tightly, letting her cry against Karma's neck. Kissing and holding her, Karma rocked her girlfriend until she calmed down. Reaching across to the nightstand, Karma grabbed a tissue and handed it to Angie.

"Sorry," Angie said. She blew her nose loudly.

"You look beautiful even when you cry," Karma said.

The two women wrapped their arms around each other and snuggled in as close as their bodies would allow. Karma grinned every time their bodies slid across each other. The massage oil would be sticky and all over the sheets by tomorrow, but Karma didn't care. She'd throw a load of laundry in before going to the bookstore. As Angie's breathing deepened and turned into light snores, Karma untangled herself and turned over onto her back. She reached over to lightly rest her palm on Angie's stomach. Closing her eyes, Karma tried to remember Jane's face, but she couldn't bring it to mind. *Soulmates*, Karma thought. *Had she ever believed in such a thing?*

When Angie's alarm went off, Karma got up

to see her off to work. Karma made breakfast while Angie packed lunches for each of them. While Angie showered, Karma grabbed the bed sheets and put them in the washing machine. As soon as the shower water shut off, she started the laundry. It felt good, being domestic. This was a nice life. She could live like this for the rest of her days. She had a business she loved and some good friends. Why not marry Angie? They could make an investment in a small house. Karma's savings weren't quite enough for a whole house of her own yet, but if Angie chipped in half of the down payment, they could easily afford something nice.

Angie came back into the kitchen fully dressed and Karma whistled. "Nice gams, lady," she quipped.

Angie twirled, showing off her stocking-clad legs. "I'm supposed to look professional, not sexy."

Karma smiled. "You look professionally sexy."

They kissed, and Angie left for work. Karma had tried to schedule her own Saturdays on the days Angie had to work. It meant they would usually get another day off together. And they both always took Sunday off.

Karma took a quick shower while the washing machine was on spin. Running naked back to the laundry, she transferred the sheets into the dryer, then ran back to the bedroom, laughing. One thing that was better at Angie's place was running around naked. Karma didn't want to be naked around her parents, and she didn't want to see them naked, either.

She threw on some jeans and a button-front shirt. Looking at her short hair in the mirror, Karma grinned. She rummaged around in her suitcase and found a tie she had recently purchased at the thrift store. Those years of helping her dad get ready for business functions came in handy. It was a little odd to tie it on herself rather than her father, but she finally managed a decent knot. She twisted and turned in the mirror, smiling. She loved looking dapper. If she squinted, she could almost believe that people would mistake her for a twenty-something.

She laughed again. As she kicked her suitcase back under the bed, she vowed to go get the rest of her things from her parents' house this week and to unpack her suitcases. It was about time she made this move permanent.

Karma half-jogged to the bookstore, swinging her shoulder bag with her lunch and the bag of cookies she had nicked from the pantry. When she got to the store, she unlocked the door and stowed her stuff. Walking through the store turning on lights, she felt the familiar rush of love. This was her home as much as anywhere else in the world. As she balanced the register, she looked up to see Callie knocking on the door. Karma held up a finger, so she could finish counting the cash. When she was done, she ran over to the door to let Callie in. "Where's Lauren?"

"She's sick and she tried to call you but there was no answer, so she sent me to work for her, so you wouldn't be short-handed," Callie said in a rush.

"It's fine," Karma said. "I think I forgot my phone at home. Why didn't she just give you her keys?"

Callie put her hands on her hips. "I am not authorized yet to have keys. Lauren would never consider giving them to me."

Karma laughed. "Okay, okay. But seriously, for next time, it's all right. I trust you both."

"I'll tell her."

Karma started to close the door, but opened it

again for Trista, the café employee. Trista said hello and rushed back to start opening the café.

They finished setting up the store and Karma unlocked the door, turning the closed sign to open. She walked back to the café to get a coffee from Trista. *I'm probably drinking myself out of my profits*, she thought.

As she walked back up to the front of the store, she noticed a slender woman with long, blond hair standing at the new releases shelf. Walking up behind her, Karma said, "Can I help you find something?"

The woman turned around and Karma's heart flipped. Jane.

Jane smiled. "Hi. I don't suppose you happen to have any copies of *Curious Wine*?"

Karma laughed. "You know, I don't. But if you're in need, I can loan you my copy."

Jane smiled. "I still have a copy, but it has a chocolate print on one of the pages."

"The horror," Karma said.

Jane laughed. "You look adorable. What happened to your hippie chic?"

Karma glanced down at her outfit. "This just kind of developed. Once I was no longer dressing for Crash, I just sort of slid into a less girly look."

"Your hair is cute, too," Jane said. She reached out to touch Karma's hair. "Still as thick and silky smooth as always."

A wave of longing swept over Karma as Jane's fingers touched her hair. She took a step back. Jane looked almost the same as she had last time Karma had seen her. Her hair was still long and blond and she was as slender as ever. Karma thought she noticed a few small laugh lines forming around Jane's blue eyes. She resisted the urge to reach out and stroke them.

"It's been too long," Karma said.

"Far too long," Jane answered.

Karma looked around the store. It was still relatively empty. She waved at Callie and mimed that she was going back to the café. "Come on," Karma said. "Let me buy you a cup of coffee."

"The place looks amazing," Jane said as they walked back through the store.

"I've put a lot of work into it. But I also have a great team."

Karma refilled her own coffee and made one for Jane. They settled at a small table near the edge of the café so Karma could keep an eye on the store.

Jane smiled and reached across the table for Karma's hand. Karma's fingers instantly wrapped around Jane's. *It's just a friendly gesture*, she thought.

"How are you, Jane? I mean, really? It's been years."

Jane held her coffee, breathing it in. Karma smiled. She remembered seeing Jane do that so many times before.

"I'm happy," Jane said. "I left Carol a while back. I don't know if David told you."

"He didn't," Karma said. "But he and Carter have been pretty busy lately."

Jane laughed. "Out of all of us, I didn't think they were most likely to end up with a kid."

Karma grinned. "Yep. I thought it would be you."

Jane frowned. "I thought about it for a time. But I figured if Carol and I were swimming in debt, how could we take care of a child as well?"

"I get it. I guess it turned out to be for the best."

"In a way," Jane said. "It would have been nice to have a child. But I'm glad I don't have to worry about sharing custody with Carol. She isn't a terrible person, but she is terribly controlling, and she needs help."

"Speaking of needing help, how's your mom?"

Jane laughed. "She found a job as an office assistant for one of the members of her church. Oddly, she's quite good at it. Now that she has to pay her own bills, she's developed quite the budget-conscious lifestyle."

Karma smiled. "It's sad she didn't get help years ago. She and your dad might have stayed together."

"I doubt it," Jane said. "Dad is so happy. I really think he's found his soulmate in Dell. And I like her— she's kind to him." She paused, laughing. "She's a good influence on him, too. She's got goddess posters all over the house."

The women laughed together. Karma had forgotten how easy it was to laugh with Jane. She squeezed her old friend's hand and Jane squeezed back. "But your mom is okay?"

"She's okay. She's renting the mother-in-law cabin at the estate of one of the church members. It took her a long time to be okay with that. She saw it as a failure. She's had a lot of therapy."

Karma shrugged. "Nothing shameful about that. I had years of therapy after leaving Crash, trying to figure out why I let myself be abused. And even then, I dated another woman for a brief time who was emotionally abusive. I think there was something broken in me."

"You never deserved to be abused."

"I know that now. And what about you? You spent a long time with Carol. I know it wasn't a happy marriage, but it has to feel odd to be on your own now."

Jane shook her head. "Not at all. Honestly, Karma,

I never even missed her. I got a tiny apartment and the long process of trying to get the divorce started. We were so in debt. We ended up selling the house and basically everything in it except our personal items. She was so mad. She dragged her feet on everything. But in the end, we managed to pay off the house, the second loan, and about half of the credit debt. We split the remainder. I've almost finished paying my share off." She took a sip of her coffee and smiled. "I'm so happy. This is how I always wanted to live. It's a simple life, but it's mine."

Karma smiled. "That's wonderful. That's what I always dreamed of. A little house of my own. I lived with my parents for way more years than I care to count."

"And now?" Jane stroked Karma's wrist with her thumb and Karma felt the shiver start in her hand and shudder through her entire body. "Is there anyone special in your life now?"

Karma paused. In this moment, it almost felt as if she and Jane had never been apart. She could picture going back to Jane's apartment with a dozen doughnuts, crawling into bed, and spending the day watching movies and eating. She fought an urge to touch Jane's hair. "There is," Karma finally said. "Angie. She's special. And I just made a commitment to her."

Jane looked down at the table. Karma wanted to reach out and hold her. She could envision their lives together, holding hands, making love, sharing a small home, maybe adopting a dog. She thought of visits to David and Carter's house and walks in the park. She saw them taking care of Karma's parents one day, making decisions about health together. Karma squeezed Jane's hand and Jane looked up. "It's silly," Jane said. "I just thought maybe I'd get lucky enough to find you single, too."

Karma touched Jane's cheek. "I think if we were meant to be, we would have happened a long time ago."

Jane nodded. "You're probably right." She stood and came around the table. Leaning down, she kissed Karma's cheek, softly, her lips just barely grazing the side of Karma's mouth. Karma felt the air leaving her lungs and she grabbed the table to quell the sudden dizziness. Jane pulled away and Karma closed her eyes, her hand automatically going to the place Jane had kissed.

"It was good seeing you," Jane said.

Karma opened her eyes, her hand still on her own cheek. "It was good seeing you, too, Jane."

Karma watched Jane leave the bookstore. Part of her wanted to jump up and stop her. But Karma had made a promise last night, and when adults made promises, they kept them. Karma squared her shoulders, trying to be proud of her decision. She didn't have Jane's number, but she thought David would give it to her. She imagined showing up at Jane's apartment or sitting on the hood of her car one day as Jane left school. She didn't know what kind of car Jane drove. Really, she didn't know much about Jane at all. How could she make a life with someone she didn't even know?

Karma went back to the register where Callie had a line of customers. Karma instantly jumped in to pick up the slack. The store stayed busy for most of the day, and Karma was relieved when the evening crew came in and she could go home.

She waved goodbye to Callie and walked into

the crisp evening air. Popping into the bakery, Karma picked up some cinnamon rolls. They wouldn't be perfectly fresh in the morning, but a few minutes in the oven would take care of that. Grinning, she thought of having Sunday coffee and cinnamon rolls with Angie. Being in love was a Hollywood creation. The true key to happiness came from mutual respect, admiration, sexual attraction, and a shared sense of humor. All those things added together had to equal love in some form, even if it wasn't the movie version.

She let herself into the apartment and ran into the kitchen. Tossing the cinnamon rolls on the counter, Karma traipsed through the apartment, shedding clothes until she got to the bedroom. Angie liked to cook on Saturdays, so Karma didn't have to do any dinner prep. She changed into sweats and a T-shirt, pulled on some fuzzy socks, and went to the living room to turn on a movie.

The front door opened, and Karma ran to greet Angie. Her arms were full of shopping bags, and Karma divested her of them and carried them into the kitchen. Karma dropped the bags on the table and turned to kiss Angie. They held each other for several moments.

As they put the groceries away, Karma debated about telling Angie that she had seen Jane. Not telling her would be a lie, and Karma had sworn to herself after spending years lying about being beaten up that she would always be honest with the people she cared about.

"Jane stopped into the bookstore today."

Angie's back was to Karma as she was putting cans in the pantry, but Karma could see it stiffen with tension.

"Oh?" Angie's voice was casual. "And how was

that?"

"It was good, Ang. It was okay, I swear. She asked if I was seeing anyone special and I said that I was. I told her I had just made a commitment to you."

Angie finally turned around. "Was she upset?"

Karma nodded. "I think so. I think she was hoping to rekindle old feelings."

"But you said no?"

"Yes," Karma said. "I said no. I made you a promise last night to be present and I meant it. I really feel we can make this relationship last. We're good together."

Angie was silent as she finished putting away the rest of the groceries. When she was done, she turned to face Karma. "We are good together. That's true."

Karma tensed. "That's a good thing," she said. "Being good together. What's wrong with that?"

Angie sighed. "It's what you didn't say, Karma."

"What didn't I say?"

Angie cupped Karma's face with the palm of her hand and looked into her eyes. "You didn't say that you told her no because you're in love with me."

Karma swallowed. "I said I made a commitment. Making a commitment takes love."

She looked away, but Angie pulled her face back. Karma lifted her eyes to meet Angie's, which were shining with tears. Karma blinked to keep from crying herself.

"I just want to hear you say it," Angie said. "I just want to know."

"To know what? That I love you? I love you. I think you're amazing."

"Karma. Look at me and answer me. Are you in love with me?"

"Do I have to be? Can we just enjoy that this feels good and be happy with that?"

Angie pulled back and straightened her shoulders. "I'm sorry, but no. I'm in love with you, but I can't find my soulmate if I stay in a relationship with someone who isn't."

Suddenly angry, Karma glared at her. "That's bullshit, Ang. There's no such thing as a soulmate. I wasted so much of my life thinking Jane was my soulmate. That's why my other relationships didn't work. It's because I held out on some Hollywood idea of a soulmate when there isn't such a thing. Don't make the same mistake."

Angie kissed her on the cheek and Karma's anger diffused as quickly as it came. She deflated, her shoulders dropping. Looking up at Angie, Karma nodded. "I'm sorry. I'm sorry for yelling."

Angie smiled. "You may not believe in the concept of a soulmate, but I do. And I don't believe that it's possible to be a soulmate with someone who doesn't feel the same about me."

Karma shrugged. "I'm sorry."

Angie reached for Karma's hand and squeezed it. "You aren't a bad person, Karma."

"I must be," Karma said. "I keep screwing up everything."

Angie smiled, but tears were streaming down her face. "You can't help how you feel. You can't make yourself fall in love with someone."

"If I could, it would be with you," Karma said.

"Let's have our Saturday night and our cinnamon roll Sunday," Angie said. "You can start moving out as soon as you're able."

"Do you need any help making dinner?"

Angie shook her head. "I've got it."

Karma kissed her and walked to the bedroom. The corner of her suitcase was sticking out from under the edge of the bed. She remembered kicking it under there this morning. She kneeled to pull it out and suddenly she was sobbing. Holding her breath so Angie wouldn't hear her, Karma leaned her head against the bed, crying into the comforter. She reached down to touch her suitcase. At least it wouldn't be hard to move out, since she had never completely moved in.

Chapter Eighteen

Jane beamed at her father. He was tanned and wind-swept and even though his hair was almost completely white now, he looked younger than Jane had ever seen him. *Happier*, she corrected herself. She reached over and tugged at the back of his hair. "You're getting shaggy."

Paul grinned at her. "That's what Dell said last night. She wanted me to get a haircut before you got here. I told her, why bother putting on airs for my own daughter?"

Jane leaned her head against her father's shoulder and he put his arm around her.

"You really love her, don't you, Dad?"

He nodded. "She's the love of my life. I always thought marriage was about having children and raising them in the church. I don't regret my time with your mother because I have you." He kissed her on the top of her head. "And I don't even regret my time with the church. But I wish I had woken up years before I did."

"It never occurred to me that you were unhappy," Jane said.

"It never occurred to me, either. I just did my duty. Go to work, support my family, go to church, tithe, go to work." He laughed. "I look back at it now and I can't believe I did it for so long. I'm not saying anything bad about your mother, Jane. She did the same thing.

Married, had a child, volunteered with the church. I think she shopped to relieve her unhappiness." He paused, squeezing her. "We lost a baby before you were born."

Jane gasped. "I never knew."

"Your mother made me promise to never talk about it again. He died a few hours after he was born. I don't know that Mary ever recovered from that."

Jane was silent, staring at the lake. Dell was out on the boat, taking Carter, David, and Suri along the shore. When Paul Edmunds invited Jane to visit and bring a friend, she had instantly thought of bringing the guys. Carter's dad had passed away a few weeks earlier, and Jane knew that everyone needed some time away. Mr. G had been a huge presence, physically and emotionally, and Carter was still half in shock. Jane couldn't blame him. She didn't spend much time these days with her own father, but she couldn't imagine not having him in the world. She leaned into him again. "Thanks for letting us all be here, Dad."

"It's a pleasure to see you all," he said. "But when I invited you, I thought you might bring a lady friend."

Jane laughed. "I don't have a lady friend. It's just as well. I made such a muck up of things with Carol."

"You didn't screw that up, Janey. You weren't meant to be."

"I know," Jane said. "And in a way, I think I knew it before I even married her."

Paul smiled. "I think you were punishing yourself for letting Karma go by marrying someone who treated you badly."

"That's deep, Dad." Jane laughed. "I'd need several years of therapy to unravel that one."

"Therapy isn't always a bad thing."

Jane nodded. "I think I married Carol because I was so used to being controlled by Mother and the church. I just moved into more of the same."

"How is your mother?"

"She's all right," Jane said. "She's surprised me. She still goes to church, of course. But she's gotten into her job. She was promoted to office manager recently. And she's paid off almost all her debt, including paying me back for some credit cards she ran up."

"The Coyles?"

"David still doesn't speak to them. He told his dad a few years ago that if he was willing to get counseling, David would agree to be back in his life in small doses."

Paul shook his head. "I'm guessing that didn't go over well."

"No. Mr. Coyle told David to go fuck himself. It doesn't matter. He and Carter are happy together and David got to experience the Gundersons for a long time."

"How is Marla?"

"She's devastated, of course. She and Mr. G were such an oddly matched couple, but so happy."

"She could have come with you," Paul said.

Jane smiled at her father. "She's not ready to face people. Carter's aunts are staying with her right now. It must be nice to have sisters swooping in to take care of her in her grief. I wish I had a sister."

Paul grinned. "I'm a little too old for that now. And I don't think Dell would be willing."

They watched Dell expertly docking the boat. Jane liked her. She was tall and solid and muscled. She looked like a tennis player with her long, thick legs. Her hair, which was whiter than Paul's, was curly and thick, and contrasted beautifully with her dark skin. Her big smile made her seem perpetually open and inviting. Jane thought Paul couldn't have found someone more different than Mary if he had tried. Watching the group traipse up from the dock, sunburned, laughing, and covered with sand, Jane imagined Karma walking with them. She would fit in perfectly. Jane turned to her dad. "Dell reminds me of Karma. Maybe that's why I like her so much."

Paul smiled. "Your first love? If I had been a better father, I would have counseled you to hold on to her."

Jane shrugged. "I thought she was my soulmate. But how can she be if we couldn't be together?"

"I know that Dell is my soulmate, Janey. And if Karma is yours, you need to find a way to be together. Fate makes the introduction, but you have to do the work."

The group reached the front porch and Jane stood to greet them. Dell threw her arms around Paul and they kissed deeply. Suri held out her foot. "Look, I stepped on a rock and busted open my foot."

"All I see is tape." Jane laughed.

"That's because Carter wrapped it up for me," Suri said. "It's awesome having two dads who can patch you up when you get hurt."

Jane ushered everyone into the house to get cleaned up. She and Paul made dinner while the rest of the group changed clothes. Suri finished first and wandered into the kitchen. Jane was so proud of how far she had come since moving in with David and Carter. Her grades were up, she was working part time, and she had started applying for colleges.

"What can I do to help?" Suri asked.

"Help me set the table, please," Jane said. "I'm going to start dishing out soon."

Suri grabbed a handful of flatware. "I wish Mr. G was here."

Jane put her arms around the girl. "He was something special, wasn't he?"

"He sure was," Carter said, walking into the kitchen. "Larger than life with a heart to match."

Suri wiped away a tear. "Even though I was already a teenager when I met him, he always treated me like I was his real granddaughter."

"You were his real granddaughter," Carter said, kissing her on the forehead. "He loved you so much. He was always bragging to David and me about how amazing you are, like we need to be told."

Jane watched them holding each other. For a moment, she regretted never having children. Suri and the guys had such a warm relationship, and she missed having that in her life.

Suri smiled up at Carter. "It won't be the same without him."

"Nothing ever is," Carter said.

Jane put an arm around each of them. "He was proud of his family."

She finished setting the table as the rest of the group filtered in. As soon as the family was sitting around the table, Jane asked if she could say grace. Her father nodded, though Jane noted he looked surprised. Jane took David's hand on one side and Dell's on the other. "I want to thank God," she grinned, "or Goddess." Jane heard Dell chuckle softly. She squeezed the other woman's hand. "Or whatever higher power for bringing this odd but wonderful family together. Amen."

"A-woman," Dell said.

Everyone laughed. Jane looked up in time to see Paul smiling lovingly across the table at his new wife. She turned to see David brushing his hand across Carter's face. She didn't regret leaving Carol. Their relationship hadn't been that loving even in the beginning.

Karma would have held her hand. Karma would have been laughing with them, telling jokes, making everyone feel happy. Jane looked at David. "How's Karma?"

"She's fantastic," David said. "Suri loves her."

"She's a great boss," Suri said. "Lauren is awesome, too. I love my job. They said I could keep working there if I go to college in town. And if not, I can work on holidays and breaks."

"You must be an excellent employee," Jane said.

"I just love it," Suri answered. "I want to be a librarian, so it's good practice to work in a bookstore."

"I have to admit I was surprised you didn't get together with Karma years ago," Paul said. "I wondered if you were having an affair with her when she sent that letter."

"What letter?" Jane asked.

"The one she sent to the house," Paul said. "I assumed she sent it to our house so Carol wouldn't see it."

"Dad, I don't know what letter you're talking about."

Paul held up his hands. "The letter from Karma. Your mother said she gave it to you."

Jane gritted her teeth. "She never gave me any letters."

"Baby, I'm sorry." Paul looked stricken, but

Jane couldn't bring herself to feel sorry for him. Her head was reeling. When had Karma sent a letter? Jane wondered if that was why Karma kept telling her no.

David took Jane's hand and she relaxed a bit. She looked back to her father. "Dad, what was in the letter?"

"I have no idea," Paul said. "I never read it. I just assumed your mother handed it to you unopened."

Stunned, Jane leaned back in her chair. It shouldn't matter. After all these years, and all these chances, if she and Karma were meant to be together, they would be. A letter shouldn't matter. Jane forced the conversation back to other topics and the group turned their attention to other things. Jane was distracted for the rest of the evening and gladly went to bed early while the rest of the family played board games by the fireplace.

In the morning, as they packed David's SUV, Paul held Jane. "I wish you could stay longer."

"So do I, Dad. I love Dell, and I love that you're so happy here."

"You'll be happy, too, Jane."

"I am happy. I love my job, I love my friends. And you know, love will present itself when it's ready." She smiled. "Or when I am." She kissed her father on the cheek. "I'll be back as soon as I can, I promise."

She turned to hug Dell tightly. "Take care of him," Jane cautioned. "He's getting a little wild in his old age."

Dell laughed, and Jane was struck again by her warmth and openness. She was leaving her father in good hands. She stood on tiptoe to kiss Dell on the cheek. "I love you, Dell," Jane said.

"I love you, too." Dell smiled.

Jane climbed into the backseat with Suri and waved out the back until they reached the end of the street. Jane slept most of the way home. Blinking, she tried to pull herself out of the fog when they turned into the Gundersons' driveway.

David insisted Carter go inside to rest. Jane helped Suri and David unload their stuff before throwing her overnight bag into the backseat of her little car. David put his arms around her as she was saying goodbye. "Don't be too hard on your mom," he said. "She probably felt like she didn't have another choice."

"We always have another choice, David." Jane kissed him on the cheek. Waving goodbye to Suri, Jane headed directly for her mother's house.

Mary Edmunds opened the door to Jane's knock. Her lips were pursed as she took in Jane's messy hair and casual outfit. "This is how they dress for Sundays at your father's house?"

Jane ignored her. "Dad told me I got a letter from Karma that you promised to give me."

Her mother took a step back. "Jane, I don't know what you're talking about. Come in before the neighbors see you dressed like a teenager." She looked Jane up and down. "Cutoff jean shorts? At your age?"

Jane flushed. Stepping into her mother's house, she made sure to slip off her shoes at the front door. Mary was living simply these days, but her house was still immaculate. She scoffed every time she walked into Jane's little apartment. Jane wasn't a slob, but now that she didn't have Carol hovering over her, insisting that she keep the house spotless, she was a little more laid-back about housework.

Mary led Jane into the small living room. Jane was amused to see slipcovers on all the furniture. She had an urge to plop onto the couch and put her bare feet up. Instead, she perched on a wooden chair. "The letter, Mom."

Mary flushed, looking away. "All of that was so long ago. How am I supposed to remember one letter?"

"How do you know it was long ago if you don't remember?"

"Why are you attacking me?" Mary sank into her chair and clutched her heart.

Jane sighed. "Mother, you've changed in a lot of ways. Most for the better. But some things never change."

"You've never taken my heart palpitations seriously," Mary said. "You're just like your father."

"I am a lot like him. I didn't realize for a long time because all he ever did was work."

"I suppose you're going to give up all decency and go live in a shack with a…"

"With a what? With a what, Mother?"

Mary held her hand over her heart. Her lips were pressed so tightly together, the blood was draining from them. Jane leaned back in her chair, suddenly exhausted.

"I'm not here to fight with you. I'm really not. I just want to know why you threw away my letter."

Mary stood suddenly. "I didn't."

She left the room and Jane heard her moving things around in the back room Mary used as storage. Jane tried to pull herself out of the chair to go help, but the weight of her body seemed to force her back into her chair. She felt as if she was moving through quicksand. She closed her eyes, listening to her mother rummage in the other room. It didn't matter anyway. Karma had made her feelings about Jane quite clear. She was happily committed, possibly married by now, to her girlfriend, and a letter she wrote years ago had nothing to do with her life today. Jane needed to move forward, stop living in the past, and get on with her life. She had made two big mistakes in her life: she had let Karma go and she had married Carol. Both of those situations were over, and she needed to let them go and focus on living for herself.

Hearing her mother's footsteps, Jane dragged her eyes open. Mary Edmunds was standing in front of her with an envelope. An unsealed envelope.

"You read it?"

Mary nodded. "I needed to know what was going on in your life. You don't talk to me."

"It's hard to talk to someone who has spent her entire life judging me and finding me lacking in just about every way."

"I wasn't perfect, Jane. But I did my best." She handed Jane the letter. Jane took it. She recognized Karma's careful lettering. Karma was so sure her handwriting was illegible. It touched Jane to see the care she had taken to make her writing so neat. Jane turned the letter over and over, looking at Karma's penmanship.

Mary cleared her throat, and Jane looked up. "Yes, Mother?"

"I was worried you might be having an affair. I didn't know why else she would write to you here."

Jane stared at her mother for a few moments, watching as Mary took a seat on the couch. The letter was shaking in her hand and Jane realized her hands were shaking. She pressed her hands to her thighs to control the trembling.

"All those years," Jane whispered.

"Pardon me?"

"All the years I lived with Carol, all the years I

spent trying to make something out of nothing. You lived with us, for fuck's sake."

Mary put her hand on her chest. "For better or for worse. That's what marriage is."

"It was all worse," Jane said. "Carol was mean to me. She treated me like a servant. She controlled me. She spent all our money. The only thing she didn't do was cheat on me, but Mother, I was so unhappy, I used to wish that she would."

Mary gasped. "You don't mean that."

"I do. I knew I didn't have the strength to leave her. I used to wish that she would cheat on me so I could leave her over it. Maybe if I had known that Karma was trying to reach out, I would have had the courage to leave Carol years before I did."

Mary closed her eyes and Jane was surprised to see tears dripping down her face. "I just wanted you to have a normal life. I was afraid of what would happen if you and Karma were together. She was so loud and she wore rainbow clothes, and I was scared that everyone would know you were a lesbian."

"I am a lesbian, Mom. And I was married to a woman. I'm pretty sure everyone knew it."

Mary opened her eyes and sighed. "That was different."

"Why?"

"You and Carol didn't act like a couple," Mary shouted. "I wasn't embarrassed to be seen with you because I knew no one would know that you were together."

Jane sat back in her chair. She stared at her mother, who was openly sobbing now. "You're right," Jane answered. "You're absolutely right. No one would have ever guessed that we were a couple." She was beyond crying about it. The only regret she had about Carol was marrying her in the first place. She had married Carol because she was a safe bet. Jane couldn't hate her mother without hating herself. After all, Jane had married someone because she wasn't afraid to be seen with her in public. Jane got to be proud of herself for coming out of the closet without really coming out of the closet. She got up and knelt on the floor in front of her mother.

"I spent so many years unhappy."

"Marriage isn't supposed to be happy, Jane."

Jane stared up at her mother. Had Mary ever been happy in her life? "Mom, I don't hate you."

Mary sniffed. "You have every right to hate me. I patted myself on the back for being so accepting of you and Carol. Really, I was just accepting of the fact that you were the straightest lesbians I knew. I could congratulate myself for my open mind without actually having to open it."

Jane patted her mother's leg. "I did the same. Karma embarrassed me back then. I was afraid everyone would look at us and see a sign flashing over our heads that screamed 'dyke' in neon letters."

Mary cringed. "I never saw you like that."

"But I am. I'm a lesbian. And it's time for me to start being proud of myself."

Mary put her hand on Jane's shoulders and kissed her forehead. "I know I haven't been a good mother, Jane."

Jane smiled. "No, you really haven't."

Mary half-snorted. "I'll try to be more accepting." She paused, looking terrified. "I'll even go to a gay pride thing with you."

Jane laughed. "Let's take it one step at a time. Why don't you just start with accepting me the way I am."

Mary nodded. "I'll try. I promise to try."

Jane stood and leaned over to kiss her mother on the cheek. "I do love you."

Mary reached out a hand so Jane could help her up. She struggled a bit, and Jane's heart melted. Her mother was getting older. If they didn't make peace now, they might never do so. She pulled her mother into a hug and they held each other for several moments.

Finally, Mary pulled away. "Okay, let's not get sentimental about it."

Jane smiled, kissing her mother once more on the cheek. "I'll call you next week. We'll have lunch."

She let herself out of the house and got into her car. Tempted as she was to read the letter right there in the driveway, she didn't want Mary spying out the window as she was reading it. Jane drove home and half-ran up the stairs to her apartment. She threw her overnight bag on the floor and curled up in her overstuffed armchair near the window. Leaning her head against the back of the chair, Jane looked out at the setting sun, holding the letter against her chest. She didn't know if it even mattered what it said after all this time.

After a few moments, she opened her eyes. With shaking fingers, she pulled out the letter. It was handwritten on stationery that Jane guessed Karma would have borrowed from her mom.

Dear Jane,

We turned thirty this year. Remember when that used to feel old? My father had a heart attack tonight and it got me thinking about wasted time and wasted lives. I think the time I spent with Crash was a lesson for me in some way. I wonder if you and I would have had a happily ever after if we had gotten together when we first met. Sometimes, I think that we need to go through bad times so we can truly appreciate the good. I've done the bad, and I know I can appreciate the good. I think of you daily and I miss you deeply. The times I spent with you were the best in my life. The first time we kissed, I felt like I had been searching for you for a lifetime without realizing it. I know it's been years and maybe you're happy with Carol now, but I still feel the call of our connection. You were the one who once called us soulmates. If that's true, how can we possibly be so out of touch with each other? Do soulmates really exist? If they do, don't they owe it to themselves to be together? Please call me, write me, or come see me at A Woman's Place. (I own the bookstore now! Long story, I'll tell you in person.) I love you forever.

Warmly,
Karma

Jane read it twice. She could hear Karma's voice as clearly as if they had talked this morning and Karma had just stepped out to get doughnuts. She traced her fingers over the letter, wishing she had received this when it was sent. She would have reached out to Karma, she would have wanted to see her, to touch her. She imagined getting the letter and taking it somewhere private to read. She saw herself telling Carol that she didn't want to be married anymore. So much might not have happened. She shook her head. Whatever Karma felt when she wrote this letter was over now. Karma had made that clear last year when Jane sought her out at the bookstore. She carefully refolded the letter back into the envelope and stuck it in a drawer.

Chapter Nineteen

Karma bounced on the balls of her feet, looking at her watch. The open house for the little place on Maryland Avenue was supposed to start at nine. It was already five past that and the realtor was nowhere in sight. Karma was happy to note that no other customers were loitering around, either. Karma had looked at this house twice and she was certain she wanted to buy it. But it was her first house purchase and she was scared. It was a lot of money to put down—almost everything in her savings account. She resumed pacing, impatiently looking at her phone every few minutes to see how much time had passed.

Finally, a woman in a business suit rushed to the front gate. She smiled at Karma. "Are you waiting for the open house?"

"Yes," Karma said. "My realtor has brought me here twice and I want to look at it one more time."

The woman nodded. "Come on in."

Karma followed the woman through the front door, marveling again at the tiny built-in bookshelves in the foyer. The house was small but well designed, with nooks and cubbies in nearly every room.

"I'm Jeannine Reef, by the way," the woman said.

"Thank you, Jeannine. Do you mind if I just wander around for a bit?"

"Not at all. That will give me time to set up my table."

Karma drifted into the living room, imagining where the couch would go. Not that she had a couch, but if she bought the house, she would buy a couch. She laughed at herself. She moved to the kitchen. It had plenty of storage space and good counters. If she added a small rolling cart at the end of the long counter, it would give her more room for meal prep. The tiny bedroom off the back of the kitchen could be set up as an office. Karma popped her head in and nodded. She remembered that this room was filled with light. Maybe someday, she would sell the bookstore to Lauren and retire to write her best-selling memoir in this sun-filled office.

The bedroom was big enough for her queen-size bed and a couple of nightstands. She stood in the middle of the room looking around. She moved to the bedroom door and stared back into the room. It needed to be painted…maybe a rich color, something in the red family. She pictured herself lying in bed at night, listening to music or waking up in the morning to the sounds of the birds. The master bathroom was large, but not ostentatious. She liked that the house had one and a half bathrooms. She never had to worry about guests looking through her medicine chest.

The house was in a quiet neighborhood and the backyard was extraordinarily big for a small house. Karma could plant a garden. Sighing, she went back through the kitchen and out onto the deck. Standing in the morning sun, she told herself to just decide. She loved this house and didn't know what was holding her back. It wasn't that it was small. It was the perfect size for her. *But is it big enough for two?*

She heard footsteps in the kitchen. Jeannine was showing the house to someone else and it spurred

Karma into action. She would make an offer on the house. She turned to step back inside, intent on getting to her car and calling her realtor.

She walked into a woman who was stepping out onto the deck, knocking a notebook out of the woman's hands. Karma instantly bent down to pick it up. The woman stepped out and bent down next to her. Karma grabbed one of the paint color pamphlets that had fallen out of the notebook and looked up. Jane was kneeling on the deck next to her. Karma handed the pamphlet over and smiled. "Hi, you."

"Karma. Hi. Hi." Jane was smiling. "Hi."

Karma laughed. "Hi."

They finished gathering the rest of the papers and Karma set the whole package on the deck behind her. She stood, offering a hand to Jane. The two women were quiet for a few moments, looking at each other.

Jane broke the silence. "You look the same as last time I saw you."

Karma grinned, straightening her tie. "Just call me Peter Pan."

Karma watched as Jane threw her head back and laughed. The urge to touch her was so strong that Karma was reaching out before she realized. She just needed to feel Jane's skin, to know she was real. Her fingers trailed over Jane's cheek and she closed her eyes. Jane was silent, but her hand closed over Karma's and held it against her cheek.

"Jane," Karma whispered. "I'm sorry for..." She didn't know whether to apologize for cutting her off when Karma was with Crash, or for not being patient with her when Jane was struggling to come out of the closet. She could apologize for not being brave enough or evolved enough to stand by Jane while she came to terms with her mother and her religion. She could apologize for sending Jane away when she reached out for her in the bookstore. She stuttered a bit before taking a deep breath. "I'm sorry for not fighting harder to be with you."

Jane blinked. "I'm sorry, too. For all of it. For everything." She touched Karma's face and Karma felt the shock through her body. She felt herself pulled toward Jane. In a moment, her arms were wrapped around Jane's waist, her face pressed into the skin of her neck. Jane responded, pulling Karma even closer. Karma could feel Jane's breath on her ear. She sighed against Jane's skin.

"I shouldn't have sent you away when you came to the bookstore."

"I shouldn't have turned you down when you wanted to be friends," Jane replied. "I think I knew that I couldn't be just friends with you."

Jane's skin felt smooth and warm under Karma's face, and she rubbed her face gently up Jane's neck to press their cheeks together. Silently breathing, the women hugged, letting the weight of the years fall away. Karma almost felt twenty-one again, holding Jane for the first time. The sense of homecoming was stronger this time. It felt hard-earned, and Karma wasn't willing to let it go without a fight. She pulled back just enough to look into Jane's eyes. "Are you seeing anyone right now?"

Jane shook her head. "No. Are you?"

Karma shook her head, smiling. She lifted one of her hands to stroke Jane's blond hair. "You're even more beautiful than you were when we met."

Jane scoffed. "I'm almost forty and it shows. You still look like a twenty-year-old."

"Ha. Please. Look at these wrinkles." Karma pointed to her eyes and mouth. "We look the same age."

Jane tilted her head. "You still look adorable. Are you butch now?"

"No. I'm just myself. I just like to dress dapper." She put her arms back around Jane's waist. "Why? Are you looking for a butch?"

"No," Jane said. "I don't want roles. I want to share everything. I don't want it to be my job to make the lunches and keep the house clean. I don't want to be made to feel like because I don't make a lot of money, I don't get a say in the household."

"I want that, too." Karma grinned. "I want to share everything. Especially sexually."

Jane ducked her head, smiling. "Yes. I don't ever want it to be all one sided. It feels so unfulfilling."

"I want to reach for my partner and I want her to reach for me. I don't always want to be the big spoon." Karma shrugged. "I also don't always want to be the little spoon."

"I don't, either," Jane whispered. "I just want to be loved."

Karma pulled her closer. "Jane, I know it's crazy. I know we barely know each other even though we were close once. But I think—no, I know—that we belong together. I was wrong when I said we weren't soulmates. I should have listened to you long ago. I should have stuck around and fought for you."

Jane curled into Karma and Karma could feel the tears on her cheek. "I think I would have come for you if I had gotten your letter. My mother never gave it to me until maybe a year ago."

Karma laughed. "That explains a lot."

Jane pulled back. "You aren't mad?"

"At your mom?" Karma smiled. "How could I be? If I'd had the guts to show up and say it to your face, everything would have been different."

"You did say it to my face, but I turned you away."

"It's because Carol showed up," Karma replied. "If we had been able to spend ten more minutes with each other that day, I would have completely seduced you."

Jane chuckled. "You might be right." She pulled away but reached for Karma's hand. "The realtor is probably wondering what happened to us."

"Nah, she's probably hoping we'll fall in love and buy the house together."

"This is my second time looking at this place," Jane said.

"It's my third," Karma replied. "I win. It's mine."

Jane laughed and squeezed Karma's hand. Karma lifted Jane's hand to her mouth to kiss it. She smiled as Jane's eyes closed. "Jane?"

Jane opened her eyes. "Yes, Karma?"

"Let's buy it together."

Jane snorted. "Are you crazy? Karma, that's…" She was shaking her head, half-laughing. Karma's heart swelled with happiness and she couldn't keep from laughing herself. She grabbed Jane and twirled her around.

"Come on. Let's do it. I know it's crazy. But you chose safety for years and where did it get you? We're either soulmates or we're not. And if we are, we are going to live happily ever after, whether we cautiously date for a year or move in together today. What do you say, Jane? What do you say?"

Jane stared at her. She was laughing, too, and Karma held her breath. "Oh, Karma. It just seems so reckless."

"Be reckless. That's what people do when they're in love," Karma stated.

Jane gasped. "Is that what you're saying? Karma, are you in love with me?"

Karma put her hands on Jane's shoulders and peered at her. "Yes." As she said it, she realized it was true. She had been in love with Jane since the first time they met, and it hadn't changed. Their lives had changed and their circumstances, but that love had never gone away. Looking at Jane now, Karma knew it never would. Jane was her soulmate and soulmates belonged together. She brushed her fingers over Jane's cheek. "Jane, I am in love with you and I want to spend the rest of my life with you. Let's buy this house and live happily ever after."

Jane smiled. "I must be crazy."

"Is that a yes?"

"That's a yes," Jane said.

Karma whooped and picked Jane up, spinning her around the deck. She was singing, and she danced Jane around the deck. Their deck. They would string up lights out here, and on warm spring nights they would dance into the night, letting the sway of their bodies build a slow burn until they had no choice but to go inside and make love.

As she swung Jane into a deep dip, she realized the realtor had stepped out onto the deck. Karma grinned sheepishly and lifted Jane back to her feet.

"Sorry, we got caught up," Karma said.

The realtor looked from one to the other. "I just came to check and see if you had any questions about the house."

"No questions," Karma said. "I want it." She didn't intend to play hard to get. She would have her realtor make an offer. The place had been on the market for a while, so they were probably anxious to sell.

Jeannine smiled. "Excellent."

Karma glanced at Jane. There was no point in making Jane uncomfortable, and the realtor didn't need to know every little detail of their decision. Karma nodded. "I'll have my realtor give you a call. I'm going to make an offer."

She shook Jeannine's hand and motioned for Jane to come with her into the house. Jane stopped to say goodbye to Jeannine as well. In the doorway, Jane paused. Karma tilted her head toward the front of the house. "Come on. We can talk about…" She trailed off, trying to think of the right word to say in front of the realtor. "The deal."

Jane turned to look at her, eyebrow raised quizzically. Karma shrugged. "What?"

Jane took Karma's hand and turned back to the realtor. "We're a couple," she said. "We're a lesbian couple. And we're going to buy this house together."

The realtor looked perplexed. "Okay. Congratulations?"

Karma pressed her lips together, trying not to laugh. She squeezed Jane's hand and pulled her toward the front door. Once on the walk, she turned to Jane, unable to control her laughter any longer. "Jane, you never cease to amaze me."

Jane pursed her lips. "When we first met, I was afraid to even think the word lesbian, let alone use it. And I want you to know right up front that I will never deny you, shame you, or let anyone think that we aren't a couple."

Karma's eyes filled with tears and she reached for Jane. Their mouths met, and she felt the soft wetness of Jane's tongue lightly moving against Karma's lips. She gently twisted her hand into Jane's hair, pulling her closer, opening her mouth to Jane's kiss. Karma slowly became aware of every part of Jane's body that was touching hers. She bent her head and kissed Jane's neck, close to her shoulder. Jane breathed in deeply, her body arching against Karma. Karma's fingers tightened in Jane's hair and her kiss turned into the lightest bite.

"Karma," Jane breathed. "My love."

Karma pulled back enough to see Jane's face. "My soulmate."

"My one," Jane said. She smiled.

Overcome, Karma held Jane, unable to speak. She closed her eyes and lost herself in the feel of her beloved.

"Karma?"

Karma opened her eyes to see Jane smiling at her. "Yes, love?"

"Would you like to come back to my apartment with me?"

"For coffee?" Karma asked.

"Coffee and doughnuts," Jane said. "We can stop on the way."

"Good idea," Karma said. "I need to call my realtor anyway."

Jane laughed. "Do you want to follow me in your car?"

"No. Let's drive together and come back for the other car later." She half-shrugged. "I don't ever want to be apart from you again."

Jane took her hand and led Karma down the path to the front gate. On the sidewalk, they turned to look back at the house.

"Welcome home," Karma whispered.

Chapter Twenty

Jane dragged herself to a sitting position, wincing at the pain in her hip. Every joint in her body seemed to pop as she put her palm on the nightstand and heaved herself out of bed. Once she felt balanced, she released the nightstand and grabbed her cane. She took a few cautious steps before trusting that her body was going to carry her without collapsing.

She paused on her way to the bathroom, looking at the wall of photographs in the bedroom. Her mother, who had passed away long ago, had a place of honor in the middle of the wall. Mary had come to be one of Jane's best friends over the years, even sometimes coming to pride parades with Jane and Karma. Jane smiled, remembering her mother's first careful forays into LGBTQ pride. When Jane and Karma got married, same-sex marriage had been legal for years. She never dreamed that those rights would be lost again to a bigoted president who seemed hell-bent on destroying the lives of millions. She and Karma had been at the forefront of fighting to legalize it again. She smiled at her wedding picture, happy that they could make it legal again in their lifetime. She touched Karma's laughing face in the photo. Karma had fought for years to change this picture—she hated her nose in it, said the way she was laughing made it look huge. Finally, Jane had taken it down, and Karma decided it wasn't so bad after all.

Laughing, she continued her journey to the bathroom. "No wonder old people are always late," she muttered. "They're always stopping to wander down memory lane." She took a couple of steps. "And they stop to talk to themselves."

In the bathroom, she paused at the mirror, smiling at the old lady with denim-blue eyes and long white hair. Some days, Jane couldn't believe that was her. How did she get so old? She debated taking a shower, but decided she wasn't feeling energetic enough. She rubbed herself down with a washcloth and combed her hair. It was still long and straight and she liked to joke that it had just one day switched from blond to white. Lifting her arms to brush her hair made her lungs hurt. She sat in the chair next to the vanity until she caught her breath. She hadn't realized how much she had come to rely on Karma for simple tasks until she had to do them herself. She took a few deep breaths, and with one hand on the vanity and the other on her cane, she stood again.

Doing the rest of her bathroom business took far longer than it should have. Finally, she hobbled to the kitchen and poured herself a cup of coffee. Sitting at the table, she looked at her checklist of things to do today. Suri would be here later to help with some of it. She was bringing her second boy, too. Maybe she'd ask him to take care of that loose board on the deck.

Sipping her coffee, she sighed. Last time she'd seen Suri had been at David's funeral back ten years. David. What a man he had been. Kind and giving and in love with Carter up until the day he died. They had a long life together. She smiled, remembering Carter's handsome face. He had sobbed when he had to give up practicing medicine after his MS progressed. He loved helping people so much. Karma was the only one who could cheer him up sometimes. She would make up stories about the wild times of their youth and get everyone laughing. Those guys both loved Karma so much. Carter had died less than a month after David. He was eighty-five by then and more than ready to go. Jane had always thought that was how soulmates would be. They couldn't live without each other, knowing they would find each other again in the next life. Fate would never be so unkind to leave one alive while the other grieved. She put her head in her hands and cried.

"Jane," Karma walked into the kitchen holding two cloth sacks. She set them down on the counter and pulled a chair up next to Jane. "I thought you were going to stay in bed until I got back from the store. I left you books and magazines and doughnuts."

"I couldn't wait," Jane said. "I wanted coffee."

Karma frowned. "You need to be careful at your age."

Jane laughed. "At my age? You're as old as I am, Methuselah."

Karma grinned, and for a second, Jane was transported back in time to the first day they met. Karma's eyes still sparkled just as much. "I may be eighty-nine years old…" Karma started.

"Ninety," Jane corrected. "Since your geriatric mind let it slip."

"Ninety," Karma repeated, laughing. "But I am not recovering from pneumonia."

"I'm fine, love. I promise."

Karma leaned forward to kiss Jane on the mouth. "Do you want to sit on the couch for a while?"

"Yes," Jane said. "It will help ease the ache of my bones."

Karma stood and held a hand out to Jane. "Come on, wife. I'll help you to the living room."

Jane took Karma's hand. Holding her cane in the other hand, she stood. They walked to the living room, mindful of the tear in the carpet at the threshold. "We'll get Henry to take care of that," Jane said. "Suri's bringing him over for our birthday."

Karma gently lowered Jane to the couch and placed a pillow behind her back. Jane knew that Karma suffered her own aches and pains, but she never let anything stop her from helping Jane. "Come sit with me, love," Jane said.

Karma sat carefully on the couch and kicked her shoes off. Turning her body, she propped her feet up on the throw pillow and rested her head on Jane's lap. Jane stroked her wife's hair softly, marveling at the softness of it. She was still compelled to touch Karma after all these years, still bathed in the warmth of her lover's touch. Karma smiled up at her. "Hey, Janey?"

"Yes, my love?"

"Remember that time you found your soulmate and then lost her?"

Jane nodded, her eyes filling with tears. She couldn't seem to stop crying these days. "Yes, I remember. It was the worst five minutes of my life."

"Five minutes?" Karma snorted. "Was that all it was?"

Jane smiled down at her. "Yes. Five minutes."

Karma pursed her lips. "Humph. Seemed a lot longer than that to me."

Jane touched Karma's face. "It was a blink, my love. It was nothing more than a tiny little wrinkle in the long fabric of our lives."

About the Author

Beth Burnett is an Adjunct Creative Writing Professor with Southern New Hampshire University and the Director of Education for the Golden Crown Literary Society. When she's not perfecting punchy prose, she practices her speed-hobbling technique on the hills of Bancroft park, runs a Lansing women's networking group, and teaches the craft of writing for the GCLS Writing Academy. She has won two Rainbow Awards and has been published in several anthologies, but her claim to fame is her writing process, which involves a twenty-pound cat sleeping on her forearms while she types. In her spare time, Beth walks her geriatric dog, has video cooking dates with her long-distance partner, and tries to figure out what she wants to be when she grows up.

Check out Beth's other books

Andy's Song - ISBN - 978-1-939062-14-7

Is there more to life than sex? Andy Ericksson is trying to find out. She's had a pretty easy life. She's sexy, she's tough, and she has a trust fund that ensures she will never have to work a "normal" job. She has a circle of adoring friends and all of the hot, casual sex she could want. It's a recipe for a great time. However, lately, Andy has started to feel that something is missing. Casual sex isn't cutting through the loneliness. Her best friend falls in love with someone else, her ex-girlfriend makes an appearance, and she meets someone who isn't willing to be a one-night stand. Andy's world is changing and she's not sure that she's changing with it. In the midst of Andy's turmoil, everyone in her life suddenly seems to be spouting new age wisdom and finding inner peace. Through the changing of one relationship and the beginning of another, Andy struggles to open her heart without sacrificing her freedom or alienating those she loves the most.

The Love Sucks Club - ISBN - 978-1-939062-50-5

Tragedy and heartbreak drive Dana McComb to a Caribbean island where she sets about to becoming a hermit. Settling into numbness seems to be the only way to suppress the psychic visions that once showed her the death of her soul mate. A failed rebound relationship leaves her even more intent on losing herself in the loneliness of her isolated house on the hill. With her middle-aged, beef jerky obsessed tomcat, Dana vows to live a life devoid of ups and downs. Making fun of her own state of mind, she and her best buddy start "The Love Sucks Club" which is really just a euphemism for sitting around bitching about their own bitterness about love. Trying to stay wrapped in her own misery starts to fail when Dana's pesky younger sister and a host of other island misfits insist on poking into her best laid plans for comfort. When a new woman shows up on the island, bringing back Dana's visions, she is suddenly besieged by night terrors, vivid hallucinations, and panic attacks. Half-convinced she's going crazy, Dana tries to shut out her past with increasing difficulty. Aware that it may be the only way to put her dead lover to rest, Dana begins a journey that could either shatter her life or save it.

Eating Life - ISBN - 978-1-943353-87-3

Carefree and irrepressible, Casey Wilde has spent her life running. Running from love, running from responsibility, and running from commitment. Megan Woodson, Casey's best friend, has spent her life building security with a long-term partner and a well-paying, highly respected position in the best ad agency in Memphis. Ben Stagg is a man who has lost everything, including the desire to live. And Brilliant Wilson is a photographer who can't quite figure out why she keeps dating women who don't love her. Faced with painful and pressing decisions, the group is forced to confront their own life choices. When their worlds collide and everything starts to fall apart, these friends must learn that the only important decision is the one to follow their hearts.

Other books by Sapphire Authors

Reclaiming Yancy – ISBN – 978-1-948232-04-3

Her bossy best friend Roxie criticizes her risky behavior, and warns that she'd better shape up before something serious happens. Her socialite mother loves when she dresses properly, but laments that the clothes hang off her strong yet unhealthily lean body.

Colorado rancher Yancy Delaney is a woman grieving past losses, escaping her past by running from any commitment—except to her beloved horses and her work at Valley View, the rural medical organization her family founded.

Enter Dr. Genevieve Lambert, the hot new medical director of Valley View's rural clinics, where Yancy is Board Director. They immediately feel the sparks of attraction, but Gen wants no part of Yancy's seduction game or her reputation for casual one-nighters. And Yancy's missteps and risk-taking may finally be catching up with her, resulting in an injury to herself and a path of broken hearts left in her dust.

Gen and Yancy embark on a journey of romance fraught with rocky rides. Can they overcome their tough trails and find true love?

Highland Dew – ISBN – 978-1-948232-11-1

Bryce Andrews, west coast sales director for Global Distillers and Distribution, is tired of the corporate hamster wheel. She needs a change.

A craft whisky trade show offers her inspiration and a chance to revisit Scotland and the majestic scenery of the Speyside region—best known for the "Whisky Trail." Bryce and her coworker, Reggie Ballard, need to find a wholly original whisky for their international distribution division by visiting a number of small distillers.

A blind curve, a dangling sign, and weed-choked driveway draw Bryce directly into a truly unique opportunity. She discovers a struggling family, a shuttered distillery, and a spitfire of a daughter called home to care for her confused father.

Fiona McDougall—the only child and heir to the MacDougall & Son legacy, had her career teaching in Edinburgh curtailed by fate…or serendipity.

When the stars finally align, the two women work together to resurrect a dream for themselves and the family business—if they can weather the storms of unscrupulous business practices in the competitive whisky market.

Lavender Dreams - ISBN - 978-1-943353-59-0

When Sarah Chase got on the ferry to Bainbridge Island, she left her lover, her job, and her past behind. She didn't know that in the course of one day she would meet a woman who might be the girl of her dreams, change her career path, create a new family, and find herself in a fairytale mansion with two of the quirkiest little old ladies imaginable.

The Treehouse – ISBN – 978-1-948232-00-5

Camilla Thompson, a Humanities college professor who never did write that Great American Novel, hasn't seen her son Nico for two years.

One morning she drives to the house where her ex, Allison, is still raising Nico. Knowing that they are away for a week's vacation, Camilla begins to build a treehouse as a surprise for the son she's not allowed to see.

But Camilla's regrets, grief, and lack of construction skills aren't the only challenges she'll face. Old friends and unexpected visitors show up to help—and complicate matters. Free-spirited Taylor, Camilla's best friend, arrives with her lover, Audrey, whom Camilla finds herself falling for. Then Wallace, Camilla's Department Chair, disrupts everything with startling news that threatens to end Camilla's career.

At first an impulsive idea, the treehouse soon promises to be an oasis for Camilla's redemption that could free her for another chance at love and family. Then again, it might simply be just a bad decision.

Meet Me in The Middle – ISBN – 978-1-943353-63-7

Veterinarian Aislin O'Shea runs a busy clinic. She wasn't looking for a relationship. She'd already had the perfect one. She certainly wasn't attracted to fancy pants executive, Ms. Zane Whitman - she wasn't her type.

Zane Whitman had it all. Stellar career, wealth, exclusive social circle, and models vying for her attention. Impulsive, emotionally charged Aislin was not her type.

Two women from the opposite side of the tracks.
Neither one expects meddling from an unexpected source on the Other side.
Neither one knows the train is coming.

Four of a Kind – ISBN – 978-1-943353-61-3

Tess Whitcomb is a struggling artist who has to work a second job at The Sloop to pay her bills. Upon her aunt's death, she is given a sealed envelop by her aunt's doctor and instructed to hand deliver it to N. Hamilton Esq., a maritime lawyer. Neither one understands why Tess has been sent to her firm. The whole meeting is odd and confusing. The only thing that is clear to each of them is that there is a strong and immediate attraction between them. Tess leaves the office certain that they will never meet again.

A valuable necklace owned by Nikki's deceased mother shows up in the most unexpected way and the truth about their entwined past is revealed. Nikki is intrigued by Tess but dismisses the meeting as ridiculous. She suspects that Tess is part of an office scheme by some of her staff trying to set her up on a date. Her heart was closed tight since the death of her beloved Jo.

Can these two women handle the truth? Can they accept that love can happen anytime and anywhere?

www.ingramcontent.com/pod-product-compliance
Lightning Source LLC
Chambersburg PA
CBHW050605190726
48283CB00007B/2286